D0823103

BY MONICA MURPHY

ONE WEEK GIRLFRIEND SERIES

One Week Girlfriend

Second Chance Boyfriend

Three Broken Promises

Drew + Fable Forever (e-Original Novella)

Four Years Later

THE FOWLER SISTERS SERIES

Owning Violet

Stealing Rose

Taming Lily

Taming
Lily

Taming Lily

A Novel

Monica Murphy

Anderson County Library
Anderson, S.C.
WES

BANTAM BOOKS
NEW YORK

Taming Lily is a work of fiction. Names, characters, places, and incidents either are the products of the author's imagination or are used fictitiously. Any resemblance to actual persons, living or dead, events, or locales is entirely coincidental.

A Bantam Books Trade Paperback Original

Copyright © 2015 by Monica Murphy

All rights reserved.

Published in the United States by Bantam Books, an imprint of Random House, a division of Penguin Random House LLC, New York.

BANTAM BOOKS and the HOUSE colophon are registered trademarks of Penguin Random House LLC.

LIBRARY OF CONGRESS CATALOGING-IN-PUBLICATION DATA
Murphy, Monica.
Taming Lily: a novel / Monica Murphy.
pages ; cm.—(The Fowler sisters ; 3)
ISBN 978-0-553-39330-9—ISBN 978-0-553-39331-6 (ebook)
I. Title.
PS3613.U7525T36 2015
813'.6—dc23   2015004749

Printed in the United States of America on acid-free paper

randomhousebooks.com

987654321

Book design by Karin Batten

To my husband: I love you.
Thank you for being you.

Those who are willing to be vulnerable move among mysteries.

—Theodore Roethke

Taming Lily

Chapter One

Max

I HATE BABYSITTING JOBS, THOUGH I DON'T KNOW IF I'D CATE-gorize this particular job as babysitting. I rarely take them on because they suck and they're boring, but the money was too good to resist. If I took every fucking job that came my way because of how much they offer to pay me, I'd be a very rich man working the absolute bottom-of-the-barrel shit jobs. Busting cheating spouses. Catching them in compromising positions. Following them, taking photos, feeling sordid and dirty as I reveal said pictures and watch my client either rage angrily or fall apart in tears.

Those types of jobs are a dime a dozen.

No thanks. I'm lucky enough that I can pick and choose. Though I felt like with this one, I didn't necessarily pick it. The job chose me.

It also intrigued me. *She* intrigued me. Not that I'd ever confess that to a living soul. I have integrity. An image to fulfill and maintain, especially when it comes to my business. I'm not one to let my dick make business decisions for me, but this girl . . . is unlike any girl I've ever seen before.

The moment I looked at her photo, I knew.

I watch her now, from my aisle seat on the plane, sitting five rows behind her. She's in the opposite aisle seat and I can get a good look at her profile if I lean forward slightly, which is exactly what I'm doing. It's wild, how she appears completely different from the photos I saw of her on the web last night while I did my research.

Whereas the endless images in my Google search featured a sexy-as-hell, scantily dressed woman doing whatever the fuck she wants all over Manhattan, this woman I'm watching now is quiet. Subdued. Wearing one of those matching sweat outfits in black with white trim, the word PINK scrawled across her very fine ass in glittery sequins. She blends right in on the plane, looks like every other woman her age. Not like the rich-as-fuck heiress she really is.

When she first boarded her hood was up and she had sunglasses on, as if she were trying to conceal her identity, though really she looked obvious as hell, at least to me. The media is always after her, always on her tail, so her incognito mode shouldn't be a surprise.

But considering she's dressed nothing like her usual self, I figure she became comfortable and eventually tugged the hood down, revealing her long, golden-brown hair streaked with bright blond highlights pulled into a high ponytail.

Offering me a tantalizing view of her perfect profile.

Dainty nose, plump lips. Long eyelashes, high cheekbones, slightly pointed chin. Every time someone passes her by she lifts her head, then immediately looks down. Almost as if she's afraid someone is going to approach her.

Like she's worried someone will realize who she is.

But no one would. She's unrecognizable. I'd bet top dollar the only one on this plane who knows she's Lily Fowler is . . .

Me.

The moment the plane touches down I whip out my phone and switch it out of airplane mode, watching as a text message appears.

Did you find her?

I answer my client with a quick yes.

Are you watching her now?

I answer again in the affirmative, my gaze fixed on Lily as she, too, grabs her phone and starts to scroll through it.

Try and grab her laptop now.

Frowning at my phone, I contemplate how to reply. I can't just make a grab while we're still on the freaking plane and run. I have to be subtle about this. I warned my overeager, over-insistent client. I don't make rash decisions. I'm not impulsive, at least when it comes to work. There's a method to my madness, and acting like a goddamn thief isn't part of it.

I finally decide to answer.

I already informed you I'm not going to move too fast.

We don't have much time.

Slowly I shake my head, glancing up to study Lily before I start typing.

We have enough. I'll get the job done. Don't worry.

The plane starts to slow as we make our way to the gate and the passengers are getting restless, including myself. My legs are cramped up. Sitting in coach sucks ass and is almost too much for my six-foot-two frame. My knees fucking ache. Even Lily shifts and moves in her seat, her head turning to glance behind her, straight at me. Our gazes meet briefly and she looks away, pretending that she never saw me.

Anger burns in my gut. Anger and lust. An interesting combo, one I've never suffered through before while working. I pride myself on keeping my distance. Work is work. My personal life is just that . . . personal. Not that I have much of one. Not that I have anyone in my fucking life, which is just the way I like it.

But this girl's rejection, as brief as it was, digs at me. Pisses me off.

My phone dings and I check it.

She's fast. Tricky. You need to take your chances when you can.

A snort escapes me. Trying to tell me how to do my job. I wish I could reply with a big "fuck you," but I don't. I have more class than that.

I'm faster. Trickier. Trust me. I'll make it happen.

You'll get what you want.

As I slip my phone into the back pocket of my jeans, the flight attendant starts talking over the intercom, telling us to remain seated until the seat belt fastened lights turn off. We're at the gate; all the passengers are poised and ready to grab their shit and disembark. I don't bother. My carry-on is sitting in the compartment directly above me. I can tell that the lady next to me is dying to leap out of her seat, but I'll make her wait. Her irritation is already a palpable thing. Like I give a damn.

I gotta move slow. The last thing I need is to catch my subject's attention. Not this early in the game.

Lily jumps to her feet the second the seat belt light shuts off, popping open the overhead compartment and pulling out a bag. A laptop bag, from the size of it.

With the coveted laptop most likely lying inside.

I curl my fingers into my palms, resting them on my knees. I want that bag. No. Scratch that. My *client* wants that bag— more like what's inside of it. So I want it, too.

And I will do anything to get it.

Anything.

Chapter Two

Lily

I FELT HIM BEFORE I SAW HIM. HIS GAZE ON ME. ASSESSING. Watching. I let him look his fill, keeping my head bent, my eyes firmly locked on the magazine lying open on my propped thighs. It's ruining my chance to get an even tan, so I'll need to ditch the magazine soon, but for now, it's the perfect ruse.

Pretending to read while I look to my left to catch him staring. He doesn't realize I know yet. And he's good. No one would be wise to his covert spying.

But I am. I've been spied upon my entire life. The media has trailed after my sisters and me, my father, and my grandmother since I can remember. We're public figures, given accolades when we do something good and torn to shreds when we do something awful.

Well. Most everyone in my family does good. I'm the something-awful one. I do stupid things on a regular basis. I should know better by now but then again, why give up my reputation? I've worked hard putting it together since I was in my early teens. Besides, it's the perfect front.

After all these years of being such a publicly mocked figure, I know when someone's got his eyes on me. It's like a sixth sense or something. And when I know people are watching, sometimes I put on a show. On rare occasions, I confront them and send 'em running—or snapping away with their cameras so they can capture me enraged with headlines like "Lily Fowler's Lost It Again!"

Bastards.

Most of the time, I pretend I don't know they exist. I act like I'm blissfully unaware some shitty photographer is ready to snap a picture of me sunbathing topless (yep, that's happened more than once) or about to kiss and grope a guy at a nightclub (that's happened, too).

This guy, though . . . he's not giving me the paparazzi vibe. He's probably older than me, but not beyond thirty. His hair is dark. Cropped fairly close on the sides though a little longish on top, with a slight wave. An alluring wave that softens all those hard, harsh lines. His jaw is firm, his expression like stone, and his lips . . . they look like they might be soft as well, but he's too far away to get a good look. Sunglasses hide his eyes, but I don't need to see them.

I can still feel them on me.

He's wearing black swim trunks with a subtle white tropical print and nothing else, sitting on a large white towel from the hotel on the scorching-hot sand, his knees bent, his looped arms resting on them, acting like he doesn't have a care in the world. His shoulders are broad, his body trim and fit. A young couple go running by him, chasing each other like they're little kids and kicking up sand as they pass and he makes a tiny grimace every time, but otherwise, no reaction. He's alone. There's no other towel beside the one he's sitting on. No woman asking him to put more sunscreen on her shoulders, no friends hanging out with him.

Weird.

Could he be a photographer? Part of the paparazzi? I recognize a lot of them by now, so I doubt it. Unless he was sent as a ruse to trick me, but damn it, I'm pretty untrickable by now.

Besides, I look nothing like my usual self, so I doubt I'm being followed. The Lily Fowler party-girl persona is back in New York where I left her a few days ago. I of course had to book my flight under my real name, but the airlines don't release that information to freaking reporters, so ha ha on them.

The minute I stepped off the plane yesterday and felt the warm air caress my skin, I took a deep, cleansing breath and felt like I'd shed my armor. Here on Maui, I am nothing but a simple girl on vacation. No makeup, no flashy jewelry, no expensive clothing, no guys trying to get in my panties, no girls trying to be my friend in the hopes I'll make them popular. I left the trappings behind, like a snake shedding its skin.

Reborn. Fresh and unsoiled.

My thoughts almost make me laugh. In fact, a giggle escapes me and I press my fingers to my lips, suppressing it. "Unsoiled," that's a joke. I gave up the goods long, long ago in the hopes that I'd find someone to love me. My beautiful mother loved me with all her heart, or so she claimed.

But she didn't love me or my sisters enough to keep herself alive. She'd chosen to be dead rather than raise her children. And that hurt. Daddy didn't love me anymore, if he ever did. I became a burden. All three of his daughters did. We were just reminders that he had a wife and she left him in the cruelest way possible.

Instead of seeking love and approval from my family, I sought it in other ways. Boys. Partying. Alcohol. Drugs. By the time I got my shit together and was ready to do right by the world? No one cared. They still saw me as Lily the party girl. So I decided to give them what they wanted and kept it up. Why disappoint them?

Glancing out of the corner of my eye, I see he's still watching me, though he averts his head quickly when I look his way. *Hmm. Interesting.* Could he be just a regular guy on vacation who thinks I'm pretty? He's alone, I'm alone; it would make sense that maybe we could get together. The resort we're at does cater to singles and young couples . . .

Huh. I doubt it. He's too good-looking to be out trolling for a woman, unless he's a complete creeper, which he might be. Is he the type who goes on vacation by himself to pick up a woman? That seems like a lot of extra effort. And I'm not here on vacation. I'm on the run. In hiding. Just for a little bit. I pissed off the wrong people—or person; I'm not sure who all knows what I did. So rather than face my problems head on, I got the hell out of Manhattan, stat.

Grabbing my cell, I go online and check that stupid fashion-and-beauty blog that seems so fascinated with my life as well as my sisters'. I want to make sure they're not talking about me. The last mention of Lily Fowler was two days ago, a photo of me with hot-pink lips, heavily mascaraed eyes, and a black lace dress, supposedly representing Fleur at a stupid party for . . . something. I'd forgotten exactly what. When I'd entered my apartment late that night and found it ransacked, I freaked. Nothing was stolen. No jewelry, no money, and I had both on hand, stashed away in my closet but not under lock and key.

The one thing I had hidden, though, was my laptop, and I breathed a sigh of relief when I found it, stashed among a stack of folded bath towels in my hall closet. Then I threw a bunch of clothes into a small suitcase, booked a flight from my phone on the cab ride to the airport, and got the hell out of there.

My phone vibrates in my hands, startling me, and I check my texts, see that it's a message from my little sister, Rose.

Call me right now!

Yikes. Can't do that. I trust no one at this moment. Not even Rose, and I adore her, but what if she can't keep her mouth shut? She could slip up and tell our father she spoke to me. The wrong person finds out where I am and it's toast time.

I can't take any chances.

So I ignore her text, shoving my phone into my beach bag before I sink back into the overstuffed lounger I'm sitting on. I rented a cabana first thing this morning and it's freaking perfect. I get endless service, someone is always checking on me to make sure I have enough to drink or eat, and the view is spectacular. The sun is blazing, there are white, puffy clouds in the startling blue sky, and a breeze brushes over me every few minutes, cooling my heated skin.

Paradise.

My gaze slides toward my watcher, who's also a part of the spectacular view. The more I stare, the sexier I find him. His shoulders and chest are so wide. There's the lightest smattering of dark hair between his pecs and while I usually go for the smooth look, there's something about the hair on his chest that appeals. Makes him look so manly. And for whatever reason, makes him appear a little dangerous.

Or maybe that's the air around him. There's an edge to him that I can't explain. He looks completely unapproachable, his expression like granite; his position is casual, but I can see all that energy contained within his posture. Like he's poised and ready to spring into action at any given moment.

I avert my head, my thoughts filled with . . . him. I'm not usually attracted to dangerous. I like easy. Fun. Good-looking and confident, even a hint of arrogance. The men I've been with are similar to me. Or the me I want everyone to see. Looking for a good time, always ready to party, to shop, wanting everyone's eyes on me.

My phone buzzes again and I check my messages, see that it's another text from Rose.

You can't avoid me forever! At least tell me where you are.

I study her message, my fingers poised above the keyboard. I want to tell her but I can't. No way. She's bound and determined to get me to respond to her and I'm just as bound and determined to ignore her.

It's not that I want to. My heart, my entire body, aches to call her, hear her voice, ask if she's okay. She's pregnant. My baby sister, the one who I resented when she was born because she took up even more of our mom's attention, is now going to have a baby herself. With a guy I went to high school with. A guy I might've kissed—and doesn't that make me feel like a complete slut—but if it doesn't bother Rose then it doesn't bother me. She's so blissfully in love with Caden, it's almost disgusting.

Just about as disgusting as when my sister Violet and her fiancé, Ryder, are together. Those two are just . . . *ugh*. I blame it all on him. Ryder exudes confidence. Sex appeal. I can see why my sister was so attracted to him, though it surprises me that the two of them *are* together. He seems more my speed, but then she spilled a couple of secrets one night after having a few too many glasses of wine. How dominant Ryder is in the bedroom.

Yeah. That sort of thing doesn't do it for me. I like to be in charge. Everything else in my life has felt so out of control, ever since I was a little kid and I lost my mom. As I grew older, I realized the only thing I can control is myself. My body. My mind. My choices.

So I'm in control, especially sexually. Forget all that growly *I will make you mine* dom shit. That sort of thing makes me roll my eyes. I mean really, who gets off on that? Maybe I haven't met the right guy, but come on.

Grabbing my boozy tropical drink, I wrap my lips around the straw and drain it, casting my gaze along the beach, watching the waves splash gently onto the shore. I want to swim. I want to feel the water swirl around my legs as I slowly walk into the ocean. I can leave my stuff here. I know it's safe. The hotel employees keep a close eye on everything, but what if my watcher is fast? What if he really is part of the paparazzi and he's just waiting for the chance to go rifling through my bag? Not that there's much in there beyond my phone . . .

And my phone is everything to me. It's password protected but if someone is determined, he could probably figure it out. I can't risk it. At least my laptop is safe, hidden in the bungalow I'm staying in at the resort, in the deep, dark recesses of my closet, sitting on the top shelf. No one would find it there.

I set my drink on the table next to me and rest my index finger against my lips, tapping them as I contemplate my next move. I don't feel my watcher's eyes on me and when I glance in his direction, I see that he's gone. Even his towel isn't there any longer, which means he's moved on.

Good. That's for the best. I don't need to worry about some weird guy staring at me. I have more important things to concentrate on.

Stretching my legs out, I swing them to the side of the chair and stand, resting my hands on my hips as I first look left, then right. No watcher to be seen. Where could he have gone in that quick amount of time? I didn't even hear him leave, so what is he? Stealth?

I'm probably worrying for nothing. He's just some player who liked the way I looked or whatever. I'm too paranoid after what happened. Hacking into someone else's life and messing with her personal shit has a way of making me feel uneasy, yet that doesn't seem to stop me. I'm doing something I shouldn't, so I tend to think everyone else is up to no good as well.

Shaking my head, I start for the water, the sand warm on the soles of my feet. A group of kids are to my right, splashing and playing along the shoreline, their hands full of colorful plastic buckets and shovels. A couple is standing waist deep in the water, the waves crashing against them, pushing them into each other's arms, and they laugh.

My heart pangs but I ignore it. I don't believe in love or couples or dating or any of that crap. Love is for fools. Despite my sisters' blissed-out lives, and their steadfast belief I can find the same, I know that's not for me.

No way would I allow anyone to get too close. Hand him the power to hurt me. And I refuse to give that up.

I walk straight into the cold water, shivering as it hits my ankles. My calves. My knees. Despite the heat of the sun and the hot sand, the water is freezing, but I don't care. I'm belly-button deep now and I bend my knees, dunking myself to my shoulders and giving a little yelp when the cold water wraps itself around me.

The rhythmic waves push me out a little farther and I fall backward into the water until I'm floating, the sun warming my face, the water swirling around my head. I can taste the salty tang of the ocean and I close my eyes, spread my arms out, and splash my fingers in the water. It feels good. Peaceful.

Until a massive wave comes out of nowhere, sending me straight underwater and slamming me into the bottom. I reach out to try and brace my fall, my hands scraping along the rocky shore, and feel a particularly sharp rock slice across my palm. The pain is excruciating and I kick away from the ground, trying to push myself above water, but another wave slams into me, sending me rolling.

Water shoots up my nose and into my mouth and I close my eyes, struggling against the waves. I want to call out. I want to throw my hands above the water and signal to someone, anyone, that I'm probably fucking drowning here, but it's no use.

I can't do it.

Another wave hits me, though this one isn't as powerful, and it sucks me farther out to sea, making me roll and tumble like I'm a ball in the wind. I kick hard, my foot hitting the bottom of the ocean, and it gives me the leverage I need, propelling me forward. I open my eyes, I can see the water above me, the light shining down upon it from the sun, and I kick even harder, determination urging me on.

Strong arms wrap around my middle, dragging me above water, and when my head pops out I take a deep breath, only to immediately start coughing. The arms are like steel bands around my stomach, firm but not too tight, as if my rescuer is aware if he squeezes me too much I'll start coughing even more. I can feel his warm, hard chest against my back as he drags me back to shore, and I drop my arm against his, clutching on to him, afraid he's going to let me go.

"You all right, princess?" His voice rasps against my ear, deep and rumbly and with a hint of a Southern accent. Despite my fear, the exhaustion, the sudden and complete pain I feel radiating from the palm of my hand, my entire body tingles at the sound of his voice.

I nod, my teeth chattering, the adrenaline and terror over what I've just experienced combining to send me possibly into shock. My rescuer readjusts his arm around my waist, his hand splayed across my bare stomach, and I glance down to study his thick, muscular forearm. His skin is golden, covered with a smattering of dark hair, and his hand . . . his hand is huge. It practically covers my entire belly, and I'm no skinny little twig.

His fingers seem to caress my skin and the air whooshes out of my lungs, making me dizzy. I let go of his arm, holding my hand out, palm up, and that's when I see it. The jagged cut open across my palm, the blood flowing freely from it.

Oh crap. That's bad.

"You're hurt." He notices the cut, too, and that seems to spur him into action. He moves faster and I go limp, overwhelmed at the sight of the cut, the blood, the pain that radiates from my palm all the way up my arm. "We need to find you help."

"I—I thought you were my help." My voice comes out a breathless rasp and I swallow hard, wincing at the pain that follows. I took in too much salt water and my throat aches, my nose burns.

"Medical help," he says gruffly as we emerge from the water.

I turn my head to the side, trying to catch a glimpse of my rescuer, but he's so tall and my neck hurts. He glances down, his eyes going wide when he sees that I'm looking at him. Shock courses through me and I part my lips, the words that follow scratchy, making my throat ache.

"It's you." Him. My watcher has turned into my rescuer.

"Hey!" I look away from him to see a hotel employee running toward us, his expression one of pure panic, and my last thought before my body goes weak and my head blanks is that he doesn't look like much help at all.

Chapter Three

Max

HOLY HELL, SHE FAINTED ON ME.

Of course, I can't blame her. One minute she was fine—beyond fine if I'm being truthful—walking along the sand, her hips swaying in some sort of feminine magical way that had me entranced, her hands going to that perfect ass as she slipped her fingers beneath her bikini bottom and tugged, as if that could help the minuscule scrap of fabric cover all that bared skin.

No, more like those fingers fueled all sorts of sordid fantasies that had my cock twitching. Of me being the one slipping my fingers beneath her bikini so I can touch nothing but warm, smooth skin. Moving a little bit farther and encountering nothing but hot, wet skin. Skin that would taste fucking unbelievable as I licked her from front to back . . .

Yeah. Lily Fowler the non-party girl is like my every fantasy come to life. Who fucking knew? I watched her from where I switched locations, standing beneath a cluster of short palm trees, keeping an eye on her as she played in the water. Her hot-pink bikini doesn't cover much and her hair is up in a sloppy bun, showing off her neck and shoulders. Her breasts strain against the tiny triangle top and I won't even go on about her ass again, because I'm starting to sound like I'm obsessed.

Which I am.

Before I could blink, the waves pulled her under and she didn't pop back up quick enough for my satisfaction. Breaking into a run, I headed straight for the ocean and dove in, catching sight of her bright bikini in seconds. She struggled and fought against the water, as did I, and when I finally caught up with her, she was almost above water. I just helped her along the rest of the way.

This was the last thing I wanted to do. Rescue my subject. Make myself obvious. I didn't want an encounter with her yet. It was too soon in the game and I couldn't reveal myself.

But I couldn't let her die on my watch, either.

Everything wore her down, though. Taking on too much water, the lack of oxygen, the cut on her hand. And now she's sagging against me, unconscious. I lay her out on the sand carefully, the panicked hotel employee helping me before he grabs the radio clipped on the waistband of his shorts and calls in her location and injury.

"Do you know her? Is she with you?" he asks as his gaze meets mine over Lily's body.

I slowly shake my head. "I don't know who she is," I lie easily. "But she was at that cabana right over there a few minutes ago." I gesture toward the spot.

The guy looks over his shoulder at the cabana before turning back to face me. "Looks like her stuff is in there."

"Good. Maybe she has ID, too." I tilt my head to the side as I take her limp hand in mine and examine the cut across her palm. It's deep. Might need stitches. I streak my thumb across her fingers, careful not to touch her injury. "Or you could look up the name of the guest who rented the cabana."

"Yeah. Right. Good idea," the dumbass employee says as he blows out a harsh breath and stares out at the ocean. He looks like he doesn't even want to deal with her, let alone touch her.

So I do. I gently press my hand against the center of her chest, where I feel her steadily beating heart. My fingers brush the side of her breast and everything within me tightens. Her skin is chilled but soft, and so incredibly smooth. Her eyes are closed, long lashes resting against her skin like dark fans, and her full lips are parted as she breathes slow and steady. "Well, at least she's breathing," I say sarcastically as I reluctantly lift my hand away from her chest.

"Help is on the way." The guy sends me a sheepish look. "I've only worked here for a month. This is the first medical issue I've had to deal with. I'm not real good with this kind of thing."

No shit. "You got paramedics coming?"

"Yeah." He nods.

I glance down at Lily, my other hand still beneath her shoulder, propping her up. Slowly I extract my hand from under her body and gently lower her to the ground, studying her as she lies there on the warm sand, still as stone. She's fucking beautiful. Her breasts are full even though she's lying down and her legs are long. She smells amazing, even with the lingering scent of salt water clinging to her, and I'm filled with the sudden urge to touch her again. Press my lips against her skin.

I give myself a firm shake. *What the hell is wrong with me?*

"She's in good hands then," I say as I leap to my feet. I need to get the hell out of here. The hotel kid stares up at me, his mouth hanging open and his eyes wide. "I gotta go."

"You can't just leave her here with me," he starts, but I cut him off with a look.

"Isn't this your job? Besides, I don't know who she is," I remind him. "I'm just a good citizen who happened to rescue a total stranger."

"You probably saved her life," he points out. "She might want to thank you when she comes to."

I shrug. I need to be as good as gone when she comes to. She catches a glimpse of me and there will be questions. Questions I don't want to answer. And I've blown it enough today, ogling her like I did. "If she asks, tell her I'm glad she's okay."

"But I don't know if she really *is* okay. That gash on her hand is pretty bad."

And this kid who's supposedly on duty for the safety of hotel guests is also pretty bad. It's just a cut on her hand. Not like she's going to die. "It's not a life-or-death situation." I almost say the word *asshole* but restrain myself. I don't need to piss this kid off. "She'll be fine. A couple of stitches and she's good to go."

I take off before he can say another word, needing to get the hell out of there. The kid calls after me but I don't look back. Just keep my head bent and my feet moving, kicking up sand as I propel myself farther and farther away from the temptation that is Lily Fowler.

I don't even think she realizes who grabbed her out of the water. At least, I hope she doesn't. And that's how I need to keep it, because no way in hell do I want her to try and thank me or talk to me.

Not yet.

Bad enough I sat near her cabana earlier while I spied on her. I think she had me figured out after a while, so that's why I left. I didn't want to be too obvious, but damn it, I needed to get close.

More like I *wanted* to get close.

Swiping a hand across the back of my neck, I head for the hotel, practically stomping my feet in the hot sand. Never before have I let a woman affect me like this, especially on the job. I don't know why I react to her so strongly. I usually know how to play it cool and calm. I don't let anything get in the way of my job.

But one glance of Lily sitting on that lounger, her skin glistening in the sun, those big designer sunglasses concealing most of her face, adding an air of mystery to the intriguing puzzle that she already is, and I wanted to get closer. Just once.

You're a fucking idiot.

Yeah, can't deny that. I've done enough things in my life to more than prove that description as accurate.

My phone rings and I answer it, knowing exactly who it is on the other line.

"Where is she?"

I decide to offer up the truth. "Laid out on the sand, unconscious."

Loud laughter fills my ear and I pull my phone away so I don't have to listen to the brunt of it. "What, you already knocked her to the ground? You work fast."

"I don't abuse women," I mutter.

"That's too bad. A good smack might do her wonders."

Jesus. My client is a world-class, top-grade asshole.

"She almost *drowned*," I stress, glancing around to make sure no one's listening to me. This is a conversation best kept private, even one-sided.

"Yeah, well she probably deserved it, the little witch." More laughter. Disgust fills me. I don't like this woman. She's not nice. Not by a long shot. And I'm still confused over exactly why she wants me to follow freaking Lily Fowler around and grab that goddamned laptop, though my client claims it belongs to her. But I'm starting to wonder if that's a lie. And I wonder if Lily doesn't have something big on this woman.

Interesting thought, and not what I would consider far-fetched, either.

"Listen, it doesn't help, you calling or texting me every couple of hours, checking up on my ass," I mutter into the phone as I draw closer to the hotel grounds. I'm near the pool and it's loud. A little chaotic, what with the Hawaiian music playing overhead and guests milling about everywhere. I need to get the hell out of here and back to my hotel room so I don't have to deal with this shit. Lily Fowler will be laid up for at least a few hours, so I should probably try and grab a nap.

"If I'm not checking up on you, who will? I paid you a lot of money to get this job done and done fast," she reminds me. "It's my right to call or text you whenever I want."

"Yeah, well, you're messing with my strategy. I'll report in once a day, got that?" I'm not going to let this woman boss me around. She may have paid me a fat chunk of change that made taking the challenging job more than worth it, but I'm still in charge of my own fucking business.

"Not good enough," she says with a dark finality that I can't help but admire, at least momentarily. This woman has balls, I'll give her that. "Twice a day. Once in the morning, once at night."

Hell. I scrub my hand across my face. "Deal," I tell her. "Want your report now or later?"

"Now." She sounds eager. "Tell me how she ended up unconscious. I want every dirty detail." She also sounds downright gleeful at the thought of Lily being hurt.

So I give her everything as requested, from my watching Lily while she lazed around in her cabana and drank two alcoholic beverages before noon, right down to her fainting in my arms and me leaving her with the scared hotel employee while they waited for a medic to arrive.

"So you just left her there?" she asks after I finish.

"What was I supposed to do? Introduce myself and let her know I work for you?"

She gasps. "My God, *no.* That would be a disaster. Bad enough that she ruins everything she puts her filthy hands on."

I have no idea what she's talking about and I don't ask. "I'll check in on her later. Ask around and make sure she's all right." Someone will tell me. I bet even the guy I left her with would let me know what's up if I found him.

"You do that," she says distractedly, and I can tell she could give two shits whether Lily is all right or not. *What a bitch.*

"I'll call you later tonight and fill you in on what's going on,"

I continue, not wanting to but hell, I have to. She's not giving me a choice.

"May I ask you a question?"

"Of course." I'm standing on the edge of the pool area with my back to it, facing the ocean. The sun is hot on my skin; my swim trunks are almost dry even though I'd dived into the ocean only a few minutes ago. I crave a beer and a burger to go along with it. I'm trapped in fucking paradise, waiting for some shrew to read me the riot act.

And it sucks.

"When exactly are you going to make your move?"

I frown. "Make my move? What are you talking about?"

"When are you going to get her laptop? That's the entire reason for you being there, you know. I'm not paying you to have a nice little Hawaiian vacation. You have a job to do," she reminds me ever so kindly.

"I know I have a job to do," I say, my voice tight. "And like I said only a couple of minutes ago, you need to trust me and let me *do* it. This isn't a smash-and-grab job. I have to work my way up to it." I'll need to earn Lily's trust. And then go in for the laptop. It's the only way.

"We're running out of time, Mr. Coleman." I really don't like it when she calls me that and I think she knows it. "Every minute that passes is another minute wasted."

"Ma'am, we only just arrived yesterday. She hasn't even been on this damn island for twenty-four hours yet," I say, my voice firm. I'm not going to explain myself and she needs to realize that. "Let me do my fucking job."

Another gasp. Like I could shock her with my language. *Give me a break.* "Don't give me that *ma'am* shit. We're practically the same age."

Christ. So that's what gets to her? And I'd bet money she's a solid ten years older than me. "I'm trying to be respectful." My mama raised me right, but this woman . . . she makes it hard to show her even an ounce of respect. "You'll hear from me later tonight," I tell her just before I end the call.

I swear I hear her sputter in protest right before the phone goes silent, and I wait for a return call or text but nothing comes.

Thank God.

I go back to my hotel room and order room service, a hamburger and a boatload of fries along with a beer. With a thirty-minute wait ahead of me, I kick back on the bed and scroll through the photos on my phone.

The photos I snapped of Lily.

There are a few covert shots of her on the plane. The photos are bad. Out of focus, quickly taken in the hopes no one would notice me. I tap my phone's screen and zoom in on her profile, studying it. The slant of her forehead, the shape of her nose, those sexy full lips. She looks on edge, a little nervous.

Vulnerable.

I swipe my finger again and again, passing through the photos, stopping at the one I caught of her in her cabana. She's sitting up, staring out at the ocean. Her lips are parted, the giant sunglasses she's wearing shading most of her pretty face, her shoulders straight, the strings of her bright pink bikini curling around her neck. I zoom in on this photo, too, checking out her breasts like some sort of pervert, admiring how they strain against the triangles of her top. My skin tightens, my dick twitches, and everything within me goes hot.

Shit.

Tossing my phone onto the bed, I run a hand through my hair, irritated. I need to get over this . . . woman. She's a distraction. I have a job to do. I can't afford to let lust get in the way of it. My client . . . she's a bitch on wheels. She'd have zero qualms about ruining me if I fail in my mission. She basically told me so when we first met. She'd tried to flirt and when I didn't respond, she went cold as ice.

A total viper.

Not that I'd let this woman scare me, but . . . *fuck*. I don't want to risk it. I need this job. I've lost everything once already. I threw my military career away all because of my fucked-up issues. I can't afford to do something like that again.

I grab my phone once more and look at the last photo I took of Lily. Of her walking down the beach, headed into the water. Her hair blows in the breeze like golden silk. She's wearing hardly anything and I can't help but admire the graceful curve of her back, the perfection of her ass. Pert and round, each cheek an ample handful. Within days, that ass will be mine.

Just not in the way I really want it to be.

Chapter Four

Lily

"W<small>ELL, WELL, YOU'RE ALIVE</small>," <small>ROSE GREETS ME, SOUNDING</small> extra grumpy. "I hope you know I've been worried sick. In fact—"

I cut her off before she can get another word in. "I need you to promise you won't tell anyone that you talked to me."

She pauses, and I can hear her suck in a harsh breath. "Why?"

"No questions. Promise me, Rose." My voice is as firm as my resolve. If she can't promise, I'm ending this call. And I won't call her again until I'm back in Manhattan.

Not sure when that's going to happen, though.

"I can't tell Violet?" she asks. "She's worried, too. I don't want to keep secrets from her."

"Especially not Violet." She'd have no problem continually calling me, wearing me down until I have to answer. And then she'd most likely heap on the guilt, and that's the last thing I want to deal with. "No one else can know where I am."

"But why? Are you in hiding or what? The gossip sites have been wondering where you've disappeared to." Another pause. "And what about Caden? I tell him everything. He's the last person I can keep a secret from."

I want to roll my eyes but don't. Besides, the effort would be wasted because no one can see me. Of course she tells her husband everything. They're so close, so madly in love and wrapped up in their own little world.

And I'm all alone in my hotel suite, my hand patched up and wrapped tightly, a little high on pain medication. Talk about a shitty start to my so-called vacation. "Not even Caden. I'm trusting you, baby sister. Only you, so I need you to promise."

"Fine." She sighs, sounding completely put out. "I promise." Her voice is small and I feel a twinge of guilt for putting her through this.

But then I push right past it.

"Okay, good. I'm calling to let you know I'm all right. I got your texts and I know you were worried but I swear, everything's fine. I'll be home soon," I tell her in a rush of words.

I can't admit the real reason I called her. That I was scared when I came to after I passed out—something I don't really remember even doing—and found myself lying on the beach, two medics hovering above me and checking my pulse, cleaning my wound and making me yelp in pain. I was so disoriented and scared and I had no one. Absolutely no one to stand by my side and reassure me that everything was going to be all right.

I was alone. I didn't even have my mystery rescuer to help me out. He'd ditched me the minute I passed out, I guess. The hotel employee didn't catch his name; he had no idea who he was and neither did I.

They put me in an ambulance and took me to a nearby hospital despite my weak protests. Luckily I didn't need stitches, just a few butterfly bandages to keep the gash closed and my hand wrapped in white gauze and a weird fishnet-looking covering that kept everything in place. They put me on antibiotics and pain meds, filling the prescriptions right there in the hospital pharmacy before they sent me on my merry way.

It had been a terrifying experience. So horribly *real*, when I rarely, if ever, have to deal with the real world. It's as if I've lived my entire life playing pretend and when shit finally got ugly and

I couldn't run, as per my usual mode of operation, I didn't know how to handle it.

That's why I reached out to Rose. I needed to hear her voice, needed her to ground me and remind me that I *do* have someone I can count on.

And right now that person is also super pissed at me.

"You're damn right I was worried. I know you've done this sort of thing before, just . . . taking off on a whim and not telling anyone, but you haven't answered my texts for *days*," she says, stressing the last word.

I hold in the sigh that wants to escape. She's exaggerating, something she's really good at. "It's only been a couple of days," I point out.

"It felt like longer. I *cried* last night, Lily. I didn't know where you were, my hormones are all over the place and Caden held me, trying his best to console me while I cried over you."

And I thought Violet would lay on the guilt. "You're not even an official mother yet and look at you. Making me feel like shit for not contacting you sooner."

"I *am* an official mother, even if this baby isn't born yet," she says with a huff. "So yeah. If I want to make you feel guilty, I have every right to do so. And just to let you know, Violet's been beside herself, too. I can't believe you won't let me tell her you called."

"You absolutely cannot tell her," I reiterate, my voice firm. I'm going all mean-big-sister on her and I don't care. I have to protect myself. "She might mistakenly tell Daddy, and then the shit would really hit the fan."

"What does it matter if he knows? What's he going to do? Demand you come back home? You're a grown woman—you can do whatever you want."

Yeah, all while spending Daddy's money. Well, it's my money, too. All three of us have our own trusts, but at least Violet works for Fleur. And Rose used to. Not me, though. I'm the lazy sister.

"Maybe," I say, my voice faltering. He's not the one I'm worried about finding out where I am.

It's Pilar that I'm hiding from. And I can't tell Rose that. Then she'll start asking questions. Questions I can't answer.

Correction: more like questions I don't *want* to answer.

"Are you at least going to tell me where you are?" she asks softly. "And when exactly are you coming back home?"

"It's best you don't know. And I'm not sure." I lean my head back into the pillows and close my eyes, exhaustion settling over me. Maybe it's the pain meds or the antibiotics. Maybe it's the scary adrenaline-filled rush I went through from the day's events. All I know is that I'm suddenly overwhelmed with the need to take a long nap.

"Oh, come on! Why are you being so mysterious?" Rose is yelling. And she never yells, not really.

"Rose, it's . . ." I can't tell her what I did. Hacking into someone else's life and then trying to mess with it. And I'm not just talking about Pilar, either—there are other people involved, not just her. "It's complicated," I say lamely, bracing myself for another outburst.

But one doesn't come.

I remember the last conversation I had on the phone and how much it freaked me out and spurred me into action. The minute I hung up I grabbed my suitcase and threw in my clothes, booked my ticket to Maui and got the hell out of there. I was scared. When I think about it, I'm still scared. I want to tell Daddy what I found but I'm afraid he won't believe me. I'm the little girl who cried wolf one too many times in his eyes. He'd believe whatever that slut Pilar had to tell him before he'd consider listening to me.

"I know we all have our secrets," Rose says, sounding much calmer. "We all have something to hide. The longer you hide those secrets, though, the more they'll consume you. And eventually strangle you."

I remain quiet, absorbing her words. Since when did my baby sister become so wise?

"Just think about that. I'm always here for you. Whenever you're ready to talk, I'll be ready to listen," she says.

Tears threaten and I squeeze my eyes shut harder, willing them to retreat. I refuse to cry. I'm not a crier; I never have been. I laugh away my pain. It's easier that way.

"Thank you," I whisper, my voice raspy, and I swallow hard. I wish I could tell her. But not yet. If I say something now, I could be crying wolf again. This could all fizzle out and be forgotten.

Probably not. But stranger things have happened.

"Lily, please . . ." Her voice drops and I know she's dying for me to say something, reveal a little piece of *anything* so her curiosity is appeased. I know she worries.

I shake my head and sniff. "Don't push, Rosie."

She practically growls when I call her that and I start to laugh. "You're so stubborn," she mutters.

"Takes one to know one," I throw back at her, and we both start to laugh. I'm so thankful for the change in conversation she has no idea.

"Tell me how you're feeling," I say before she can try and get something else out of me.

"I'm fine. Just sick of feeling nauseous. This baby is mean."

"Sure. You're going to love and spoil that baby so much when he or she is born," I remind her, relieved that we're talking about the baby. My chest warms and the tears fade. I'm filled with a sense of peace at the thought of becoming an aunt in the near future.

A baby to hold and love—and then hand back to Rose when the little munchkin starts fussing or becomes stinky. It's the perfect situation. I can love on a baby but it's not *my* baby.

"I think it's a boy." Rose's voice drops lower. "I hope it is. I want a sweet baby boy who's handsome like his daddy."

"Gag," I tell her, making her giggle. "Get over your man. He's just all right."

"Whatever, you jealous hag."

She's teasing me. We've called each other far worse, but there's something about her words that hurts. Cuts me straight across the heart.

Maybe because what she's saying isn't too far from the truth.

"I didn't know getting married would turn you into such a bitch," I jab right back.

"Please. You'd better clean that potty mouth before your nephew is born. I'll have to bust out the swear jar," she threatens. "Between you and Caden, the child's ears will burn from all the cursing."

"Give me a break. You're no saint."

We continue on like this for another ten minutes and it feels good. Normal. I don't feel so lonely, holed up in my hotel room in the middle of a tropical island, hopped up on pain medication and depressed.

The phone call comes to a halt when Caden arrives home, though. I can hear his deep voice, hear him ask how she's feeling, and then everything becomes muffled because he's kissing her. He's kissing her and she's enjoying every minute of it and I can hear their little murmurs of love and my heart lurches. It feels like it's going to leap out of my chest and run off in a jealous rage, which is the stupidest thing ever, but there you have it.

Long after we hang up, long after I take another dose of pain meds and crawl into bed in nothing but my panties, wincing when I try and pull up the comforter with my injured hand like an idiot, I stare at the ceiling and ponder over all the mistakes I've made in my life so far. There are a lot of them. A ton.

And I wonder if I can ever find even a glimmer of what my sisters have.

Chapter Five

Max

SHE'S AT THE POOL.

That long, sleek body is stretched out like an offering to the sun. Mirrored aviators cover her eyes, which should look ridiculous on her but somehow she makes them sexy.

Lily Fowler has a way of making everything sexy.

She's completely on display, surrounded by people and not hiding in her private cabana like yesterday, allowing me to watch her blatantly. Her hand is wrapped from her mishap in the ocean, and I'm glad to see she doesn't look too banged up. Considering what she went through, I figured there would be a few bruises and scrapes, but I don't see a mark on her beyond the wrapped hand.

In other words, she's fucking flawless.

There's so much skin on display, I don't know where to look first. The bikini she's wearing is a joke, a strapless scrap of brightly covered fabric that barely contains her full breasts. Her dark blond hair is piled on top of her head in a messy topknot, loose, silky strands teasing her elegant neck, the smooth slope of her shoulders on display, her skin turning golden from the sun. She shifts her legs, drawing my attention, making me wish I were sitting right next to her, touching her . . .

Memories from yesterday hit me like rapid fire. Diving into the ocean after her without thought, without concern that she'll figure out who I am. A risky move, it reminds me now of how I used to be when I was in the military. How that abrupt, spontaneous behavior got me into trouble more times than I can count. Most of the time those moments worked out, but when they didn't . . .

I failed spectacularly.

But seeing her tumble in the waves like a rag doll, her arms and legs flailing, the look of pure panic on her face, I knew I was doing the right thing by going in after her. Somehow I fought against the waves and grabbed her, pulling her above the surface in seconds. I'd been fucking grateful to hear that first big gasp of air, just before she started to cough.

Scary, but at the same time the entire experience had been exhilarating. I might have saved her life. It wasn't the first life I've saved but it felt damn good to come to her rescue, and I hadn't rescued anyone in a long time. What if I hadn't seen her? What if I hadn't got to her in time?

She could have drowned.

Once the terror and adrenaline had lessened its hold on me, I realized just how soft she felt in my arms. I pressed my hand and splayed my fingers on her trembling stomach and couldn't help but notice the way her curves nestled perfectly against me. And then she turned her head and saw my face. Looked right into my eyes and recognized me just before she fainted.

Big mistake on my part, letting her see me. Huge. She passed out within minutes of saying something, though, so she probably doesn't remember.

At least, I hope she doesn't remember. It's pointless to relive those moments from yesterday and worry about her reaction, because what's done is done. I can only hope it all works out in the end.

I try my best not to look at her but it's impossible. I'm drawn to her, and not just because she's my assignment. Feeling like this . . . letting my attraction to her distract me is risky. Stupid.

But I can't seem to help it.

Returning my gaze to her, I watch as she lifts her arms to grip the back of the lounger, the position thrusting out her chest. I can see her nipples pressing against the thin fabric that covers them and I swear my mouth is watering. The way she's sitting, she's going for the bored look but she seems restless. Uneasy. I wonder what's bothering her.

I'd love to go to her but there's no way that I can. Not yet. Hell, it's like I can't even move. All I can do is stare.

She's so fucking beautiful it almost hurts to look at her. Her nonchalant pose isn't working. Her entire body is tense. She's on high alert. Why? What has her so on edge? She's on the run, so maybe it's getting to her. The relaxing setting of this Hawaiian resort isn't doing its job. Maybe she feels the need to run some more.

Frowning, I rub the back of my neck, peering at her over my sunglasses, trying to ignore the uneasy feeling bleeding through me. My instincts are usually spot on and over the years, I've honed them. Learned to trust them. This girl . . . she's giving me a vibe and it's not a good one. She looks ready to make a run for it.

And I can't lose sight of her. Not now. It was a lucky break that my client knew Lily bought the plane ticket to Maui. How she did that, I'm still not sure, but I'm not one to ask questions when it's none of my business.

The late afternoon sun is intense and I grab the iced tea I ordered earlier, chugging most of it before I set the glass onto the small table beside me. A shadow falls across my legs and I glance up, my entire body going still when I see who's standing in front of my lounge chair.

Lily Fowler.

"You're my rescuer." The words come out a statement, not a question, and dread consumes me, makes me wish she would have never looked back, never seen me yesterday.

Did that incompetent kid tell her I was the one who rescued her? Probably not, considering Lily looked right at me before she passed out.

Shit.

When I don't say anything, she continues.

"I wanted to thank you," she says, her voice light and sweet, her eyes sparkling and friendly. She tilts her head to the side, a little smile curling her lips. I'm thankful her sunglasses are sitting on top of her head so I can really study her. Her eyes are clear, her cheeks are rosy from the sun, and she looks fucking gorgeous. Getting a testosterone spike is so not what I need right now. "For saving me," she adds.

Jesus. I need to say something. Not stare at her like some sort of tongue-tied asshole. I clear my throat. "Just doing what any other man would've done."

"Please. I'm not so sure about that." She rests her hands on her hips, smiling, then wincing when her wounded palm makes contact with her skin and the tie of her bikini bottoms. My gaze drops to that tie and the matching one on her other hip. Two tugs and I could have her mostly naked.

Not the right direction for my mind to stray.

I sit up straight, swinging my legs wide so I'm straddling the lounger. Her head drops, her lips parting slightly, and I wonder if she can feel it. The attraction that vibrates between us, like a living, breathing thing. My fingers literally itch to touch her again and I clench them into tight fists.

Jesus, get your shit together!

"Well, you're welcome. You're lucky I saw you," I say, hating how rough my voice sounds, how my temperature spikes at having her so close. This—attraction between us is strong.

"Of course you saw me. You're not only my rescuer, you're

my watcher, too." A delicate eyebrow lifts as she settles her sunglasses over her eyes, shielding herself from me. I can't help but be impressed with the way she calls me out.

The girl isn't timid, and I don't know if this is a good trait or not. It's probably half the reason she gets herself in so much trouble.

Who'd have known it would be such a damn turn-on?

"Not sure what you're talking about." Curling my lips, I lean back against the lounger once more, straightening out my legs and crossing my feet at the ankles like I plan on staying here a good long time. Playing dumb and enjoying her company far more than I should.

"Really. You *don't* know what I'm talking about?" She sounds skeptical.

I shrug. "Don't quite understand what you're getting at, either."

"Yesterday. On the beach. You were staring at me while I was in the cabana. Or maybe you don't remember?" The question is more like a challenge.

As if I could forget. "Can't a man admire a pretty girl when he sees one?" I smile sheepishly, going for the *oops, busted* look, and I see her expression soften the slightest bit.

Almost got her.

"Well." She clears her throat and stands up a little straighter, thrusting her chest out. *Damn*, the woman is going to kill me with that smokin'-hot body, I swear. "Now that we got the awkward part of the conversation out of the way, I want to thank you again for rescuing me. I got pulled under the water and started to panic and . . . I'm not sure what would've happened if you hadn't come along." The worry in her voice is blatant and tugs at something deep inside me. But I need to play it off, resisting the urge to wrap her up in my arms and clutch her tight.

"It's a good thing I did then, huh?" I offer a smile, a big one this time, not my usual style. I've spent far too much time walking around with a permanent scowl on my face and I swear the muscles in my cheeks are already trembling with exertion. "Glad I could help you."

"Can I ask you a question?" When I nod, she continues. "Why didn't you stick around? After I blacked out?" She crosses her arms in front of her, plumping up her breasts the slightest bit, offering me a glorious view of her cleavage. I try not to look, but it's damn difficult. "Didn't you want to make sure I was all right?"

"I knew you were in good hands." An exaggeration if there ever was one, since that kid who worked for the hotel was an utter failure.

"Really." Her gaze drops to my hands, which are currently resting on my stomach, fingers linked, pose casual. "Because I thought *your* hands were pretty good."

Her words stun me silent. Now I'm the one who feels tense, restless. Having her this close, listening to her lyrical voice, seeing the light sheen of sweat that coats her skin, inhaling the scent of her, heady and sweet . . .

Fuck. It's taking everything inside of me to keep from grabbing her and hauling her into my arms.

She's staring, looking like she's waiting for me to say something else, so I fill the silence. "Plus I had to leave."

Her arms drop to her sides and I swear she looks the slightest bit defeated. "Oh. Of course. Back to your wife?"

I glance at the empty lounger right next to mine. "No," I say slowly, wondering what she's getting at.

"Your girlfriend, then," she suggests, her tone flat. First she flirts, now she fishes.

"Don't have one of those either." I shake my head. She's not coy. Her bluntness is surprising, but then again, not. That she wants to see if I'm here with someone is . . . interesting.

And allows me an opportunity.

"So you're here alone."

"Yeah." I let my gaze trail over her, from the top of her head on down, lingering on the good bits, which there are plenty of, though she can't tell what with my sunglasses on. "How about you?"

She smiles. "I shouldn't admit shit to you."

I laugh, surprised again at her brutal honesty. "Smart move."

"Hey, I learned about stranger danger in elementary school." Her smile is blinding. Pretty, straight teeth flash at me for the briefest moment and I'm a little dazzled from the sight.

Keep your head on straight, asshole.

"Well, my name is Max." I sit up once more and hold out my hand to her.

She takes a tentative step forward and slips her hand into mine, the bandaged one. Despite the barrier, her touch is like an electrified jolt to my system, and I clasp her hand gently, not wanting to hurt her. "Lily," she offers softly.

I grin. Don't let go of her hand. "I guess this makes us not strangers anymore, huh, Lily?"

Her answering grin sends a surge of lust straight to my cock. She carefully extracts her hand from my hold. "I guess you're right."

"Care to join me?" I indicate the empty lounge chair next to me with a slight inclination of my head.

Her gaze shifts to the chair briefly before returning to mine. "I'm afraid I have to decline."

Say what?

"But it was great meeting you." She offers me a little wave before she starts to turn away. "Bye, Max."

I watch her retreat, my gaze dropping to her ass, watching the material of her bikini bottom rise and offer me a glimpse of her perfectly round, perfectly smooth cheeks. My hands itch to touch her there.

Touch her anywhere.

"See you around," I call after her, but she doesn't look back.

As if she knows I'm watching her, lusting after her, wishing I could have her, yet she can walk away so easily. Like I'm no big deal. Like I don't affect her whatsoever.

I think I might, though. And now that we've met, know each other's names, I'm not going to waste time. I need to make my next move.

Tonight.

Chapter Six

Lily

MY WATCHER GAVE UP WATCHING OVER ME.

I think.

Last night I ate dinner alone, in too much pain and too woozy from the medication I took to go out. Tonight, the thought of another lonely meal by myself in my room—yes, fine, it's a gorgeous bungalow with an amazing view of the ocean, but still—depressed the hell out of me. So I dressed up and decided to take myself out.

And couldn't find Max anywhere. I wandered the resort grounds, numerous couples walking hand-in-hand passing me by and making me envious.

Me. Envious of couples, of other people having someone to love. The girl who doesn't believe in relationships, who has a daddy complex because he's so selfish, is wishing she had someone, at least for tonight.

If my sisters were here, they'd be beside themselves in shock.

After searching around the resort for almost thirty minutes and about ready to give up, I accidentally stumbled upon a discreet nightclub tucked away behind one of the hotel towers. My earlier boredom evaporated the moment I saw the club and all the people milling about in front of it. I'd been so restless since the moment I walked away from Max, regret hitting me full blast when I went back to my bungalow. I knew I would go out looking for him tonight.

And most likely get myself into trouble.

Adults only, the sign reads by the club's door, the loud thumping bass of the music pounding from within the dark, cavernous room, the sound seeming to throb deep inside my body. Pausing at the door, I peek my head in and see that the place is full of people.

A man materializes in front of me, large and imposing, and I take a step back, craning my neck to look up at his face. He's huge, his face like an impenetrable mask, his mouth drawn into a thin line as he crosses his arms in front of his massive chest. His head is shaved, his skin dark, a sleeve of tattoos covers each arm, and he's wearing a tight black T-shirt that conforms perfectly to his muscular chest. I stare at him, at a loss for words. His eyes narrow as he glares at me.

"How old are you, sweetheart?" he grunts.

Okay, I can't remember the last time I was carded, but every club I hang out at in Manhattan knows who I am, so I'm surprised. "Old enough," I answer, lifting my chin and resting my hands on my hips. I probably look younger than I am, what with the lack of makeup on my lightly sunburned face and the simple bright pink cotton dress I'm wearing. It's not my usual style.

But I'm trying to deviate from my usual style while here on Maui. It's refreshing, not having to keep up the pretense.

The man looks me over, not in a creepy, sexual way, but in an assessing, I-don't-believe-you-at-all manner. He probably deals with fake IDs every night.

He flicks his head at me, the glare softening in his gaze. "Let me see your ID."

Slightly irritated, I reach into my tiny purse and pull out my identification card, handing it over to him. He takes it, staring at the card, his gaze lifting to take me in for a long, tension-filled moment before he resumes his study of my ID.

I shift on my feet, worry coursing through me. I hope he doesn't recognize my name. I'm here to avoid the Lily Fowler persona, not embrace it. Not that I think I'm that recognizable or whatever, but I'm trying to avoid the bullshit that comes with people knowing who I am.

"You can go in," he finally says as he offers my ID back to me. I take it from him and stuff it in my purse before I flash him a quick smile.

"Thank you," I toss over my shoulder as I enter the club. I blink against the darkness, my eyes adjusting slowly as I take everything in. I'm surrounded by people, the women scantily dressed and overly made up, the men clad in Hawaiian shirts or tank tops, many of them sporting fresh sunburns, their skin gleaming red against the flash of multicolored lights coming from the nearby dance floor.

I can feel the men's eyes on me as I walk past them, checking me out. I'm sure they see me as fresh meat. I knew the resort caters to the singles crowd versus families but I've seen nothing but couples since I arrived, save for my watcher.

Damn it, I still want to kick myself for leaving him like I did earlier. Why didn't I take him up on his offer? I could have sat on that empty lounge chair and talked to him. Flirted with him some more. He certainly is handsome, in that rugged, manly way that I don't normally find attractive. But I caught myself before taking it too far.

I stop at the edge of the thick crowd that surrounds the giant bar, standing on tiptoe to see just how deep the throng is. The club is hot. I'm dying of thirst and wouldn't mind getting my buzz on if I'm really going to stay here for a while, which I so am. It's not like I have any major plans. And unfortunately, I haven't spotted Max. Though I'd love to. Despite the warning bells clanging in my head, I'm half ready to go with my impulses.

How would one night of hot sex with a stranger hurt? I need to do something to take the edge off.

"Care for something to drink?"

Startled from my thoughts, I turn at the sound of the deep voice coming from behind me, ignoring the disappointment that settles in my stomach when I see that it's not Max. Of course it's not Max. He probably wouldn't frequent a club like this.

Would he?

This man, he's very attractive, in a slick, well-kept way. He looks a little older than me, mid to late thirties, with a confident smile and interest lighting his pale blue eyes.

"Are you offering?" I flash him a flirtatious smile, grateful for the attention, almost starved for it despite my reluctance to capitalize on my last name while I'm here. I was starting to feel invisible, and that flat-out never happens to me.

"You look like you could use a helping hand." He inclines his head to the right, toward the crowd clamoring for the two bartenders' attention. "I have the inside track."

I raise a brow. "Really? Friends with one of the bartenders?"

"Friends with the owner," he says, his smile growing with a shade of arrogance.

"Nice." I don't mind a little arrogance in a man. It usually means they're confident, and I find that attractive. "I'd appreciate the help, considering it looks like it would take about an hour for the bartenders to move through that crowd."

"They're faster than they look." He chuckles. "What would you like?"

"Hmm." I tap my finger against my lips, notice that his attention goes right to my mouth. He is definitely on the prowl. I'm not sure if he's my type, but a little flirting never hurt anyone. "I'm not sure."

"Do you have a preference? Something you like in particular?" He steps closer, his voice lowering as he reaches out and settles his hand on my bent elbow. I feel nothing at his nearness or his touch and I'm disappointed. I'd love to feel a spark, a zing, anything.

But there's only one man who seems to have my interest on this island and he's nowhere to be found.

"You choose." Though I don't usually like to give up control, when I first meet men, I know they love showing off in any way possible, including picking out something to drink for me. "Surprise me."

"All right. I will." He releases his hold on my elbow and offers his hand. "Russ."

"Lily." I take his hand and shake it, careful of my still-wrapped palm. Again, there's no spark, not even a pleasant buzz, and I struggle to keep my smile in place. I shouldn't get so hung up on a man who I clearly rejected only a few hours ago. It's my own damn fault I'm alone tonight, chatting up another guy I have zero interest in.

"Give me a few minutes. I'll be right back." Russ releases his hold on my hand, his gaze intense as it locks with mine. "Lily."

He leaves me standing there on the fringe of the crowd surrounding the bar and I glance around, searching for a face that I just can't find.

So stupid.

Within minutes Russ is bringing me a glass of white wine—not a lot of thought behind the choice, but I'm impressed enough by how quick he was so I can't complain. I take the glass from him with a coy smile and a murmured thanks, noticing how close he stands next to me, a beer bottle clasped in his hand.

"Have you been to this club before?" he asks, dipping his head so his mouth is close to my ear. Almost too close.

I take a step back. "This is my first time," I say just before I take a sip from my glass. The wine is almost bitter and I make a face. Did he buy me the cheapest shit they have or what?

"Ah, so you're a virgin." The sly smile he offers makes me laugh.

"Not quite," I say, making his eyebrows rise. "I haven't been called a virgin in a long time."

"Well, you're a virgin to Vice." He invades my space once more; his voice is low but I can still hear it above the din of the crowd. "And I'm looking forward to popping your Vice cherry."

Ew, gross. What the hell is he talking about? I shift to the side, giving us some breathing room. And I need it, what with how strong his cologne is. "What sort of club *is* this place?"

"Have you never heard of Vice?" When I shake my head, he continues. "It adheres to the meaning of its name quite closely, if you know what I mean. Your every immoral, wicked fantasy come true."

Oh. I try my best to keep my expression neutral because I don't want him to know I'm shocked. I've been to a few, hmm . . . alternative clubs in my past. I've never partaken in anything, though. More like I'm always an observer.

"Kinky," I say with a hint of laughter, making him chuckle as well.

"You're not shocked?" he asks just before he takes a sip from his beer.

"No. I had my suspicions, what with the name of the club and all," I say breezily. I'm really good at faking it when I need to. And right now? I'm totally faking it.

"So what's a beautiful woman like you doing in Maui all alone?" he asks, his voice casual, his gaze . . . predatory.

A shiver moves through me, and not the good kind.

And what is it with men being so surprised at a woman traveling alone? "I needed to get away." I don't say anything else. I've discovered over the years the less said, the better.

"From life?" He smirks. It's vaguely smarmy and I tell myself to knock it off. He's just being friendly. I'm making too big a deal over this.

"From stress." I smile and sip from my wine. It really is terrible, with that bitter aftertaste that still lingers in my mouth. I don't really want to finish it, but I also don't want to be rude.

"Ah." He nods, like he completely understands the need to get away from it all. "Stress. It's a killer."

"It is," I agree. "So can I ask you why you're in Maui all alone?" A pause. "You *are* here alone, aren't you?" If he's married and the wife is down at the beach or pool or whatever, I'm going to smack this asshole upside his arrogant head.

"I'm here on business." He chuckles when I send him a skeptical look. "A retreat of sorts. Training and meetings all morning, then fun in the sun during the afternoons."

"Nice. You must work for a great company."

"They're pretty good." He shrugs, looking ready to burst. I know he wants to tell me what he does for a living or who he works for. He's dying to show off.

"What do you do?" I ask, keeping my voice casual.

"I'm a real estate broker." His smile turns the slightest bit smarmy again. I can tell he's impressed with himself. *Ugh.* "In Beverly Hills."

"Ah." I look him over as discreetly as possible, not wanting him to think I'm interested. I note the perfectly cut light brown hair, the Tommy Bahama shirt, the fact that there's not even a single line or wrinkle in his face and I'd bet big money he's at least ten years older than me, maybe more. Probably uses Botox. And the Rolex on his wrist is ostentatious. Big and bold, with the face trimmed in diamonds.

Hmm. He may look designer, but I bet he doesn't have much cash in his bank account. Probably in debt to his eyeballs, trying to impress any and every silly woman he meets.

Like me.

"What do you do?" he asks as he rests his hand once more on my elbow, his fingers cupping my skin. When I send him a questioning look he clarifies, "For work."

"Oh. I'm, um, in computers." Not far from the truth. I am into computers. I just don't get paid for it, not usually.

Well, there were those few times back in my late teens when Daddy would cut me off financially. I'd end up doing some IT jobs for people, work one of my good friends from high school would find me. I'd also secretly do some sneaky hacking work, but those jobs were few and far between because I didn't want the trouble.

It's one thing to be a teenager and change up your friends' bad grades by hacking into the school's computer system. It's another thing entirely to fuck someone's life up by, say, depleting the person's bank account. Or forward that extra-sexy email from a mistress to the man's wife. I've had those sorts of requests more than once but I never took them. Not from strangers, and not for money.

Once I turned twenty-one and received my trust fund, I didn't have to worry about picking up odd jobs anymore. Now any hacking work I do is for fun.

Or revenge.

And that's what typically gets me into trouble.

"Beauty and brains, huh? Sounds like you're the full package." He runs his fingers down the length of my arm. My immediate instinct is to jerk away from his touch, but I don't. I shouldn't be so hung up on Max, especially since I'm the one who walked away from him. I need to focus on Russ. Pretend that he interests me.

Despite every instinct screaming inside of me to run away, I stay. I'll give him another chance. But if he does one more thing that creeps me out, I'm gone.

"Why do men always assume if a woman is attractive, she must be dumb?" I keep my voice light as I ask the question, but I can see the quick flash of anger in his eyes.

He looks offended. "I never said you were dumb."

"Ah, but you did say beauty *and* brains, as if you were surprised," I point out.

"Well, I have to admit, I *am* surprised. You really are the full package. Hot. Smart." He lets his gaze dip to my chest as he checks me out. Blatantly. The full-body disgusted shiver is hard to contain and I wonder if he notices.

Worse, I wonder if he thinks I'm shivering in anticipation. *Ick.*

I say nothing. I'm afraid if I open my mouth, I'll probably insult him and piss him off. Luckily enough, he continues on with the conversation.

"So where are you from?"

"The East Coast." I don't want to say anything else personal. The less information I give him, the better. Glancing at my glass, I decide I'm not going to drink anymore. I need to get out of here. This guy gives me the creeps.

"My, uh, ex-wife is from Connecticut," he offers, and I want to roll my eyes but don't. Of course he was married. Now that I'm studying him a bit closer, I can see he has that *I just got divorced and I'm on the hunt* look to him.

Probably has kids, too. Most likely he cheated on his wife or he was a total workaholic or a combination of both, and they ended up involved in a nasty divorce that resulted in a horrific custody battle. And now he's paying her alimony and child support through the nose, bitter every month as he writes out the check.

I've met his type before. They're all the same. Yet here I am getting mad at his generalizations and I'm doing the same exact thing to him. I need to get over myself.

"Hmm, how nice." I set my glass down on a nearby cocktail table and turn to smile at him. "It's been great talking to you, but I'm afraid I have to go."

"What's your hurry?" Russ grabs hold of my upper arm, his fingers pressing into my skin. It's a possessive hold that makes me uncomfortable, though I try my best to play it off.

"I've had a long day of too much sun. And I hurt myself yesterday, so I'm still dealing with that." I offer him a view of my bandaged hand but he doesn't even glance at it. His gaze is entirely focused on mine, his body looming over me, his expression serious. Too serious.

"I got you a drink," he reminds me.

I try to withdraw from his hold but he tightens his fingers. "And I thanked you for it."

"It's not like you have any other plans. You're here alone, right?" He glances around as if wanting to make sure no one's paying us any mind, and I'm sure no one is. The place is packed, the music loud. Everyone's in their own little world and I'm stuck with a creep who looks like he wants to maul me. And not in a good way, either.

"You should come back to my room with me," he suggests. "We could get to know each other better."

"I don't think so." This time, I get out of his hold and I step away, ready to bolt. But he's quick and he reaches out, locking his fingers around my arm again and jerking me toward him.

"Women like you are all the same," he says, his beer-laced breath hitting my face, and I wrinkle my nose. How much has he had to drink? Why did I talk to him anyway? Why do I always get myself into these awful situations? "You flirt, you give me the look, you force me to buy you a drink and then you won't put out."

"You think with a few words and a free drink I'll put out?" I try to jerk my arm out of his grip but it's no use. The guy is strong. "You're disgusting."

He leans in even closer, his mouth practically touching mine, and I lean my head back as far as I can. "What the hell did you think, coming to a club called Vice? Give me a break with the innocent act. It's a bunch of shit."

My mouth pops open, I'm about to hurl an insult, when I feel an ominous presence behind me.

"If you're smart—though I'm wagering you're not—I'd suggest you let her go before I rip your fucking fingers off."

I glance over my shoulder, my knees going weak when I see *him* standing there, tall and broad, wearing a white linen shirt in a sea of Hawaiian print, a stark contrast against his tanned skin.

It's my watcher.

Chapter Seven

Max

I FOLLOWED HER INTO THE CLUB, THOUGH SHE WASN'T AWARE I was tracking her. What a sight she was, too, in that hot-pink dress that fell to the tops of her thighs, the skirt swishing and swirling with that captivating walk of hers. The dress, while simple, showed a lot of flesh. Her shoulders, her back, all that sun-kissed skin on display and driving me out of my ever-lovin' mind. I couldn't stop staring.

More like, I didn't *want* to stop staring. The fact that she rejected me yesterday, leaving me in the dust without a backward glance, kind of pissed me off. It shouldn't, because the fact that I'm interacting with her, wanting to get closer to her, is risky. I need to get her laptop, but I can go about it in different ways.

Certainly don't need to flirt with her, that's for damn sure.

Lily's not very observant, though. I learned that quick enough. She seems fairly savvy in some ways yet she's completely oblivious in others. And that makes me worry for her safety.

For example, this dickwad has such a tight hold on her I can see his fingers pressing into her flesh. From the moment he approached her—which was seconds upon her arrival—I could tell he was no good. I stood on the other side of the bar in the shadows, observing their interactions, ready to spring into action if she needed me. Lily appeared distracted most of the time, as if she wanted to be anywhere but with that guy, not that I could blame her.

Has she ever frequented a club like this one before? Hell, I know I haven't. I didn't even know this place existed at the resort. Vice is unlike any club I've ever been to before and I'm intrigued. The moment I walked in, the vibe was overtly sexual. Women studied me with interest in their eyes as I passed by them. The music that filled the space had an incessant, primal beat. An energy hummed in the air, pumped in my blood, and I knew I could easily find a woman tonight if I wanted one.

And I do want one—Lily.

As fucked up as that is, it's the damn truth.

"Who the hell are you?" the guy asks, his nostrils flaring, eyes wide and filled with anger. He doesn't let her go and that infuriates me. Makes me want to smash his face in, but I need to show some sort of restraint.

"Doesn't matter to you. Just do as I say and let her go," I demand, my voice loud, causing more than a few people to turn and look in our direction. Reluctantly, he releases his hold on her and she springs away from him, absently rubbing her arm at the spot where he touched her. "Come here, Lily."

She hurries over to stand just behind me, never protesting my command, and I'm thankful. I don't want any trouble, but I feel like everywhere this girl goes, she's a walking, talking disaster. To keep her out of danger I'll have to put her under lock and key.

And why does that thought appeal so damn much?

"What, is she your bitch?" the man asks as he starts to laugh. I lunge for him, my hands gripping the front of his shirt, close to his collar, as I yank him up almost to his toes and thrust my face in his.

"Don't you ever call her that again, do you hear me? Or I'll fuck up that pretty little face of yours," I murmur, my voice low so only he can hear me.

He blinks up at me, the anger in his eyes turning to fear, and I let go of his shirt, pushing him away from me so he nearly stumbles and falls. He bumps into a small crowd of women and they all shout out in protest, calling him names as he scrambles to his feet and takes off, the women's laughter trailing after him.

I turn to Lily, about to ask her if she's all right, but I find her gaping at me, a shocked expression on her pretty face.

"You defended me," she says, her voice full of awe.

I brush at the front of my white shirt. Despite how dark the club is, the lights are almost fluorescent and my shirt seems to glow. I didn't mean to be so damn obvious. I also didn't mean to end up at some sort of deviant club, defending Lily Fowler's honor, for Christ's sake. "Of course I did. That asshole had his hands all over you."

She takes a few cautious steps toward me, those plump, sexy-as-hell lips still parted in surprise, and my fantasies go into overdrive. I can imagine tracing them with my finger. Slipping my dick between them, hearing her sigh in pleasure just before she licks the head of my cock with her wicked tongue . . .

"No one's ever done that for me before. Thank you," she says sincerely.

Now I'm the one who's shocked. I push all dirty thoughts out of my head and concentrate on the stunned woman in front of me. "What the hell are you talking about, no one's ever done that for you before?"

"Rushed to my defense," she explains, tilting her head to the side, as if she's observing me in a whole new light. "I'm usually left on my own, having to take care of myself."

Guilt nails me in the gut and I try to ignore it, but I can't. I hate her admission, hate thinking of her all alone, all the time. I shouldn't feel sorry for her. I shouldn't give two shits about this girl, but . . . I do. Why? I don't know her, not really. She's bound to be more trouble than she's worth. Only a couple of days in and I've already rescued her twice.

Leave. Just turn around and go.

But my feet stay firmly in place.

"That guy . . ." My voice drifts and I stare at her hard. She's the one who puts herself in these types of situations. It's as if she looks for trouble. "He could've hurt you if I hadn't stepped in."

"I know. It was dumb. I shouldn't have talked to him, let him get that drink for me." She moves even closer, and I can smell her. Honey and sunshine. Sweet and warm. "You're like my white knight."

"I'm no one's knight, princess." I want to say more, but the words get caught in my throat when she wraps her arms around my neck and presses that hot, tight little body against mine. I can feel her, every single inch of her, and my cock twitches in response at the same exact time my brain short-circuits.

"You're mine," she whispers, her hand curling around the back of my neck and tugging my head down to hers. "At least for tonight."

And then she presses her mouth to mine, her lips sweet and insistent, the faintest sigh escaping her when my lips gently part beneath hers. No tongues are involved, just lips and breaths and her fingers tightening around my neck, her mouth so damn soft and damp and fucking delicious. I don't touch her, just let her guide the kiss, let her have all the control, though it goes against everything I normally do when I'm kissing a woman. I restrain myself from taking it deeper. Harder.

It's the most difficult thing I've done in a long-ass time.

When she pulls away from my mouth, her hand loosening its grip on my neck, I stare down at her, wondering what her motives are. I need to remain suspicious. This girl is the enemy. Hell, more like I'm working for *her* enemy. I can't lose focus. "Why'd you kiss me?"

She smiles, managing to be sweet and sexy all at once. Her breasts are nestled close to my chest, the deep V of her dress allowing me a fine glimpse of her cleavage. I could slip my hand beneath the neckline and touch warm, bare skin in seconds. I'd bet good money she's not wearing a bra. "Aren't all princesses supposed to kiss their white knight as a way of saying thank you for rescuing them?"

I slip my arm around her waist and tug her closer, her eyes going wide when she feels just how much she's affected me. She wants it bold? I'll give it to her bold. "Like I told you, I'm no one's white knight, princess. No matter how badly you want me to be."

The sassy look on her face tells me she likes the challenge. "I like it when you call me 'princess.'"

"And I don't like it when you call me your white knight." I splay my fingers wide at the small of her back, touching just the top of her ass. I want to smooth my hand down lower and cup her flesh but damn it, we're in a public place.

A public place called Vice, you idiot. You can do just about anything you want in a club like this.

"Maybe I should call you something else." Her smile grows. She sure is receptive after nearly getting into a dangerous situation with a complete jackass only minutes ago. "Maybe with that slight drawl of yours, I should call you 'cowboy.'"

I lift a brow. "Drawl?"

"Your accent," she explains as she slides her hands down the front of my chest, so slow I'm wondering if she's trying to memorize the sensation of my body beneath her palms. I know I'm sure as hell trying to memorize the feel of her gentle touch. "You're from the South, right?"

"Maybe," I say, stretching out the word, letting the Texas back into my voice at full force, liking the spark that lights her eyes.

"Tell me where you're from," she demands.

Fuck it. I cup her backside and haul her in as close as I can get her, her eyes going wide, her fingers curling into the fabric of my shirt so I can feel the light scrape of her nails against my skin. "Awfully demanding, aren't you?"

"I've been known to get my way a time or two," she practically purrs, her lids lowering as she stares at my chest, her fingers loosening their hold on my shirt.

I squeeze her ass tighter, making her squeak. It would be my absolute pleasure to mark that pretty, pale skin tonight with my bare hands but she probably won't let me. Bossy thing. "Tell me why you wouldn't sit with me earlier." I shouldn't ask. It's as if I'm trying to torture myself and I might not like the answer.

Her head lifts, her gaze meeting mine, wide and full of regret. "Because I'm stupid," she admits, her voice the softest whisper.

"You're definitely not stupid. It was probably the smartest thing you could've done," I tell her, my voice just as soft. Leaning in, I press my cheek to hers, my mouth close to her curved lips. "And it's Texas," I whisper.

She turns the slightest bit, her lips brushing the corner of mine, and I keep the groan that wants to escape from slipping out. "You're from Texas?"

"Yes, ma'am," I say in my best good-ol'-boy drawl. "Never was much of a cowboy, though."

Lily laughs, the sound melodic. My heart lightens just hearing it, which is the craziest thing ever. Being with this girl . . . she makes me forget what I should be focusing on. "I find that surprising, considering you're from Texas," she says as she pulls away. I let my arms drop from her waist. "Want to get a drink?"

"You think that's wise?" I glance around, notice that the club has become even more crowded, the music somehow louder. Beams of multicolored light flash, illuminating a couple standing close by, locked in a passionate embrace. The man's hand is beneath the woman's top and her hands are gripping his ass as they kiss.

No one holds back in this place. And I bet as the hour gets later, it gets even dirtier here.

"I want to check the club out, see what else is going on." She takes my hand and starts to walk, leading me toward the back of the building, where the dance floor is. "Or maybe we should dance first."

"Princess, I don't dance," I protest, but she ignores me. Her fingers entwine with mine as she pulls me through the crowd and I keep hold of her, not wanting to let her go. I see the way the men look at her as we pass and it gets my hackles up. They want her and I can't blame them. She's fucking gorgeous.

Yet she doesn't seem to pay much attention to anyone but me.

"I'm not going out there and making an ass of myself," I tell her as she heads toward the dance floor.

Lily turns on me with a pout, her eyes wide as she blinks up at me. "Come on, cowboy. I want to dance." She starts to sway her hips and my mouth goes dry. *Holy fuck,* I could watch her do that all night. "All you'll have to do is just stand there. I'll do the rest."

"No way." I shake my head. It's never that simple. I don't dance; I never really have. But damn, she tempts me. Watching those hips move, the inviting look on her face, in her eyes . . .

"Please, Max?"

Hell. It's the "please" that does it. Reluctantly, without a word, I let her lead me out onto the dance floor, thankful that she has us stand on the edge. The music is loud, the crowd moving as one to the beat, and I stand there and watch her, our gazes locked as she starts to move. Within seconds she's lost to the music as she lifts her arms, her hands in her hair, and she lifts it away from her neck. She closes her eyes, her body fluid, and I want to grab her. Pull her into me, and feel that sexy body move and shake.

But I don't. I just stand there like she wanted me to, my muscles tight, my skin heated. It's hot as hell out here with all the gyrating bodies and I can feel sweat start to form on my forehead. She's driving me out of my mind, and all she's doing is dancing.

I can't imagine what she'll do to me if I ever get her beneath me, naked, wet, and willing. My head would probably explode.

"You need to loosen up." She wraps her arms around my neck again, just like she did earlier when she kissed me, but this time she grinds her lower body against mine. The song changes, this one a little slower, a lot sexier, and she moves with it, her lids lowering, her lips pursing into a sexy pout, driving me out of my mind with wanting her.

I slip one arm around her and lift my leg so it wedges between her thighs. She takes the opportunity to dip low, and I swear to God I feel the silky rasp of her panties against my knee.

Holy shit.

Pressing my face against the side of her head, I whisper in her ear, "Turn around."

"What?" She withdraws so she can blink up at me.

"Turn around," I say again. "Your back to my front."

Without protest she does as I ask, her ass brushing against my erection, and she flashes me a knowing smile over her shoulder. I grab hold of her hips, my hands loose, letting her sway and move against me. Those plump ass cheeks work my cock as she continues to dance and I let my hands drift down, toying with the hem of her dress. She arches her spine, her head going back at the exact moment I slip my hands beneath her skirt and touch the bare skin of her thighs.

Glancing around, I see no one's paying any attention to us. Other couples out on the dance floor are getting just as grabby as we are. One man has his hand blatantly between the legs of the woman he's with, her eyes closed in ecstasy. Another man has his hands tucked within a woman's tank top, fingers moving busily over her breasts as he devours her mouth with his own.

Lily lifts her arms and reaches for my neck as she turns her head to the side, still moving to the music. I move with her, slowly establishing my rhythm, thrusting against her ass along with the pounding beat. She pushes her chest out as I glance down, captivated by the way the fabric of her dress slides over her breasts, her nipples hard. I race my hands up the outside of her thighs until my fingers encounter the thin, lacy strap of her panties.

All I want to do is rip them off her body. Dive my fingers between her legs and see just how wet she is for me.

I bet she's fucking soaked.

"Max." She moans my name as she tilts her head to the side, exposing her neck to my gaze. I lean in and kiss her there, lick and nibble her skin, and I hear her whimper. Feel the tremble move through her body.

I don't know what the fuck we're doing, but I'm playing a dangerous game. One that's going to get me in a lot of trouble.

For the first time in a while, I don't really care.

"I don't even know you," she whispers as I toy with the flimsy band of her panties. Her skin is so soft and I touch her lightly, drift my fingers across her flesh, slide them over her hip. "Yet I'm letting you touch me like this in public."

"You've never done anything like this in public before?" I kiss her just behind her ear, noting the tiny heart tattoo that's etched there. The heart is broken, a jagged line going down the middle, and I wonder at that.

"Maybe . . ." Her voice drifts, confirmation that she has done this sort of thing before. Not that I care, considering she's with me tonight.

Her past doesn't matter.

"You want me to stop?" I breathe deep her delicious honey-eyed scent. Her hair tickles my face and I study the giant diamond stud in her ear, wondering if it's real.

Of course it's real. Lily Fowler is worth millions. Maybe even billions.

She shakes her head, her hair catching on the stubble on my cheek. "No," she whispers.

"Making all your secret dirty fantasies come true then?" I ask as I carefully shift my hand to her front, my fingers tracing along the edge of her underwear.

"Almost," she chokes out when I swipe my finger across the front of her damp panties.

My hand goes still. "Almost? What do you mean by that?"

She rubs her butt against my cock and I remove my hands from beneath her dress, settling them on her hips. "I have another fantasy. A much . . . darker one."

Everything within me stills, with the exception of my heart. It kicks into high gear, pounding within my chest, roaring in my ears. "What is it?"

Lily looks back at me, a wicked smile curving her lips. "Wouldn't you like to know?"

I rest my hand against her belly and then slowly slide it up, between her breasts, along her chest, her collarbone, until my fingers are resting against the base of her throat. I can feel her pulse beat mightily beneath my thumb, hear the slight catch in her breath when I stroke her skin. We're not dancing anymore but no one cares. No one's paying attention to us. It's like we're in our own little private world and all I can see, all I can hear and focus on, is Lily. "Tell me," I murmur, ducking my head so my mouth is close to her ear.

She melts against me and I bring my fingers up farther, so I'm clasping the front of her neck, my hold feather light. I may want to possess her but I would never want to hurt her, and she needs to know this.

I hope she realizes my intent. I don't want to break her. Just . . . tame her. At least for tonight. Then I have a job to do.

Lily shifts her ass against my cock, lifting her head as if she's giving me better access. She doesn't say a word, doesn't tell me to let her go, and I know she likes the way I'm touching her.

Interesting.

"You'll think I'm a freak," she finally whispers in response, her hand dropping to rest on the outside of my thigh. Her fingers burn where she touches me.

"No, I won't." I tighten my hold on her neck, making her gasp. "Tell me, Lily. You like it when I touch you like this?" She nods but doesn't say a word. "I want to know what else you like."

"I want . . ." Her voice drifts and I can feel the delicate movement of her throat when she swallows. I press my face against hers, my mouth at her temple as I wait to hear what she has to say next, anticipation riding me hard. We're playing a game, Lily and I. I have a feeling whatever her secret desire is, I'm the one who's going to fulfill it.

Tonight.

"I've never admitted this to anyone before, so it's hard," she says, and I breathe deep, dying to know what she's about to say next.

"Take your time, baby girl," I coax, my voice low, my mouth right at her ear. I stroke the fragile skin at her throat, my other hand resting on her stomach. I can feel her tremble beneath my touch and everything within me goes hard.

She swallows again before she speaks, her voice hesitant. "My favorite fantasy is a man breaking into my room." Her words are low and carefully chosen, her head bent forward, as if she doesn't want to look at me or meet my gaze for fear she'll see nothing but judgment there. "I'm sleeping. I have no idea he's in the room with me."

With my free hand I reach up and brush her hair away from my face, pressing my lips against her temple. "Tell me what happens next."

She takes a deep breath. "I can sense that he's there but I pretend I'm asleep. I like . . . I like knowing that he's watching me."

Arousal punches me in the gut and makes my dick even harder. She likes knowing I watch her, too. "So you want to trick him."

"No. Not necessarily." She shakes her head, seeming at a loss for words. I can't believe we're having this private conversation in the middle of a crowded nightclub, but I'm so attuned to her, she's so attuned to me . . . she is everything I see and feel and hear. "More like I want to savor the moment."

I close my eyes and breathe deep the scent of her hair, thrusting my cock slow and easy against the curve of her ass as I slide my hand back down her throat, caressing her delicate collarbone and then lower, the erratic thump of her heart pounding against my palm. We would be so fucking good together. I shouldn't do this. It goes against every work ethic I have, messing around with my subject, with anyone related to my work, but I think that's half the thrill.

Knowing that being with her is . . . forbidden.

Wrong.

"Then what happens?" I open my eyes and tilt my head down just as she turns to look at me from over her shoulder. I see the arousal in her gaze, feel the shiver that steals through her. She sinks her teeth into her lower lip as she contemplates what to say next.

"I . . . I don't know. I never get that far in my fantasy." Her gaze drops to my mouth and lingers there for a long, tension-filled moment. I wonder if she's afraid to push the fantasy farther in her thoughts. Most people don't want to know how far they'd go for sexual satisfaction. "You think I'm weird, huh."

"No." I drop my hand from her chest, resting both of my hands at her hips. "I think you're brave for revealing that to me."

Slowly she turns in my arms, staring up at me as if I've sprouted two heads. "Really?"

I nod. "Everyone has dark fantasies they're uncomfortable sharing."

Her expression fills with interest. "What's yours?"

Pressing my forehead to hers, I whisper, "I sneak into a beautiful woman's room and watch her while she sleeps. She doesn't know I'm there and that makes me . . . hard."

"Oh." Her eyes go dark.

"You want to hear more?"

There's no hesitation. "Yes, please."

The girl definitely gets off on this sort of thing. "So I take off all my clothes and sneak into her bed, only to discover that she's naked, too . . ." I let my voice drift off.

"What happens next?" she asks eagerly.

"Well, maybe I'll show you." I lift my head away from hers so I can gauge her reaction.

Her eyes go wider. "How?"

Smiling, I murmur, "Wouldn't you like to know?"

Chapter Eight

Max

I'M FUCKING CRAZY. I HAVE STRAIGHT-UP LOST MY MIND AND I need to leave before I do something really stupid and risk my career forever.

Yet here I am, standing in front of Lily's bungalow after I snuck into the exclusive area by hopping over the gate, my hands shoved deep into the pockets of my black cargo pants, the warm tropical wind whipping around me and making my hair fly into my eyes.

I push the hair away from my forehead and scratch the back of my neck, contemplating my next move. It's late. Past midnight. I waited on purpose, walking Lily to the entrance of the bungalow area after we left Vice, giving her a soft, chaste kiss before I whispered in her ear, asking her which bungalow she's in.

"Number eight," she murmured, looking disappointed when I didn't say anything else, didn't make a move to kiss her again. "Do you . . ."

I shook my head, cutting her off. "Maybe I'll see you later," I tell her pointedly, hoping she got the hint.

But the disappointment was still there, written all over her expressive face. She didn't want me to leave. She wanted me to come back to her bungalow and get naked. *Hell,* I haven't even really tasted her mouth yet, though I felt her wet panties, the heat emanating from her pussy.

The moment I went back to my hotel room, I wanted to jack off. My cock was aching, my mind filled with thoughts of licking Lily all over her body, driving her wild with my tongue, making her come and fucking her hard.

But I held back. I did nothing but take a cold shower and will my erection to go down. Dressed in all black and sneaking out like a thief in the night, my thoughts wild with the prospect of having Lily naked and beneath me soon.

I'm a man desperate for a woman. And only one woman will do.

Glancing about and making sure no one is near, I skirt around the premises, ducking along the side of the building and out of view of the windows. I go around to the back of Lily's bunga-low, opening a tiny gate that's unlocked and leads to the beach. The moon is full tonight, shining its silvery light so that the sand is bright and the whitecaps of the waves stand out stark against the swirling dark blue sea. It's a beautiful evening, not one on which I should be sneaking into Lily's room and possibly scaring the shit out of her.

But she wants it. It's her deepest, darkest fantasy and I'm hell-bent on fulfilling it. What if she freaks out? What if she was feeding me a line of bullshit and she calls security on my ass and I somehow end up getting arrested?

That would ruin everything. Not that I've been following my plan to get into that laptop and destroy whatever's inside it. My fascination with Lily shot that to hell. I've never been so dis-tracted on a case before and I can only blame her.

If everything fell apart, Pilar would want to kill me. My cover would be blown, my reputation trashed. I shouldn't risk it.

I should turn back right now. Go back to my hotel room and hope like hell I run into her in the morning. I know I would, because we always find each other. And I could come up with some sort of excuse, tell her I'm sorry, that I fell asleep and maybe I could make it up to her? I bet she'd understand. I bet I could convince her to understand.

You sneak into her room and you have instant access to the laptop. It's gotta be in there. Get inside Lily and then grab the laptop. Everything you want, all at once.

Right. I have to do this. There's really no other choice.

I sneak onto the lanai, holding my breath as I approach the French doors. They'll be locked, but I can peek through the glass and see if there's any movement inside. Leaning in close but not touching anything, I do exactly that, squinting against the reflection of the moon off the clean glass, trying to see something, anything that'll make me turn tail and get the hell out of here.

There's nothing. No lights on, no movement, no Lily in sight. She's in her bedroom. She's asleep.

I can almost guarantee it.

Cursing under my breath, I stride across the lanai, following along the building until I reach the sliding glass doors. One side of the curtains is drawn back, allowing me a glimpse inside the bedroom. The bed is huge, covered in white, and I see the form of a body beneath the comforter, tucked in tight.

Blissfully unaware that I'm watching her.

I reach out and curl my fingers around the handle, close my eyes, and count to three.

One . . . I shouldn't do this.

Two . . . I need to walk. Now.

Three . . . My hand tugs on the handle and the screen door glides open, whisper-soft.

Almost as if I never opened it at all.

I take a deep breath and step inside the quiet room, pulling the screen door closed behind me. It doesn't even make a sound—nothing like the screen door at my parents' place, which screeches on its hinges like an old witch's laugh.

The sound of soft breathing reaches my ears and I stand at

the foot of the bed, staring down at the figure lying on her side, buried beneath the fluffy white comforter. The air conditioner is on despite the open screen door and it's frigid in the room. A fan swirls overhead, stirring the ice-cold air, and I shiver, stuffing my hands in my pockets as I stare at Lily.

She shifts, almost as if she knows she's being watched, and I take a couple of steps back, panic nearly making me run into the dresser. She throws her leg over the comforter, nudging the fabric so it's tucked between her legs, and I realize she has nothing on.

Lily is fucking naked, just like I described in *my* fantasy.

I swipe a hand across my face, leave it covering my mouth as I stare at her, contemplating my next move.

Go, asshole. Before you do something really stupid and scare the shit out of her. Next thing you know she's calling security, they're calling the police, and they're arresting your ass for stalking—and you're fucked for life.

But I don't leave. Instead, I step closer to the bed, coming around to the side closest to where she's sleeping, my gaze never leaving her. The moon's light shines into the room, illuminating her in a soft glow, and I'm fascinated. I watch the rise and fall of her body as she breathes deeply, her parted lips plump and alluring even when she's asleep. I listen to the sound of her soft, even breathing. Her eyes are closed, thick eyelashes like dark little fans lying across her skin.

She looks peaceful. So beautiful that the urge to go to her, to slip beneath the covers and join her, is so strong I almost do it.

But not yet. I need to rationalize this first. Though it's nothing close to rational, being in this room with her uninvited. I'm breaking the fucking law. I should leave.

I don't.

My cell phone is set on silent and my wallet is in my back pocket, my room's key card tucked safely inside. I brought nothing else with me beyond the clothes I'm wearing and the shoes on my feet. I could easily strip in silence and climb into bed with her like some sort of nut job, explore her body with my hands and mouth and fucking teeth, waking her up in the best possible way. Then I'd finally slide deep inside her, fuck her hard, fuck her deep until we're both coming with low groans.

I'd have to be quiet. Stealthy, if I'm really going through with it.

No way are you going through with it, asshole.

My smug side rises up, ready for the challenge.

Watch me. It's what she wants. You've got nothing to worry about.

I really hate that guy sometimes. He gets my ass in trouble.

Deciding the hell with it, I take off my shirt and toss it on the floor. Undo the button snap on my cargoes and carefully pull down the zipper, thankful it's quiet. Until I'm standing in her bedroom with just my blue boxer briefs on, my entire body on fire at the thought of what I'm about to do.

I go around to the other side of the bed, the one that's empty, and I carefully, quietly pull back the covers. She doesn't move. Her back is still to me and I can definitely confirm that she has nothing on. She sleeps naked.

Approval wholeheartedly given.

Without another thought I slide into bed with her, pulling the covers up over me. I lie there for a minute, stiff as a board, holding my breath, not wanting her to wake up and freak out. Because she absolutely should freak out. She has to, despite what she said to me earlier. No way did she really mean that, wanting me to sneak into her room. Maybe it was more like a dare, her wanting to see if I'd be crazy enough to make her supposed fantasy come true.

Like the dumbass I am, I fell for it. This girl . . . makes me do stupid shit. I'm a thinker, a planner, and she's turned me spontaneous. Something I never believed I could be.

She shifts in her sleep, sticking her ass out straight toward me almost provocatively, and all rational thought seeps out of my brain. I become nothing but primitive urges, resting my hand on her ass, smoothing my palm over her soft skin, intoxicated with the feel of her, the smell of her, the knowledge that she's lying next to me, oblivious and vulnerable to whatever I want to do to her.

How dangerous that is. How lucky *she* is that I'm a relatively good guy who snuck into her room, ready to fulfill her every fantasy, and not some violent asshole that's hell-bent on hurting her.

Yeah. My rationalization for my actions wouldn't fly with the law. I don't know who I'm trying to convince.

Maybe yourself?

A soft, feminine sigh lingers in the air and Lily is pushing her ass into my hand, almost as if she knows it's there. I caress her skin, swear I can feel the heat of her pussy, and then she's humming, a sweet little sound that definitely indicates she feels my touch.

And she likes it.

"I've been waiting for you," she whispers and I go completely still, wondering if I should jump out of the bed and get the fuck out of here. What if she calls security? What if she already did? Or worse, what if she tries to wrench off my nuts?

"I knew you'd come back," she continues as she scoots closer to me, her back to my front, her bare ass brushing against my cock, which happily rises to the occasion. Only the thin barrier of my underwear prevents me from slipping inside her and I grit my teeth, tell myself to get it together.

I say nothing and Lily lifts her arms behind her so they come around my neck, her hands at my nape, and I automatically wrap my arms around her waist, my fingers resting against the soft skin of her stomach. "You're pretty bold, you know, sneaking into my room."

So she's really okay with this? "You wanted it," I say, as a sort of test. I skim my hands up her stomach and she arches forward, my palms cradling her breasts.

A laugh escapes her and she squeezes tighter around my neck. "I did. I still do," she admits softly, a little moan escaping her when I run my thumbs over her nipples, back and forth over the beaded points. "God, your hands are so big."

"I'm a crazy motherfucker for doing this," I tell her. She needs to know what a risk I took, sneaking in here. What a risk *she* took by leaving her door unlocked for any old asshole to walk in and attack her. I should spank her ass for doing something so careless.

I wonder if she'd like it if I tried to spank her ass.

"I have a thing for crazy motherfuckers," she admits, her breath catching in her throat when I pinch her nipple hard. "Are you really here to make my fantasy come true?"

"Yes." I lean into her and nibble on her ear, making her gasp. "Are you going to do what I say, no questions? I need total submission from you, princess. No protests. No arguing."

She nods, her hair brushing against my face. I love the smell of her. I could inhale her all damn day. "Whatever you want me to do. I'm yours."

Her words sound way too good. She shouldn't make promises she probably can't keep.

"So when I tell you what to do, you'll do it? I won't push you too far. I'll make sure and give you everything you want, baby girl." She shivers when I call her that, and I caress her breasts, holding them in my hands. I'm dying to suck her nipples into my mouth and really taste her, feel her squirm beneath me and beg me for more. "I promise."

"I promise, too," she whispers. The purr of satisfaction in her voice is raw and unfiltered. I want her falling apart in my arms. I want her gasping, unable to breathe, unable to fucking think.

I probably want too much from a woman I barely know but

damn it, that's exactly what I need to experience, too. It's been too long since I've lost myself inside a woman. I've been too wrapped up in other shit. Stupid shit that holds me back and fucks with my head.

"Then let's get started, princess." I release her breasts and pull away from her, her hands falling from around my neck. Placing my hands on her back, I give her a gentle push. "Lie on your stomach."

She does as I say, no questions asked, no protesting, kicking the comforter away from her body so all I see is naked flesh as she rolls over onto her stomach. She folds her arms underneath her head, resting her cheek on her entwined hands so she can watch me. Her eyes glow in the dim light and my skin tightens the longer she looks at me.

"You have too much clothing on," she observes.

I glance down at my underwear, my cock straining against the front like it wants to burst free, a tiny spot of wetness from leaking pre-come. "I get naked and I'm bound to fuck you."

Her eyes heat and her lips curve in a tiny smile. "But that's exactly what I want."

"I'm sure." I hover over her, pushing her hair away from her neck. "We'll get there," I murmur against her skin just before I kiss her nape. Lick her, her salty sweetness dissolving on my tongue, making me crave more.

Without moving away from her neck I shift so I'm completely over her, my knees on either side of her hips, my mouth still at her nape, my hands curling around her front. She lifts up, allowing my hands to slide between her body and the mattress, and I cup her breasts, kneading them, running the heel of my palms up and down, teasing her nipples.

I lift away from her nape and that's when I spot a tattoo. High up on her neck, almost hidden completely by her hairline, is a bird—a flock of them, at least five, seeming to try and escape into her hair. "Nice tattoo," I say.

"You found my birds," she murmurs as she bends her head, allowing me a better glimpse. I trace each bird with the tip of my finger, enjoying the hide-and-seek game we're having with her ink. "I never get to see them."

"That's what happens when you get a tattoo on the back of your neck." I drop a kiss on each bird, making her shiver. "Do you have more?"

"You'll have to search my body and find out."

Her words are just the invitation I want to hear. I slide down the length of her, my lips mapping her skin, making note of the spots where she jerks away because she's too sensitive or where she moans when I find a spot that must feel particularly good. She's ticklish, especially around her ribs, on the back of her thighs, behind her knees. I even kiss her feet, the soft soles, lightly tonguing her toes. She giggles and I find another tattoo, this one on the side of her left foot, a pretty little pink flower.

"A hibiscus," she explains when I trace the delicate design. "I've always had a thing for them."

I don't say a word, just continue to kiss my way back up her body until I'm gently flipping her over at her waist and she goes willingly. Lifting up, I straddle her hips, staring down at her, my gaze zeroing in on her breasts. That's when I spot yet another tattoo, this one curving just beneath her right breast. A scattering of stars, like a constellation. I trace them with my finger, goose bumps forming in my wake.

They represent something, a part of her. What, I'm not exactly sure, but there must be a meaning for the tattoos she chooses.

I want to find out those meanings. The meaning of Lily. There's more to her than she leads on. She's not just some sexy rich girl out looking for a good time, no matter how hard she tries to push that image. It's a front. There's something deeper playing behind the scenes. There's a reason she's on the run, why Pilar hates her so damn much, why Lily's hiding.

I want to discover all of her secrets. Fuck the job. Fuck what I'm supposed to take from her, this woman who's naked and beautiful and wants me just as much as I want her.

At least for tonight. All I want to do, all I can think about, is fucking Lily.

"Are there more?" I cock a brow.

Her smile is mysterious. "Search and see for yourself."

That means there are definitely more. And I can't wait to find them.

Chapter Nine

Lily

HIS BIG, WARM HANDS ROAM ALL OVER MY BODY AND SET MY skin on fire everywhere he touches. I really like his hands. Those long, skilled fingers that are slightly calloused and the wide palms—one of them alone can practically span the width of my ass and that's kind of amazing.

He's palming my ass now, rubbing it, slapping the side of one cheek and watching it jiggle. I jolt when he slaps it again, harder this time, and I mumble a shocked "That hurts."

I've had guys spank me before but I didn't enjoy it. At all. More like, the spanking irritated me. It felt like they were trying to claim me as their own personal piece of property to do with whatever they wanted. Oh, I'd always put on a show for them, gasping and squealing and acting like it turned me on.

It never turned me on. But the way Max is touching me, smoothing his palm over my stinging flesh just before he slaps it again, well . . .

I'm aroused. Wet. I lift up on my knees a little bit, pushing my ass into his hand—again—and he takes the hint, slapping it so hard the sound reverberates throughout the quiet room, and I swear I hear a grunt of satisfaction come from him at the exact same time I moan.

"You like that, princess?" He's caressing the spot where he smacked me, his fingers so gentle my heart flutters. "I can see how pink your skin is even in the dark."

The moon is bright, painting the room in silver, gilding his sharp features, his beautiful mouth. I watch him from over my shoulder, my arm resting beneath my head, my ass in the air. "I like it," I admit, my voice quiet. I say nothing else because I'm scared I'll say the wrong thing. Or worse, that I'll say too much and make a fool of myself.

"Interesting." His hand moves to my other butt cheek and he taps it, lightly. "You have the most perfect ass I've ever laid eyes on."

I start to laugh, then clamp my lips shut when I see the serious glow in his eyes. "I'm glad you like it," I say, feeling ridiculous as I turn away from him.

"I like everything about you I've uncovered so far." My gaze returns to his, shocked by his admission, but he says nothing more. He slips his fingers between my cheeks, skimming over my damp folds, and his eyes narrow as he dips his fingers deeper. "Damn, baby girl, you're soaked."

I should be embarrassed. Overabundant wetness is something I rarely have to worry about when I'm with a guy. I mean yeah, they've aroused me, a few have given me orgasms, or I touch myself and make sure I gain my satisfaction when they do. But with this man in particular . . . I'm aching. My clit is throbbing and my pussy feels . . . empty. I want to know what it feels like to have his cock move inside me. I won't be satisfied until that happens, and I hope to God it does.

I'm desperate for it. For him.

"You must really like it when I spank you," he says almost reverently. He sounds downright fascinated by the possibility and I'm more than a little mortified. He's probably not *really* into that sort of thing . . . Wait a minute.

Maybe he *is*. He did ask for my complete submission before we started. And he crept into my room like some sort of sexy thief, sneaking into my bed and touching me while he thought I slept. The entire scenario had been amazingly hot, fueling the long dormant fantasies I'd kept hidden from the world.

I'd been awake the entire time, waiting for him. I knew he'd show up and when I heard the screen door slide open, I had to bite my lips to keep from saying something.

It had been difficult, staying still while I could feel him watching me. I'd never felt sexier, never felt so alive and excited and terrified. My heart had pounded in my chest so hard I swore he could hear it and my entire body was overcome with shivers. I'd loved every moment and when I surprised him? I'd felt triumphant. Sexy.

In control.

But he took the control away from me within seconds, something that has never happened before. I don't like anyone telling me what to do. I never have.

Until Max.

"Touch me," I urge, spreading my legs farther, inviting him to continue his exploration.

He does exactly what I want, his deft fingers searching my folds, one long finger pushing deep inside my aching pussy. I whimper, savoring his invasion but wanting something more. Something bigger, thicker. Longer.

"I want inside you so fucking bad," he grits out, that sexy low growl I'm starting to love coming from deep inside his chest. He sounds tortured, which is good because I am 100 percent tortured and I want him feeling everything I am at the same time.

"I want you inside me, too," I whisper, moaning when he adds a second finger, then another. He's fucking me with three fingers, I can hear my wet pussy as he pushes them in and out, and I close my eyes, bite my lip to keep from crying out. He plunges deep, touching a spot inside of me that makes me gasp, makes me tremble, and I want more.

"You ready for me?"

I nod, hoping he can see the frantic movement of my head. I can't speak, I'm so overcome with the sensation of his long fingers thrusting inside me, his thumb coming around to press against my clit, and then I'm coming, unintelligible words falling from my lips as my entire body is consumed with shudders. My inner walls grip his fingers again and again and I collapse on the bed because my body's too weak to hold me up. He withdraws his fingers from my body before he grips me by the hips and turns me over again so I'm on my back.

He's flipped me around over and over since he showed up as if I weigh nothing and God, I like it. The way he takes full ownership of my body, pushing me into position, driving me wild. He's commanding, a little rough, a little crude.

A lot sexy.

"Well, well, well, look at this." His fingers trace just above my pubic hair. "Another tattoo."

I say nothing, my heart is still pounding too hard and I'm afraid if I try to speak, nothing will come out but a rusty gasp of breath. He brings his fingers, shiny with my juices, to his mouth and licks them, the sight of his tongue making everything inside of me twist with yearning.

He hasn't even really kissed me yet and I'm dying to feel that tongue of his slide against mine.

"What does it say?" he asks, flashing me a satisfied grin. He knows what he just made me do, how hard he just made me come, and I can see the pride etched all over his handsome face. He's on a power trip and I'll give it to him. I have to.

"Get a little closer and find out for yourself," I finally encourage him breathlessly. My heart is racing as though I just ran twenty miles and it's hard for me to concentrate, I'm still so blissed out.

Max does as I tell him to, his mouth hovering above my pussy, his eyes glued on the tattoo he's just discovered. He traces it with his finger again, over every curve of every letter.

" 'Keep me wild.' " He lifts his head, his eyes meeting mine. "What exactly are you referring to, princess?"

I reach for him, grabbing his hand and pulling him up so he falls on top of me and I whisper against his lips, "That's what I want from you," just before I kiss him.

The kiss is dirty. Rough. Primal. Tongues and teeth and bites and sucks, no romantic softness, but I want none of that. I prefer this. Raw and uninhibited, our breaths come fast, our mouths frantic. My hands are in his hair and his are in mine, tugging and pulling and making me whimper, making him growl. Our legs are entwined and his cock is brushing against my belly, leaving wet streaks in its wake because he's so aroused he's leaking pre-come everywhere.

I wish I could taste it.

He rears up just as I grab for his cock, my fingers curled tight around the base. It throbs against my fingers, hard steel covered with velvet, and I lift my lids to find him watching me, his jaw tight, his mouth grim, his eyes glittering.

"I need a condom."

"Did you bring one?" I ask, stroking him, squeezing my fingers around all that hot, silky skin.

His eyes close and a shudder courses through his body. I continue my paces, stroking him up . . . and down. Up and down. "I have one in my wallet," he whispers, the last word hissing out.

"Then go get it." I release my grip on him and he leaps out of bed, going to where he left his clothes on the floor and rummaging through them until he finds his wallet. I lift up on my elbows, staring at his fine ass, the muscles that ripple and flex as he moves.

My mouth waters and I wonder what he might do if I bit him there.

He flips open his wallet and pulls out the wrapper, flashing me a triumphant smile before he climbs back onto the bed, joining me with condom in hand.

"Can I put it on?" I ask innocently, dying to touch him again. I'd suck him into my mouth if he'd let me, but I'm also eager to know what it's like to have him deep inside my body. Taking me. Fucking me . . .

"Only if you promise to ride me when you're finished," he says, pulling me from my thoughts.

"Deal." I smile and he withdraws from me, lying on his back, folding his arms behind his head as if he has all the time in the world.

Oh, this is going to be fun. Never taking my eyes from his, I tear into the wrapper slowly, pulling the rubber ring out and tossing the trash onto the floor. He smiles at me, sucks in a harsh breath when I run my free hand down the center of his firm chest, scraping my nails against his skin as my fingers travel down, down . . . past his navel, tangling in his dark pubic hair until I'm encountering his giant cock.

"You're big," I tell him.

"The better to fuck you with," he says with a mock leer.

A giggle escapes me. I don't giggle. Not for real. I put on acts, laughing with guys like they're the funniest thing ever when they are so . . . not. But this man, he might actually have a sense of humor hidden beneath that rough and rude exterior. "Like the big bad wolf?" I ask.

"Oh yeah, princess. Do I need to start calling you Little Red?" He grins and I shake my head, fighting my smile.

"I think you'd like that. Me pretending to be the scared little girl hiding behind my cape while you chase after me and finally take me down," I taunt him, noting the way his eyes heat as he stares at me.

"I already caught you." He grabs hold of my wrist, stopping me from stroking his cock. "Put the condom on."

I do as I'm told when he lets go of my wrist, my fingers shaking as I fumble to slip the circle over the head of his cock. He watches me the entire time, making me nervous, and I lift my gaze to his as if seeking approval.

By the satisfied smile on his face, I think he likes my obedience. And for some strange reason, I like that I pleased him. "Come here," he whispers as he drags me over his body so I'm straddling him, my legs draped over his hips, my pussy poised just above his cock. I can feel him nudge against me, teasing my folds, and I grip hold of his shoulders, closing my eyes as I brace myself for his welcome invasion.

Within seconds he's giving it to me, his ragged exhale making my entire body clench in anticipation. "Look at me, princess," he murmurs.

My eyes flash open and he tilts his head, indicating I should look down. I do so, all the breath rushing out of me as I watch his cock slide slowly inside my body. I move in closer to him, wrapping my arms around his neck, his face at my throat as I start to ride him.

He feels good. So big and thick, invading me completely. The man knows just what he's doing, too, flexing his hips and pushing deep as I rotate and shift, making sure he hits all of my secret spots. His lips are damp, his breath hot on my neck, and I tilt my head back, squealing when he sucks on the skin right at my pulse at the base of my neck. His hands are on my hips, guiding me, holding me still so he can lift his hips and thrust deep inside my pussy, and a shuddery moan escapes me.

"You like that?" he asks and I nod, too overcome to speak. Too afraid I'll say something and ruin it. So I keep my lips shut, letting my moans and my whimpers and my body do all the talking for me.

"You're tight as fuck," he continues, his voice raspy as he starts to pick up the pace. "Squeeze around me, princess. Let me feel you."

I clench my inner walls around his cock, pleasure rocketing through me when he groans. I like the way he holds me down. I like how tight he grips my hips, how brutal his thrusts are. He's using me and I love it. I want to be used. I'm the one who's always using, who's always entertaining and putting on the show, and I'm so fucking sick of it.

I just want to be free. To fly. To lose myself and let this man do whatever he wants to me. I just want . . . to feel nothing.

And everything. All at once.

Tilting my head, I curl my fingers into the damp hair at his nape and pull his head back, sealing my mouth over his. The kiss is a wreck, smashed lips and seeking tongues and nipping teeth, but I love it. He reaches between us and palms my breast, nimble fingers working my nipple as his cock works my body and his mouth works mine. Our bodies are slick with sweat, I can hear the squeak of the box springs as we move and bounce on the mattress, and when his hand slips farther, his fingers brushing against my clit, I almost lose it.

"Sensitive?" he murmurs against my lips. His touch becomes more purposeful, his finger tracing over my clit again and again, and I can feel the orgasm building. I don't want to come yet. I want to savor this. Enjoy it. The way his cock moves inside my body, the drag and pull as he thrusts again. And again. And again . . .

"Oh God," I gasp just as my orgasm hits full force, even stronger than the one he gave me earlier. It vibrates just beneath my skin, rippling through my veins, settling deep in my body, and I clutch him close, my mouth at his ear, my panting breaths in time with the spasms taking over me.

Still he continues to thrust, his own orgasm coming soon after mine, his entire body going so still I lift my head, staring into his eyes just as the first wave sweeps over him. His hand grips the back of my head as he pulls me in, crushing his mouth to mine. I swallow his groans, run my hands over his shoulders and back as if I can soothe him through the shudders and the gasps and the moans.

Not that I really want to soothe him. I'm not fooling myself into thinking what we just shared is something . . . more.

This is nothing. Just one night of terrific, hot sex. That's all it can be. I'm not built for relationships, for caring about some-one. I'm too selfish. Daddy's told me that time and again.

And he's right.

Chapter Ten

Max

"You're costing me too much money."

I yank up my pants over my ass, wincing at the sound of Pilar's shrill voice directly in my ear as I slip through the opening in the sliding glass door and shut it, hoping like hell Lily didn't hear her screaming at me over the phone. Every time she calls I feel like she's yelling at me, even when I know she's not. The woman speaks at a constant high volume.

"What the hell are you talking about? How am I costing you too much money?" I charged her my normal flat fee for my services, including covering my predicted expenses, and I haven't gone into overtime yet. Though she's the one who added a bonus incentive, not me. I haven't cashed that check yet, wouldn't let myself. The way I've been falling down on the job, I don't deserve to cash that damn check.

The woman is fucking nuts. She likes to complain just for the hell of it. And I take it because she has every right to complain. I'd rather do anything else than take that damn laptop.

I rub the back of my neck as I settle heavily into one of the plush, overstuffed chairs that are scattered all over Lily's lanai. The view is fucking amazing and I pause for a moment to take in the breathtaking sight of the sun coming up. The sky is hued with streaks of pink and orange, the water a gentle shimmery blue, and the salty scent of the ocean is in the air. This is way better than the shitty view I have from my hotel room.

"Time is money, Mr. Coleman, and so far, you've wasted a lot of my time. You promised me thorough and quick. So far, you haven't lived up to either promise." She sniffs, sounding disgusted.

It's late, or early, depending how you look at it. Dawn is creeping in, turning the sky the lightest pink, and I yawn, wishing like hell I could go back in the room and collapse into bed. Gather a naked, warm Lily in my arms and let my dick do all the talking. She responds well to it, that perfect ass nuzzling against my rigid cock. Not that I can fuck her again. Turns out we got lucky. I had two condoms in my wallet and we used them both.

But you don't need a condom to have some fun. I made her come with my mouth twice. And she returned the favor once. We've been messing around all night and I'm exhausted. Though that wouldn't stop me from crawling right back into that bed and feeling Lily up until she's awake. I don't care that she's tucked in like Sleeping Beauty and down for the count. I know she'd be raring to go for another round.

I glance through the sliding glass door and see that she hasn't moved a muscle. My ringing cell phone didn't disturb her, thank Christ. Leave it to my client to call me at dawn, but what the hell does she care? She's six hours ahead of me. She got her beauty sleep.

"Give me a couple days. I need more time," I tell Pilar wearily, irritated with how she pushes. The woman is nonstop. Completely unsatisfied. I'd hate to be the poor sap tangled up with her.

It's my own damn fault, though. I'm the one putting her off and failing at my own job. Why don't I just do what I'm supposed to and get the hell out of here?

You don't want to leave Lily, asshole. You like her. You're insanely attracted to her.

True. I could be fucking everything up, all for a girl. A beautiful, sexy-as-fuck, sweet-as-hell girl.

"Three days tops," she reaffirms. "Get that goddamn laptop and bring it back to me. I don't care what you have to do to get it, just do it." She ends the call before I can say another word.

Fucking woman irritates the shit out of me. I open up the browser on my phone and start a more extensive search on my client, Pilar Vasquez.

I did the requisite search when she first approached me, inquiring about my services. A quick name entry on Google told me everything I needed to know. Her age, what she looked like, where she worked. There were a few photos of her on Forrest Fowler's arm, but nothing looked out of the ordinary. Once I found out exactly what Pilar wanted me to do, I figured she was out for revenge against Lily because of Fowler family politics.

But Lily doesn't work for Fleur. She never really has, minus a few summers as a teenager. The minute she graduated high school she did her own thing, unlike her younger sisters. Traveling around the world, partying, dating a variety of men, making the rounds on the tabloids and gossip blogs, looking like a hot mess most of the time. Yes, I did thorough research on my subject, but not enough on my client.

That's where I failed. And I rarely fail.

Tell that to the guys who died on your watch.

I'd had my shit together. Joined the military right out of high school, eager to follow in my dad's footsteps, to see combat, to fight this war and serve my country. I didn't expect it to be so damn hard. To be so mentally and physically crushing. To lose my friends, men who worked with me, defended me, to friendly fire and to fight against the injustice of it all.

The moment I was given my evaluation results and they expressed worry over my mental state, I knew my career in the army was done for good.

Banishing the old memories that love to haunt me at the

worst time, I focus on my Google results for one Pilar Vasquez. As one of the top employees at Fleur, she gets plenty of mentions, including a recent article in an online business magazine noting a promotion, accompanied by a photo of her standing beside Forrest Fowler in what looks like a boardroom.

There's another photo of her at a social event, hanging on Fowler's tuxedoed arm while wearing a body-hugging gold, glittery dress. I study it closely, noting the way she's looking at him, how his arm is wrapped tightly around her waist.

They're an item. A couple. And I'm a fucking stupid, blind asshole not to have realized this before.

I scroll through more images, noticing there are quite a few older photos of her with a guy who looks a lot younger than her. Good-looking guy, angry expression on his face most of the time while she clings to him, looking like the cat that just licked up every last drop of the cream.

The name is familiar: Ryder McKay. I immediately enter him in the search box and hit the images tab. Up come dozens of recent photos of McKay in London with none other than Violet Fowler, including mentions of an engagement and close-up photos of a giant rock on Violet's finger.

Interesting—and freaking strange.

What sort of twisted relationships make up the Fowler family? It appears that Pilar at one time was with McKay. But now McKay is with Violet Fowler and Pilar is with Forrest Fowler. Talk about odd.

And what does Lily Fowler have to do with any of this? Pilar mentioned in our initial meeting that Lily tried to damage her reputation. I can only imagine that Lily has information on my client and is using said information to blackmail her. Pilar won't go into detail, which makes me believe that the information Lily has is pretty damaging.

I'd like to know exactly what that information is.

After a few more searches on other Fowlers—Violet and

Rose, to be exact—I find out nothing else major and give up. Setting my phone on the tiny glass-top table right next to my chair, I lean forward and rest my elbows on my knees, running my hands through my hair. What the fuck should I do? I have my subject lying in bed, sleeping like the dead after I just thoroughly fucked her, and I need to somehow, some way, search her room and get that damn laptop Pilar's so insistent I take from her.

Your opportunity is now, asshole. Why not take advantage of it?

I sit up straight and crane my neck over my shoulder, studying the sleeping Lily once more. Her back is to me, her hair wild from the constant fucking, the white sheet wrapped tight around her sexy naked body. I bet those sheets smell like her, are drenched in her. I should have her come to my room for the next round so she can rub her sexy scent all over my sheets. I probably wouldn't have the maid change them out for days.

You're a sick fucker.

Yeah, I am. It's like I'm fucking addicted to her. The sounds she makes, the taste of her skin, her sweet little tongue, her even sweeter pussy . . . damn. Being inside her is heaven. Feeling her pussy clench and tremble and squeeze all around me. The gush of wetness that coated my cock when she came drove me out of my mind. I couldn't hold back with her. She makes me crazy with wanting her.

And she's the last woman I should want.

Heaving a big sigh, I stand and open the sliding glass door, thankful it glides shut so quietly. I stand at the foot of the bed, studying Lily lying on her side, the sheet loose around her breasts, giving me a teasing glimpse. I want to go to her. Kiss her all over her body until she slowly awakens. I want to spend the morning in this bed with her naked.

I can't, though. I have a job to do.

Her tiny purse sits on the dresser and I go to it, peering inside. There's not much in there. A lip gloss. Six crisply folded twenty-dollar bills, two sticks of gum, and her room key. I pull out her ID and study it, surprised at how completely different she looks in the photo that was taken—I squint at the fine print—two years ago.

She's blonder in the picture. Lots of makeup on her face, especially her eyes. Her lips are curved in this almost mocking smile and her lids are heavy, looking like she just woke up and was nursing a wicked hangover.

The Lily Fowler on her ID card looks nothing like the Lily currently lying in the bed not ten feet away from me.

Shoving the ID back in her purse I turn and study the room, contemplating where I should look next. The mirrored closet door is shut and I go to it, carefully sliding it open, breathing deep to calm my racing heart. Adrenaline pours through me, pushing me to the edge, and I peer inside. There's nothing in there—no clothes on the hangers, no shoes scattered on the floor. Her suitcase sits on the other side of the room, on top of one of those folding metal stands that hold luggage.

I'll search the top of the closet first and if the laptop isn't there, the suitcase is next. It's gotta be stashed around here somewhere. I saw it with my own eyes on the plane.

Well, I saw a bag that looked suspiciously like a laptop case but I never actually saw a laptop. For all I know, I could be chasing a mythical object that doesn't even fucking exist.

The air conditioner clicks on, a blast of cold air hitting me, and I shiver. I snoop around in the closet, reaching along the top shelf, where no one ever puts anything—unless maybe they have something to hide. I gently slap my palm along the smooth wood, encountering nothing. Until I reach deep into the recesses of the farthest corner and my palm makes contact with something. It's hard and cool to the touch, like metal.

There it is.

Excitement ripples through me as I pull it down off the shelf, glancing toward the bed to make sure Lily's still asleep, which she is. She owns a MacBook, top of the line, nothing less for the Fleur heiress. Holding the laptop close to my chest, I crack it open and wait for it to start up, not surprised at all when the password screen appears. I fumble with the laptop and set it carefully on the dresser, then pull my phone out of my pocket, opening it up to my email and scrolling until I find the one from Pilar with the subject line "Possible Lily passwords." She had her suspicions and sent a list along to me.

I try them all, but not a one of them works.

Damn it.

Carefully closing the laptop, I shove my phone back into my pocket before I slide the laptop back into its hiding place in the closet, making sure I disturb nothing. If Pilar knew I was putting the laptop back where I found it, she'd come unglued. Hell, I wouldn't blame her.

I should grab it and leave. Fuck Lily Fowler. Fuck the shit I left in my hotel room. It's a few changes of clothes and toiletries, nothing else. I could leave it all behind and not miss it. Deliver the laptop to my client and be done with the job. Hands clean. Money earned.

But my hands wouldn't be clean and neither would my conscience. I had sex with her last night. My subject. Lily. I kissed her, fucked her, slept with her, her body nestled close to mine, like we were lovers. The very last thing I should have done, yet I did it anyway like a complete asshole.

I'm in too deep and I need to find my way out. I can't let her suck me in any deeper, despite how much I want to be sucked in. I like the woman. I enjoy spending time with her. Every time our eyes meet, it's like a current of electricity runs through my veins. And when she touches me, kisses me . . . *damn.*

I'm done for.

But I can't let any of that affect me. I need to re-strategize. Come up with a new plan, one that allows me to spend more time with Lily.

You're a fucking idiot.

Fine, I am. An idiot who wants at least one more night on this island with Lily.

I'll earn Lily's trust. Hell, I'm probably more than halfway there already. I'll discover the things and the people that mean something to her, try to figure out exactly what went wrong between her and Pilar. And then I'll get into that laptop and find out exactly what Pilar is looking for.

Chapter Eleven

Lily

My eyelids are heavy and i don't want to open them. plus the room is bright with the rising sun—I can see the glow even behind my closed eyes, and I know the second I open them I'll want to hiss and groan like a vampire.

More than anything, I'm reluctant for this night—morning, whatever—with Max to end. What if he utters a casual "It's been real," and then bails on me? I don't think my mind—or my heart—could take it. I know what happened between us can be nothing but casual. I get it.

So why am I feeling like this? Like I don't want him to go? Like I want to spend the rest of my vacation with him, exploring the island, going out for dinner, splashing in the pool or better yet, in the ocean, and then letting him take me to new heights of pleasure every night?

Because you always want what you can't have.

Isn't that the truth?

My body aches in the best possible way and I stretch my legs out, wincing at the dull pain I feel between my thighs. Not an agonizing pain, no. More like a *you've been well used and you'd like more of it right now, please* type of pain.

"You okay, princess?" A large, warm hand slides down my

back just before I feel Max press a soft, lingering kiss to my bare shoulder.

I squeeze my eyes shut, both loving and hating how tenderly he treats me. I'm confused. I don't know what I want from him. Worse, I don't know what he wants from me.

He slides into the bed, pressing his hard, hot body flush against mine from behind. His arm comes around my waist, his hand resting almost possessively on my stomach, and I sigh contentedly, enjoying how good he feels pressed next to me.

"I should go soon," Max murmurs just before he drops a kiss on my neck, behind my ear.

I want to scream out, *No! Don't leave me!* But I contain myself. "Got some things to do?"

"No, not really." His mouth is at my ear, his warm breath making me shiver. "I should go back and take a shower. Get some fresh clothes on."

"Oh." I rest my hand lightly over his, curling my fingers so I can draw patterns on top of his hand. "I should take a shower, too."

"You smell delicious." He squeezes me tight, his face in my hair.

"I'd rather not leave this bed." I hold my breath, waiting for his answer.

"Aren't you hungry?"

Starved, but I'm hungrier for him. "I'm all right."

"We need condoms."

Oh. That we do. "Valid point."

"I could go back to my room, take a shower, get dressed, and pick up a box at the gift shop in the lobby," he suggests. "And then we could meet in a few hours and go do something. Together."

"Like what?" I smooth my thumb over the top of his hand, my entire body going tense in anticipation when he slides that hand down lower, over the slope of my belly.

"Let me surprise you," he says, his fingers tangling through my scant pubic hair so that he ends up cupping me between my legs.

My hand falling away from his, I spread my thighs open, allowing him entry, whimpering when his fingers sink into my damp folds. His touch is slow. Assured. Confident. Back and forth he strokes me, teasing my clit, thrusting one finger shallowly inside my body before removing it. Toying with me, driving me wild, making me shiver and shake in anticipation.

"I love how wet you always are for me," he whispers close to my ear, the slick sounds of his fingers in my pussy loud in the otherwise quiet of the room. "And I love how easily you respond to me."

I'm already mindless with wanting him. I can't speak, I can hardly think at his touch and I lean back against him, my head on his shoulder, my limbs weak. I close my eyes and focus on his sure fingers working me toward orgasm.

"You want to come, baby girl?" he asks and I nod, a moan escaping me when he pinches my clit. "Say it."

"I want to come," I whisper as I tilt my hips up, looking for his fingers to touch me in a particular way.

He stills those magical fingers between my legs. "Beg for it."

The man is mean, in the absolute sexiest way possible. "Please let me come. Please. I need it."

"You need what?"

"To come." He flicks my clit, a teasing glance that makes me clamp my thighs around his hand to keep him there.

"Who can do that for you, baby?"

"You." Yes, him. The sensitive skin between my legs tingles with anticipation and I feel like I'm drowning in desire.

He bites my earlobe, emitting a low growl that sends a shiver through me. "Say my name."

"Please, Max. Make me come."

"You want to come in my mouth or on my fingers?"

My legs go so weak at his words, at the images they conjure, I swear they feel like jelly. Thank God I'm not standing or I'd drop to the floor. "I . . ."

He removes his hand from my pussy, making me moan at the loss. "Tell me what you want, Lily."

"I want your mouth."

"Hmm, let's do this, baby." He swivels me around, yanking me on top of him so we're in a sixty-nine position. My feet are on either side of his head, my knees at his shoulders, my backside in his face. I brace my hands on the mattress, his hips between my arms, his majestic cock thick and ready in front of my mouth. Just as I feel his skilled mouth land on my pussy I draw his cock between my lips, sucking the head of him, the salty essence of his pre-come coating my tongue.

He moans against me, his low voice sending a ripple of sensation across my sensitive skin. I pull him deeper into my mouth, licking him slowly with my tongue as he licks at me. His fingers come into the mix, teasing my entry as his tongue circles my clit and I lift up away from his cock, lost to the feeling of his mouth on my pussy, taking me higher and higher . . .

"That's it, baby, grind on my face," he encourages me and *oh God,* I do. Shamelessly. I can feel his stubble-covered chin brush against my folds and it drives me wild. His tongue slides all over my skin, like he wants to taste every inch of me. His fingers . . . oh my God, his fingers are moving up, pressing against my ass, teasing me there, sending me straight over the brink . . .

I'm climaxing on a gasp, his name falling from my lips as I come all over his face, just like he demanded I do. His hands reach up to grip my hips, steadying me as I grind and shudder all over his lips and tongue. He doesn't stop licking me, touching me, his fingers playing with an area I've never really allowed anyone to touch before. The sensation of his finger pressing at my ass, his lips wrapped tightly around my clit, has me coming again. To the point where the moment the shudders leave me, I'm trying my best to get away from him, my skin is so sensitive.

"Stop, please. I can't take it anymore," I tell him on an agonized moan, and he releases his hold on me so I can climb away from him and fall at his side. I press against him, my arm going across his stomach, my fingers resting close to his still-hard cock. "I failed you."

He starts to laugh, sounding rusty. Makes me wonder if he doesn't laugh much. "How?"

"I didn't finish you off." I trace my finger around the head of his cock and it twitches beneath my touch. "And you definitely finished me off. Twice."

Max kisses my forehead, his hand going to my breast, fingers playing with my nipple. "We still have time. I don't have to leave just yet."

I slide between his legs, lying on my stomach, his cock poised and ready at my lips. "Then let me help you with this." I grip the base of him and lift up, slipping my lips around his thick cock and sucking him deep.

So deep, I feel him touch the back of my throat and I swallow, trying to relax the muscles there. He's big. He tastes salty, his musky scent filling my nostrils, swimming in my head. My pussy clenches, as if I didn't just come twice already, and I can't believe how sucking him, touching him, is getting me off, too.

"You taste so good," I murmur after I withdraw him from my mouth. I smile, run my tongue up and down the length of him, putting on a show, knowing how much guys love to watch.

And Max is just like any other guy. They can't help it; it's in their DNA. He reaches forward and sweeps my hair away from my face, holding it in his fist as he studies me intently. My gaze never leaves his as I lave attention onto the head of his cock, my fingers gripping his base as I lick him up and down.

"Suck it harder, princess," he grits out and I do as he asks, my cheeks hollowing when I suck him deeper. Harder. "That's it. Fuck, your mouth feels like heaven."

Pleasure ripples through me at his compliments. I brush his thigh with my hand, feel the muscles jump beneath my touch, and I remove his cock from my mouth with a smile. "I like touching you."

"Keep sucking, baby," he orders, and I flash him a wicked smirk before I rear up and drop little kisses all over his flat belly. The muscles quiver beneath my lips, his cock twitches against my chest, and he releases his hold on my hair so that it falls all around me, tickling his skin.

"Fuck," he grits out when I lick and nip his skin, teasing him. "You're making me crazy."

"Just returning the favor," I murmur, my tongue searching the path of dark hair that stretches from below his navel to his cock. "You made me feel like I was losing my mind only a few minutes ago."

"You liked it," he mutters, and I laugh because he's right. I loved it.

"You like this, too," I whisper, brushing the hair out of my face so I can see him. He's watching me, his gaze intense, his mouth drawn in a thin line and sweat forming on his forehead. He looks like he's doing everything possible not to fall completely apart and I love that, too. It's a heady feeling, knowing I have so much power over him.

That I'm capable of giving him so much pleasure.

"Don't stop," he urges and I return my attention to his cock, bobbing up and down on him, moaning when he sinks his fingers into my hair and guides me, thrusting deeper, fucking my mouth. He's uttering an endless string of harsh curses, using me for his satisfaction, mindless with it, and I let him, murmuring around his cock, gripping him tight, sucking him deep.

"Gonna come," he rasps as a warning but I don't move away from him. More like I sink him deeper into my mouth, and the first spurt of semen on my tongue makes me moan in tandem with his bone-rattling groan. I pull away from him slightly so he doesn't flood the back of my throat, but I don't waste a drop, either. Men love this sort of thing and normally I don't swallow.

But there's something about this man that makes me want to do . . . anything for him. Give him as much pleasure as I possibly can. Do whatever he wants me to do.

Let him do with me whatever he wants, too . . .

"OKAY, I REALLY SHOULD GO NOW," MAX SAYS HOURS LATER AS he sits up in bed, swinging his legs so he's seated on the side of the mattress, his feet planted firmly on the floor. He runs a hand through his hair, then turns to look at me.

I'm lying on my side, completely uncovered and not really caring. I'm comfortable in my nudity, I always have been, and this intimidating, delicious, sexy man is not going to get to me, no matter how intently he stares.

Besides, I like the way he stares. And kisses and touches and licks and sucks . . .

"Why?" I ask when he doesn't say anything more. Though I already know the answer. He gave me a long list of things he needed to do hours ago. Before he proceeded to attack my pussy first with his fingers, then his mouth. It's all we've been doing, getting each other off with lips and fingers and tongues. No condoms mean we have to get creative.

And I've discovered that Max is extremely creative.

"I still need to take that shower. Get some fresh clothes on.

Find a giant box of condoms." He grins ruefully, and the sight of it sends a zing of pleasure straight between my legs. "Trust me, princess. It's hard for me to leave with you looking like that. You're too damn tempting."

"Should I take that as a compliment or an insult?" I'm confused, which is dumb. And I'm also feeling a little unsure. This isn't my usual thing, making small talk and plans to see a guy again after a sex marathon.

Stretching out my legs, I sigh, my muscles aching deliciously. I feel gently abused since he just finished bringing me to orgasm for the third time since I woke up. I swear my body is still trembling from the force of that last climax.

I honestly don't think I've come so many times before in my life.

"It's definitely a compliment." He reaches out and runs his fingers down the side of my thigh, making me shiver. His hand drops and he gets up, reaching for his clothes where he left them on the floor and offering me a very fine view of his very fine ass. "I gotta get out of here. I won't be able to resist you like this," he says.

I raise a brow. "Like what?"

"Naked and sexy as fuck." He turns and faces me with a grin, and dodges when I toss a pillow at him.

I settle back against the remaining pillows, pulling the sheet up over me as he gets dressed. The late-morning sun is blazing through my bedroom window and I glance at the clock on the bedside table, shuddering when I realize just how late it is. We've fucked the morning away completely.

Not that I regret it.

"You covered up," he says, sounding disappointed.

"I'm a distraction, remember?" Sitting up, I plump the pillows and lie back down, a yawn taking over me so fast I don't quite cover it up with my hand.

"And you're a sleepy distraction." He's fully dressed as he

comes back toward the bed and dips over me, dropping a kiss on top of my head. "See you around, princess."

"Wait a minute." I grab hold of his hand before he can escape. "Are we still meeting later?"

He raises a brow. "You still want to? Or are you having second thoughts?"

Is he projecting? Maybe he's the one having second thoughts. "I want to," I admit softly, swallowing hard against the lump in my throat. Honest admissions aren't easy for me. They make me uncomfortable, like I'm putting myself on the line. Making myself vulnerable.

He smiles, and the sight of it steals my breath. It's not cocky or full of amusement. It's tender. Real. "Good. I still want to, too." He gives me another kiss, this time on the lips, soft and sweet and unlike any kiss he's delivered. All the others have been full of passion. Raw. A little rough.

Not this one. My lips are tingling and I reach up and touch them, watching as he goes to the door, flashes me one last grin over his shoulder, and then opens the screen door, sliding through it and shutting it with barely a sound.

The room is depressingly quiet without him there and the air conditioner clicks on. A blast of icy air hits me, making me shiver, and I tuck the sheet tight around my neck, letting out a trembling sigh as I close my eyes, waiting for sleep to take over.

But it doesn't. I can't sleep. I've been up most of the night, occupied by Max's insistent hands and mouth and body, and I should be exhausted. My body is sated and tired. My brain, though, is wide awake and full of disturbing thoughts.

Like how lonely I am. Despite spending hours with a man who knew just how to touch my body to make me respond in the most outrageous way, I feel alone. Hollow.

Empty.

I didn't want Max to leave, which is dumb. I couldn't ex-press that to him. He'd think I'm a psycho with a dependency problem. I barely know him. I shouldn't have these sorts of expectations because they're unrealistic. How I view the world is totally unrealistic. Skewed. I am the quintessential poor little rich girl and I've worn the role for so long, I almost prefer it to anything else. I'm in my comfort zone, wallowing in my lonely existence.

Stupid.

Gazing up at the wall, I will myself to fall asleep, regretting I didn't bring my sleeping pills with me. I didn't want to depend on them and look where it got me. Wide awake when I should feel sated and sleepy and content. I got what I wanted.

Supposedly. But they always leave. Men. Not that I really want them to stay, because I have no idea what it's like to have a real relationship with a man. A one-night stand? Oh yes. I've got those down pat. A few nights of constant fucking with one guy? I can do that, too. But nothing lasting, ever.

Nothing real.

Everyone leaves me eventually. It's been a pattern throughout my entire life. My mother killed herself because we weren't enough for her. We didn't make her happy. Daddy would rather work than deal with his daughters, leaving us to be raised by nannies. Grandma preferred Violet because she was a good girl or Rose because she was the pretty little sweet baby.

And then there was me. There *is* me. No one likes me. Not really. My family tolerates me because they have to. And I took advantage of that. Expected them to always stand by me, to look the other way when I made yet another mistake. They were all good, so I was allowed to be bad, right? One black sheep in the family is allowed.

That's me. I could always count on them, if not for their support, at least for them to still talk to me despite everything I've done.

But I don't know how they'd respond to me now. If they knew I'd hacked into Pilar's computer at work and found all of the dirty email between her and fucking Zachary Lawrence. My sister's ex-boyfriend, the biggest creep on the planet. Violet finally kicked the cheating scumbag to the curb and Daddy sent him to travel around Fleur stores in Europe, training them on the latest projects.

Getting him out of Violet's—and supposedly Pilar's—hair.

But they still talk. Or at least, they did. I thought the email evidence was bad enough, but then I found something worse. Something so bad, it scared me. Sent me straight into a panic and made me run. Not before I drank a giant glass of wine for courage and then sent Pilar an email from her business account to her personal Gmail, letting her know I was on to her.

I know what you've been up to . . .
Kisses,
Lily

We talked that one time on the phone when she threatened me, but she'd only referenced the emails with Zachary the asshole. She never mentioned the other stuff.

And neither did I.

I want to call my father. I want to tell my sisters. But how? Will they believe me and want to help me? Or would they think I'm full of it again? Causing trouble again. I don't even realize the tears are slipping down my face until I taste them when I lick my lips. A sob escapes me and I grab a pillow, pressing it down hard over my face as I scream into it. My voice is muffled, reflecting exactly how I feel.

Muffled. The real me unseen. Unheard.

Throwing the pillow to the floor with a huff, I climb out of bed and stalk to the bathroom, goose bumps covering my chilled naked skin because of the incessant air conditioning blowing through the rooms. I turn on the shower, twisting the knob to almost scalding hot before I hop in and let the water run over me, washing away my sins, my thoughts, my emotions.

Until I am completely numb.

Chapter Twelve

Lily

I FEEL AS GIDDY AS A SCHOOLGIRL—A SAYING I'VE HEARD BEfore and always thought sounded stupid. But I'd never been that girl while in school, excited over boys who might like me. I went after what I wanted, no hesitation. I was brash. A brat. A complete rebel who couldn't bother to give a shit most of the time since the boys all flocked to me.

In my own head, I sound like a shit and that's because I was. Nothing was a challenge. I think that's why I took to hacking so quickly. It challenged me, forced me to think in a different way, filled me with the overwhelming need to figure something out. Who knew that it would be intricate code and not fashion or cosmetics? That hacking into someone else's computer, system, whatever, was also breaking the law gave me an additional thrill. I've always been looking for a thrill.

Still am.

Right now, though, for once in my life, I'm giddy. Over a *guy*. My insides are fizzing with excitement as I enter the openair lobby of the hotel. A warm tropical breeze flows over me, lifting my hair, and I glance over my shoulder, taking in the view of the ocean, the swaying palm trees, hearing the music playing over the speaker—all of it combined makes me feel like a real tourist.

Not some crazy woman on the run.

"Do you need some help, miss?"

I stop short at the man who appears in front of me, clad in khaki-colored linen pants and a subtle Hawaiian print shirt, the standard uniform of the hotel resort employees. He's young and handsome, with short, dark hair and flashing brown eyes, a pleasant smile on his face.

I smile in return and shake my head. "Thank you, but I'm fine. I'm supposed to meet a friend in the lobby."

A knowing look crosses his face. "Ah, are you Lily?"

I blink at him in surprise, wondering how he knew who I was. "Um, yes. I am."

He offers his arm. "Follow me. Your friend requested that I go in search of you. He's waiting for you outside."

Taking the man's arm, I let him guide me through the grand double doors that lead to the front of the hotel. I glance around the circular drive, watching as a group of people wearing jeans and sweaters and looking like they traveled a great distance unload from a shuttle van. A line of taxis sits on the other side of the drive, eager to take tourists wherever they need to go.

But there's no Max to be found anywhere.

The hotel employee releases my arm and I turn to him. "I, uh, don't see my friend anywhere . . ."

He points behind me. "There he is. Have a good afternoon, miss."

I whip back around to find a shiny black Jeep parked in front of me, the engine idling, Max sitting in the driver's seat and watching me with a smile on his face. The passenger-side window rolls down and he ducks his head to meet my gaze. "Wanna go for a ride?" His flirtatious, sexy tone sets a thousand butterflies alight in my stomach.

"I was always told not to take rides from strangers," I call to him, sending him an innocent look when he scowls at me.

Max exits the car and comes around the back of the Jeep, his long-legged stride eating up the ground until he's standing directly in front of me. Wearing a dark gray T-shirt and black cargo shorts, he smells fresh and clean, as if he just got out of the shower. I want to say something clever, something funny, but my throat has gone dry, all because he's so close. My hands literally itch to touch him and my lips tingle, I want to feel his mouth on mine so bad.

He grabs hold of my hands in both of his, as if he has to restrain himself and me so we don't grab at each other like oversexed freaks. He leans in close, his mouth at my ear, his breath warm as it caresses my skin, making me tremble. "Considering I had my mouth on your pussy and made you come with my tongue only a few hours ago, I definitely wouldn't classify us as strangers, princess," he murmurs just before he softly kisses my cheek.

Thank God he has ahold of me because my knees go weak at his blunt choice of words. "Max," I breathe, unable to say anything else, my cheeks growing hot.

With a grin he leads me to the Jeep and opens the passenger door, giving me a boost with his hand on my ass since the tires are oversized and the entire vehicle is lifted. A typical man car, something I would never consider driving, not that I have my driver's license. When would I ever need it?

"Where are we going?" I ask when he climbs back into the Jeep.

He flashes me a mysterious smile and throws the vehicle into drive. "You'll have to wait and see."

"I hope I'm dressed all right." I glance down at myself. I'm wearing a green tank top and white shorts, my skin golden from all the sun I've been getting.

"You got a swimsuit on under there?" he asks as he makes a left onto the main road.

"No." I bite my lower lip, regretting that I didn't put one on. What was I thinking? Maybe he's going to take me to a secluded beach.

"That's too bad. Guess you'll have to go swimming naked," he suggests, that sexy Texan drawl back in his voice.

"I'm sure you'd like that," I say, my panties growing wet when he shoots me a hot look out of the corner of his eye.

"I'd love it," he agrees.

We make idle small talk on the drive, commenting on the beauty of the island, the fabulous views of the ocean, how much it must cost to live there. Max is not only easy on the eyes, but he's also easy to talk to, a great conversationalist who knows how to fill a quiet moment without making it seem like a bunch of endless chatter.

He's confident behind the wheel and as I watch him drive, I become aroused. Everything he touches he does so with such command. His every movement is controlled and efficient. He doesn't waste words or energy, and I can't help but sit and watch in quiet admiration.

The men I've been with in the past pale in comparison. I can't even consider them as real men. Boys playing at being a grown-up is a more apt description.

But Max? He's all man. Mature and responsible and sexy, with just a touch of cocky self-assuredness I find incredibly attractive.

"You're quiet," he accuses after a few minutes of silence. "Makes me think you're scheming."

"Who, me?" The man is also incredibly perceptive. Not that I'm necessarily scheming, but I have been known to do just that more often than not.

"Yes, you." He sends me a look. "Mad that I won't tell you where we're going?"

"I figure you're taking me to some remote tropical rain forest or something along those lines," I tease him. We keep climbing and climbing, the road becoming narrower, the view more and more beautiful the higher we go.

"You're not too far off the mark," he says as he slows down and turns left, onto what looks like a private and rarely used road. "Hold on to the 'oh shit' handle, princess. The ride's about to get bumpy."

I do as he asks, reaching up to grab the handle that's right above the door, a little squeal escaping me when we go over a particularly large bump. He stops the vehicle and hits a button, switching it into four-wheel drive. Shooting me a wicked grin, he lets out a whoop like he's about to ride a bull out into the center of a rodeo ring and presses hard on the gas, sending the Jeep flying down the narrow, bumpy road and making me scream.

Never in my life have I experienced a ride like this one and it's both terrifying and exhilarating, all at once. The road stretches along the side of a lush green mountain, and one wrong move or turn of the steering wheel will send us flying over the edge of a cliff and straight into what I can only assume is a canyon. I grip the handle above my head with both hands, my butt literally lifting away from the seat with every bump and rut he drives across. Max is laughing, I'm screaming and laughing at the same time, and I close my eyes when I feel the back wheels scramble to grip the road when he makes an extra-sharp turn.

I've never been the praying sort, but this experience is making me whisper all sorts of promises to God as long as we make it out of here in one piece.

When he finally brings the Jeep to a full stop, he murmurs, "Open your eyes, princess."

Slowly I open them, all the air escaping my lungs when I see what's in front of us. A view of the ocean unlike anything I've witnessed before. Nothing but blue skies dotted with white, puffy clouds and the glittering Pacific spread out before us.

"What do you think?"

I don't take my eyes off the ocean. It's as if we're hanging right on the edge of the earth—which we might be for all I know. "It's beautiful," I murmur. "How did you know about this place?"

"I asked around, talked to some locals." He touches me and I turn to look at him, pressing my lips together when he runs his index finger down the length of my arm. "Come on, I have more to show you."

He hops out of the Jeep before I can say another word, rounding the vehicle and opening the door for me like a gentleman. I take his offered hand and exit the Jeep, letting him escort me along the gravelly dirt road until we find a rough path that leads straight down the cliff.

"Uh, are we really going to try and walk that?" I ask cautiously, tugging on his hand to make him stop.

He turns to look at me, his brows lowered. "It doesn't look that bad."

I hold out my foot toward him, my sandal dangling away from my heel. "I'm in flip-flops."

Max laughs and shakes his head. "I'll pick you up and carry you the rest of the way if you can't handle it."

"Oh, I can handle it." I lift my chin, not one to back down from a challenge.

And neither is he. His eyes sparkle as he looks me up and down, probably silently mocking my choice of pristine white shorts for a trek through the Hawaiian jungle. How was I supposed to know what he had planned for us? "Then what are we waiting for? Let's go."

The problem is that after a while, I really can't handle it. At least, my shoes can't. They slip and skid over the steep, rocky terrain and a couple of times, I lose an entire shoe, the flip-flop flying down the trail, rescued by my watcher. Twice I stumble, thankful Max is directly in front of me so I can brace my fall by gripping his solid back or tugging on his shirt. The path curves sharply, going deeper and deeper into the lush, thick trees and bushes, and I hear things move among the branches, see birds flying away with squawks of surprise when we come upon them.

I just know there are unknown critters everywhere, studying us. I hope there aren't snakes, or other creatures with poisonous fangs. God, what if a bird gets pissed off and attacks our heads? Does that sort of thing actually happen?

"I can practically smell your fear, princess. Don't worry, nothing's going to get you," he says teasingly.

I glare at his back. He has a really nice back, too, broad and strong, the skin smooth and warm. I hope he takes his shirt off soon. "What about snakes?"

"From what I've learned, there are no snakes native to the Hawaiian Islands," he answers.

I follow after him for a bit, pondering what he said. "What about snakes that were brought here?"

"Yeah, there are probably a few of those."

Max turns when he realizes I'm not following him, resting his hands on his hips as he squints up at me. He's not wearing sunglasses and the sun shines right in his eyes. "What's wrong?"

"What if there really are snakes on this trail?" I ask him.

"I already told you there's nothing to worry about."

"But . . . snakes." I throw my hands up into the air, not sure I can explain to him how much they scare me without sounding like a complete loser.

"Are you telling me you're afraid of snakes? A badass like yourself?" He raises his brows in question.

"I am so not a badass." I roll my eyes.

"You have to admit, you kind of are."

I shake my head, pleased that he thinks I am. "You're the one who calls me 'princess.' "

"That's because you're pretty as a princess." He starts to approach, my gaze dropping to his legs as he makes the trek back up the steep incline, his calf muscles straining as he walks. Since when are calf muscles so sexy? I sort of want to fan myself just staring at them. "And you're also feisty. Like a badass princess."

I start to laugh as he stops in front of me, his hands going to my waist, his fingers pressing into my skin. "You want me to keep all the snakes away, baby girl?"

His words, the tone of his voice, the way his fingers slip beneath the hem of my tank top and touch my bare skin, send me reeling. "I really, really hate snakes. I can't stress it enough."

"I'll save you." He releases his hold on me and turns around, bending forward the slightest bit and holding his arms out away from his body. "Hop on."

"What?" I frown, wondering what he's getting at.

"Hop on my back. I'll give you a piggyback ride." He waves his hands at me. "Come on."

"But . . . I'm kinda heavy." No way can I jump on his back on this steep trail. I could knock him forward and both of us would go stumbling down the freaking mountain.

He glances at me from over his shoulder. "You weigh nothing. I had you on top of me last night, remember? I think I can handle you."

My cheeks warm at the memories of last night. Of how I rode him hard, his hands all over my breasts, gripping my hips as I bounced up and down on his cock.

"Now stop blushing and hop on," he teases.

Sticking my tongue out at him, I take a few backward steps so I can get a running start. I launch myself toward him, jumping on top of his back and gripping hold of his shoulders as he grabs me behind my knees. He holds me on top of him and with a low grunt readjusts me, my arms sliding around his neck, my legs wrapping around his middle so my entire body is clinging to his back.

"You won't drop me, will you?" I ask, gripping his neck tight.

"As long as you promise not to strangle me," he says, making a little noise like I'm cutting off his circulation.

I start to laugh, relaxing my hold on him. "Sorry. No one's really carried me like this before."

He starts to walk, acting like my weight slung on his back doesn't affect him at all, not one huff or puff escaping him. "No one? Not even your dad?"

"Especially not my dad." The silence that follows after my snarky remark is almost deafening. "He wasn't the hands-on sort."

"Gotcha." He's quiet for a moment longer. "Not even with a high school boyfriend, huh?"

"We never messed around or played any sorts of games like . . . this." Everything was much more sophisticated and grown-up where I come from. In high school my friends and I drank the finest liquor money could buy since we pilfered it from our parents' locked liquor cabinets. We bought the most expensive cocaine or weed because usually one of us had connections to a top-of-the-line dealer.

No searching the dirty streets for a dime bag for us private school girls and boys, no way.

"I'm sure you played other games, right?"

"Sure." I don't want to go into detail. I really don't want to share my past with him. I've done a lot of things I'm not proud of. I was a total spoiled bitch who demanded certain things and . . . always got them.

In other words, I was horrid.

"How about skinny-dipping? Ever do that?"

My entire body tingles at the casual suggestion. "Are you saying that's what we're going to do? Don't tell me we're going to hike down this entire mountain to the ocean." We're still a long way from the water. I can't imagine he could carry me much farther.

"Nah, I have a better spot all picked out." He turns right, down a trail I didn't even notice. It's mostly covered by overgrown shrubs, vines and low-hanging tree branches, and we have to duck as we make our way along the new trail.

"Where exactly are you taking me?" I ask, squeezing my legs along his sides.

He huffs out a breath. Finally, he sounds tired. The man can just go and go. It's almost nice to see cracks in his perfectly fit veneer. "Another few minutes and you'll find out."

I remain silent, enjoying the sensation of his big hands gripping the back of my legs, how solid he feels between my thighs. The scent of his hair is intoxicating, as is the feel of his body moving and shifting beneath me. He's so strong, so hard . . . everywhere. Just knowing this man had me every which way last night into this morning is enough to leave my body buzzing and desperate for more.

He rounds a corner, past a particularly thick group of trees, and I hear it before I see it. A dull, steady roar, the sound of water splashing. Then it comes into view, like a shining oasis in the middle of a desert, a gorgeous waterfall cascading down the side of a mountain and falling into a channel of swirling water.

"We're here," he says as he loosens his hold on me and I slide down his back, making sure I brush against every available body part of his that I can. I straighten the hem of my tank top as he turns to look at me, a satisfied smile on his face as he waves a hand in the direction of the waterfall. "Was that worth the hike or what?"

"It's beautiful," I agree as I start walking toward it. The water is falling so rapidly I can feel it mist in the air, bathing my warm skin in cool sprinkles. I go to the water's edge and kick off my flip-flops, dipping my toes into the water. "And cold."

"Yeah?" He approaches me, stopping right by my side. He tugs off his shirt, revealing that mouthwatering chest, and my greedy gaze drinks him in, not sure where I should settle my eyes first.

All of it is just too delicious to take in.

"Are you jumping in?" I ask as he toes off his shoes.

"Hell, yeah. It was hot, packing you down that mountain."

I slap his arm, grimacing at the impact. His biceps are rock hard. "I told you I was too heavy."

"Nah, I'm just giving you shit." He reaches for the button of his shorts and undoes it, then slides the zipper down, taking off his shorts and his boxer briefs in one push. He kicks them off, flashes me a wicked smile, and starts walking into the water.

Breathless, I watch him, my gaze glued to his ass. It's firm and muscular, just like the rest of him, and stark white compared to his tanned skin, as are the back of his thighs. I giggle, clamping my lips shut when he gets waist deep and turns to look at me.

"What are you laughing at?" he asks.

"Your ghostly white butt," I tell him, deciding to be honest.

He splashes water at me, getting my feet and ankles wet, and I jump back a little. "I bet your pretty little ass is just as white. In fact, I know it is."

I remember that he became real up-close-and-personal with my ass this morning and my skin tingles at the memory. "Care to see it?"

"Absolutely," he says without hesitation.

I grab the bottom of my tank and yank it up and over my head, tossing it to the ground. I'm not wearing a bra and I swear I hear him mutter, "I knew it," under his breath as he watches me strip.

Smiling, I continue, taking off my white shorts, a small part of me hoping like crazy that they don't get too dirty while crumpled on the ground, leaving me only in a white lacy thong that is completely see-through.

Exactly the reason I wore it.

His expression slackens and that arrogant smile disappears. He's gazing at my panties like they're the solution to all of his problems and I start to wade into the water, hissing in a breath at the cold temperature. "Like what you see?" I ask innocently.

"Not going to take off the panties?" he asks, his voice a little rough.

"I thought keeping them on made things more interesting." Slowly I approach him, the roar of the waterfall becoming louder and louder as I come closer to Max. The water is waist high, then chest high, and he grabs me, hauling me to him, his hands automatically going to my butt as he slides his palms up and down my curves.

"Very interesting. And flimsy. Though I thought we were skinny-dipping," he murmurs just as he bends his head, his mouth connecting with mine.

I run my hands up his wet chest, parting my lips, allowing his tongue entry. A moan escapes me when he hauls me in close and I wrap my legs around his waist, feeling his erect cock poking against my backside. "Take them off then," I encourage when I break away from his hot, delicious mouth.

One hand goes to the thin band of my thong and he tugs, tearing the lace away from my body. A gasp escapes me and he's pulling the ruined panties off me, balling them up in his hand and tossing them over the water, where they land on the shore, right by my flip-flops.

I stare at the balled-up underwear on the ground before I turn back to look at him, my lips parted, gaping at him like an idiot. He smiles and grabs hold of me, pulling me farther into the water, and I have no choice but to swim with him.

"Let's go fuck under the waterfall," he says, and I laugh at him, shaking my head.

"We don't have a condom. Unless you have one tucked under your balls," I tease, making him chuckle.

"That I don't. I have one in the pocket of my shorts, though."
He glances at the shore once more, where his shorts lie in a heap.
"Guess we'll have to improvise."

"Guess so," I say, my heart racing at the thought.

Can't wait to see what he comes up with.

Chapter Thirteen

Max

LILY LOOKS LIKE A WATER NYMPH, SEXY AND NAKED, DROPLETS of water scattered all over her skin and clinging to her eyelashes and her hair slicked back. Her breasts bob in the water, offering me teasing glimpses of her dark pink nipples, and they're hard as diamonds, tempting me to lick and suck and make her crazy out of her mind with wanting more.

She likes it when I suck her nipples. She likes it when I do anything to her. She's so damn responsive. I know she liked it, too, when I tore her panties off her body. They probably cost a fortune but I don't give a shit. It felt good, showing such aggression, showing her what I can do.

Hell, I felt like a show-off carrying her down the trail to this spot. She complained she might weigh too much, but give me a break. She's light as a feather. And despite how hot it is, it still felt good having her pressed so close to me. Her mouth at my neck, her breasts crushed against my back, her legs clamped around my hips. She's warm and soft and fits perfectly in my arms, against my back . . .

Too damn bad the condoms are stuffed in my shorts pocket and I was too stupid to remember to grab one and bring it with me into the water. Now I can't fuck her properly like I want to under the waterfall.

Guess we really will have to improvise. Eventually I'll carry her back to shore, grab a condom, and fuck her in the shallow end. Hell, if I can stand it. I'm afraid she might wear me out by the end of the first go-round.

She splashes water in my face and pushes her body beneath the surface, headed toward the waterfall. I follow after her, my arms slicing through the water as I easily catch up with her. She's a good swimmer, a talent I figured she was lacking considering what happened when I rescued her out of the ocean.

"So you really can swim," I say when I capture her in my arms and haul her in close to me.

An indignant gasp escapes her and she slugs my shoulder. "What makes you say that?"

"After your little tumble in the ocean a few days ago, I figured you were a beginner at best." I grab hold of her injured hand and examine it. The bandage is gone and it looks like the wound is healing nicely. "Still bother you?" I ask.

She slowly shakes her head. "It's a lot better."

"Good." I bring her palm up to my mouth and kiss it, noting how her eyes fill with heat when my lips touch her skin. "That was a scary moment."

"Tell me about it."

"What happened, anyway?"

"I don't know." She shrugs, turning her head to stare at the waterfall. "One minute I was fine and the next, I was being swept away, along with the tide. I couldn't get my bearings, I couldn't rise above the water, and I started to panic."

The worst thing that can happen when something goes wrong while underwater—panicking. "Glad I was there," I say, knowing we've had a similar conversation already but feeling like it needs to be said. She'd come close to death that afternoon.

"I'm glad you were there, too." She returns her attention to me, her voice going soft, as does her body, since she seems to melt into me. I gather her closer, my gaze dropping to her breasts, the way they're pressed firmly against my chest, water drops making wet paths all over her abundant flesh. "I'm glad you're here now."

"Yeah?" I skim my index finger along her temple, her cheek. Her skin is sleek from the water and chilled, her cheeks and lips redder than normal.

"Oh yeah." Her smile turns sultry and she circles her arms around my neck, her fingers diving into the wet hair at my nape. "You've made my solo vacation infinitely more interesting."

"Same goes, princess." I lean in and kiss her, her lips parted and wet, the inside of her mouth hot compared to her cool skin. I sweep my tongue inside, tangle it with hers, and she clutches me closer, her legs curling around my thighs.

I grab hold of her legs and lift, groaning when they wrap around my hips and I can feel her hot pussy press against my erect cock. I'd give anything to drive myself inside her, but I can't. Not without protection. I'm not about to do something stupid and fuck her bare.

She rubs against me, little whimpers sounding in the back of her throat as she grinds her body on mine, and I know she's trying to get off. No way am I going to let her find her satisfaction just yet. "Slow down, baby girl," I tell her, my hand going to her ass and giving one cheek a firm squeeze. "You're moving too fast."

"I can't help it," she murmurs, wiggling her hips and nearly making my eyes cross. "You feel so good."

"It'll feel even better if you can find some patience." I squeeze her butt harder, wanting her to get the hint, but it seems to only get her off more. "If you don't stop squirming, I'm going to drop you."

She sends me a challenging look. Brows raised, lips curved in a smirk, eyes full of doubt. Slowly, boldly, she rotates her hips, slips one hand between us, and grips my cock tight. "You really want me to stop?"

I release my hold on her, shocking her so much her fingers spring free from my dick, and I push her legs away from my hips, putting some much-needed distance between us. Damn it, when she moves like that, touches me like that, I can hardly think straight. And I'm always thinking straight. I'm the one who's in control, not her. She tends to forget that.

So I guess I need to remind her.

"What the hell are you doing?" she yells, splashing water at me with both of her hands.

I swim away from her, drawing closer and closer to the waterfall. It's so damn loud I can hardly hear myself think and the water is colder, helping my erection settle down some. "Trying to get you to slow the fuck down. Haven't you ever heard of anticipation?"

"Haven't you ever heard of a quickie?" she yells back, looking completely irritated.

And hot. Definitely hot. There is nothing better than watching a naked Lily Fowler swim around in a freshwater lagoon, all those lush curves on display, her expression full of rage. That I'm getting off on her like this shows what a sick fuck I am.

"Baby, you were rubbing against me like a cat in heat," I taunt, because for some twisted reason, I enjoy riling her up, pissing her off.

"It's all your fault, you know. You're the one who makes me feel like a cat in heat." She starts for me, diving beneath the water and swimming fast, straight toward me like a bullet. I turn onto my belly and put some effort into it, swimming as fast as I can, until I find myself directly beneath the waterfall. The water pummels me deeper and I struggle to swim away from it, opening my eyes to see Lily zoom past me like she's some sort of mermaid.

Impressive.

She pops her head above water at the same exact time I do, about fifty feet away and glaring at me like she could slice me to bits with just her eyes. "You're an asshole."

"You're only just now realizing this?" I push my wet hair away from my face with both hands. "I thought you had that all figured out when I took you on that death ride to get here."

"Do you want to drive me away? Because I don't get this." She waves a hand at me, flicking water in my direction. "What you're trying to do. Put a wedge between us? Act like an arrogant prick? I'm confused, Max."

I tread water, watching her, her words repeating themselves in my muddled brain. She just called me out on my shitty behavior, something that hasn't happened in a long time. My mama used to do it when I was still living at home, but that stopped once I went into the military and straightened my ass up.

Until I didn't have my ass on straight and made a spontaneous move, trying to save the men in my squad and losing more than half of them in the process. I lost all control, something I rarely do, and it cost me my military career.

I disappointed my family, especially my father. I fucked up. Swore I would never do something stupid again when I became a civilian once more, grateful for my friends who rallied around me and invested in my new business. I took their unwavering faith as them investing in me, believing in me.

And I needed that. Desperately.

The business has done well; it's been almost two years and it's grown steadily. Since the doors opened I've taken on a steady stream of clients, treated them well, done what I needed to do and kept on the right track.

Until Lily. She's fucked me up all over again. I shouldn't be here with her. I shouldn't be doing this. I can tell myself all damn day I'm trying to get close to her so I can get that laptop, but it's complete bullshit.

I like her. I'm attracted to her. Hell, I think I might be addicted to her pussy, to her mouth, to the fire that blazes within her. I want her.

And it has nothing to do with the laptop, with the job, with Pilar Vasquez.

It has everything to do with Lily.

Without a word I swim to her, never taking my eyes from hers, seeing the troubled doubt, the anxiousness, the worry in her expression. The fire is there, too, blazing in her beautiful hazel eyes, and I know she doubts me. Is probably tempted to shove me away and tell me to go fuck myself.

I'd deserve it, too.

I stop just before her, water splashing all over my head, the roar of the waterfall making it hard for me to hear or be heard. Clearing my throat, I yell, "I'm sorry."

There's no need to explain myself to help her figure out why I just reacted the way I did. I need to finish out today and be done with it. Be done with her. That's what I tell myself, at least.

I don't know if I can do it.

She watches me, her gaze, her expression, softening the slightest bit. But she says nothing, which fills me with the need to say something.

"I'm a dick." I shake my head, sending water droplets flying, and she floats away from me, like she needs the distance. "I don't want to ruin this."

Lily frowns. "Ruin what?"

"Today. This afternoon. What we're doing." I come toward her, relieved she doesn't move away. "I'm having fun."

"I was, too," she says, the sarcasm heavy. "Until you went all asshole on me."

"I can't say I won't do it again." I slip my arms around her slender waist and she drifts toward me, her legs circling my hips once more, her hot pussy pressed up against my lower belly. Breathing deep, I place my mouth at her temple, the scent of her shampoo, the feel of her skin, making me hard once more. "But I'll try my best to not be a dick for the rest of the day."

She starts to laugh, her arms coming around my neck, her breasts once again lodged against my chest. I love how her body feels close to mine. We fucking fit. "Well, that was the most honest apology I think I've ever received."

I kiss her because I can't resist her laugh, can't resist the way she's touching me. The kiss turns deep in an instant, our tongues tangling, the two of us moaning, our bodies melding as close as they can get. I start to steer us both closer to the water's edge, on the other side of the waterfall, so I can at least stand.

Within seconds, it's shallow enough for me to find my footing and I reach between her legs, making her gasp. She's so hot, she coats my fingers with her creamy essence and I kiss her hard while I work her harder, sinking my fingers inside her body as I press her swollen clit with my thumb. She moans into my mouth, her teeth nipping my lips, her tongue circling mine, and I know she's already fucking close.

Hell, I'm about to explode, all from arguing with her, kissing her, touching her. She works her hips against my hand and I add another finger, then another, fucking her with three, getting a little rough as I thrust as deep as I can get.

But this girl, she can take it. She likes it when I take over, when I'm not gentle. It's a rare thing, to find a woman who seems to get me immediately. When I was young I fought my urges. Figured they weren't normal. Now I run with them, though I usually have some restraint when I'm first with a woman.

Not Lily. I sensed she would like what I could give her. And I was right.

She breaks away from my mouth and takes a deep breath, her head slung back, her lips parted on a silent moan, her eyes squeezed closed. She's holding on to me so tight with her legs that I'm able to take my free hand and reach into her wet hair, gathering it up and tugging hard, making her face me once more. "Open your eyes," I demand and she does, though her vision is hazy, as if she's completely lost in her pleasure. "Watch me."

Lily never looks away as I continue to push my fingers into her body. She's obedient, compliant, and the satisfaction that roars through me is overwhelming. I press my forehead to hers, my hand busy between her legs, my fingers loosening in her hair, and I push it away from her shoulder. "Keep your eyes on mine, princess. I wanna see it when I push you over the edge."

She nods, a little whimper escaping her. "Please."

That I'm making her beg for it pleases me even more. "Work those hips, baby," I whisper, encouraging her. "You close?"

Her hips twist and she clamps her knees on either side of my hips, locking herself in place. I pull my fingers from within her body and cup her pussy, her moan of frustration sending a sick thrill through me. "Don't stop," she whispers, tugging on the hair at my nape.

"You need to learn something," I tell her, pleased when her eyes widen. "When it comes to this . . . whether I'm fucking you with my cock or my fingers or my mouth, I'm *always* in control."

Her lips part as if she's going to protest and I cut her off with my mouth, thrusting my tongue deep at the exact time I push my fingers back inside her. Her inner walls clamp hard, her entire body shakes, and then she's crying out against my lips, her body consumed with shudders as her orgasm slams into her.

Damn it, I didn't get to watch her face, see that exact moment when I push her to the edge and she hangs there for an agonizing moment before she falls. I wanted that, needed it so damn bad, and even though she's trembling in my arms, my name falling hoarsely from her lips, I feel strangely disappointed.

Meaning, I need to do that to her again. And the next time—which is gonna happen in hours, if not minutes, if I have anything to say about it—I'll study her face so close I'll see every nuance. Every flicker in her gaze, every tremor beneath her skin, see the flush rush up her cheeks, her lips quivering, her eyelashes trembling . . .

It'll be fucking amazing.

And it'll happen all because of me.

Chapter Fourteen

Max

"Tell me something about you. something you've never admitted to anyone else."

Lily's softly whispered request makes my entire body stiffen and I will myself to loosen the hell up. She's stroking my chest with her fingernails, her naked body half draped over mine as we sit on the sandy shore, our legs still submerged in the water. Not ten minutes ago I'd been inside her, pounding away, making her beg and plead and cry out incoherently, and now she's trying to find her way inside *me*. Inside my thoughts, my past, my secrets.

No way can I let her in. I say one wrong thing and my cover is blown. Bad enough how much I've put myself at risk. Fucking around with my subject when I should be following her, plotting my next move so I can get what my client wants.

Instead, I'm plotting ways to get inside Lily Fowler's body again. Talk about messed up.

"There's nothing to tell," I say, keeping my voice deceptively casual. More like there's nothing I *want* to tell.

"Oh, come on." She lifts her head, her gaze meeting mine, steady and true. She's so pretty like this, her skin still flushed from our lovemaking, her hair in disarray, her lips swollen from my kisses. "You can't give me a little something? Just a hint? I feel like I hardly know you."

"Isn't that the point of a vacation fling?" I swear I see hurt flicker in the depths of her eyes just before she looks away and I immediately feel like an asshole. "You know what I mean," I say, my voice softening.

"Yeah, I know exactly what you mean." She rolls away from me and stands just as I sit up, her ass practically in my face. She walks over to where we hastily tore off our clothes and slips on her shorts—sans panties, since they're probably still floating in the water somewhere—then jerks on her tank, messing up her already wild, damp hair. "I just thought . . ." Her voice drifts and she shakes her head, a small laugh falling from her lips though she doesn't sound happy. "Never mind."

"You thought what?" I stand as well and go to her, grabbing my clothes from the ground and casually putting them on. Her back is to me, her shoulders stiff, as she steps into her flip-flops. "That we've had sex a few times and now we should play true confessions?"

Lily whirls on me, indignation flaring in her eyes. "Yes, okay? You're right. Is that a crime? I thought—I don't know what I thought. All I know is I like you." Her expression doesn't change when she says that, though I can feel mine changing, I'm so shocked by her admission. "I wanted to maybe, I don't know, find out a few more things about you besides that you're from Texas and you're an expert kisser. Oh, and an expert rescuer. That's all I have. All I know about you."

Expert kisser? I figure Lily Fowler's kissed a bunch of guys— and no, the thought of her kissing a bunch of guys doesn't make me jealous at all.

Not really.

Keep convincing yourself.

Nice to know that I rate highly at least. "Isn't that enough?"

I ask her softly. I don't want her to know anything else. I thought she preferred the casual fling, the anonymity of a revolving door of lovers. That's how they make her look in the press.

Maybe they're wrong.

"Not really, but I guess it'll have to do." She rests her hands on her hips, drawing my gaze to her shapely body, the way her tits look beneath the tank top without a bra. High and firm, I can just make out the outline of her hard nipples poking against the thin fabric and just like that, my cock twitches back to life.

Unbelievable.

"Why do you care?" I ask with a shrug, trying to figure out her motives. Does she have suspicions? Is she faking me out with the *I like you* speech because she has a hunch that I'm up to no good?

Because her hunch would be correct.

"Do I really have to explain myself again?" She crosses her arms in front of her chest, plumping up her breasts so they curve above the neckline of her tank top. "Didn't you hear me the first time? I like you, Max. I'm trying to get to know you beyond the—sex stuff."

"Did you just stumble over the word *sex,* baby girl?" I tilt my head. "After I just made you come all over my cock a few minutes ago?"

She shakes her head, a little smile curling her lips. "Stop teasing. You know what I mean."

I leave her alone. May as well turn this around and work it so I'm the one asking questions, not her. "So what more do you want to know?" I throw my arms out wide, then let them fall at my sides. "There's not much. I'm a pretty boring guy."

"I find that hard to believe." She arches a delicate brow. "But I know what you mean. I'm incredibly boring, too."

"Uh-huh." *Give me a fucking break.* She's had a crazy life, traveled everywhere, has all the money she could ever want, and is a constant figure in the media. And what is she? All of twenty-five? "Tell me about the belly ring," I demand. If we're going to play this game, she gets to give up information first.

"What do you want to know?" She briefly glances down at her stomach before returning her attention to me.

"How old were you when you got it? Why did you get one?"

"Sixteen." Her voice softens and I take a step closer to hear her better. "I did it to make my dad mad."

"Did it work?"

"Oh, yeah He was furious. Grounded me and everything, though that didn't work. I still snuck out and saw my friends." Her cheeks color the slightest bit, and I'm surprised that I made her blush. "It was stupid. And the piercing hurt like crazy. Got infected because I didn't take care of it at first, I was so ignorant about the entire process. Just . . . a really dumb move on my part."

"Typical teenage rebellion, more like." I pause. "Yet you kept it."

"I like it." She shrugs. "It's fun to find pretty stones to wear, change them out."

"I like it, too." I smile. "I think it's sexy." Nothing I like better than teasing the dangling stones with my tongue, feeling her belly quiver when I do.

Her cheeks turn even pinker. Probably remembering how much I like to play with it. "Okay, your turn."

"My turn?" I press a hand to my chest.

"Well, yeah. I just shared a little piece of me, so now you need to share a little piece of you."

"What do you want to know?" I ask warily. All I asked about was her belly ring and it turned personal in a snap. Whatever she's going to ask me has the potential to do the same. And I don't like it.

"Your tattoo." She reaches out and touches my arm, drifting her fingers across my biceps. "When did you get it?"

"After I came back from Afghanistan." I take a deep breath and my lungs seize up, just like they always do when I talk about the time I served over there.

I've been told by enough therapists and caring family members over the years to know it's not good to keep all the memories locked inside, but . . . who the hell wants to talk about death and destruction? About an unnecessary war and the killing of innocent people? Of soldiers and strong men and women who were fighting for their country?

And how I blame myself for so many of my friends' deaths? *Fuck,* that's not fun. It's miserable. Depressing. "It's so I never forget the friends I lost over there," I admit, noting the slight tremor in my voice. I wonder if she noticed.

I hope she didn't.

"Oh." Her eyes grow sad and she touches me again, her fingers caressing my forearm. "I'm sorry."

"Yeah, well, that's life." My words sound flippant, meaningless, even to my own ears, and I immediately regret them. "We should probably get going and hike back to the Jeep. It's getting late."

"Yeah. Okay." She nods, her hand falling away from my arm, and I miss her touch. "Let's go."

She follows me back up the trail, never complaining once, though the hike is steep and the ground uneven. She doesn't say a word, either, and after a while, her silence is unnerving. I wonder what's going through her head. I wonder if she regrets being with me.

I also wonder why the hell I'm thinking like this when I know what I'm doing with Lily isn't right. I should say something extra shitty to push her away. Make her regret ever meeting me.

But I don't. I can't make myself do it, no matter how much I know I should.

"So, where are you from?" I ask out of the blue, making her pause. I know this because I don't hear her footsteps against the gravelly trail any longer, and I turn around to find her watching me, her mouth gaping open. "What's wrong?" She probably didn't like my question, but tough shit. I want to see just how forthcoming she'll be with me.

"I—" She shakes her head, flashing me a fake smile. "Did you say something?"

"Yeah, I asked where you're from." I wait, anxious for the lie I'm sure is coming. No way is she going to be honest with me now. It's like I want her to lie, just to prove to myself that I shouldn't feel guilty for what I'm doing. I'm lying? I'm tricking her? Well, guess what, she's doing the same thing.

"New York." Her smile fades. "Born and bred."

Guess she's going for the truth. And now I feel even more like shit. "Tough city girl," I tease, and she shakes her head, waving a hand as she starts walking again. I fall into step beside her. "Not quite sure what you see in a simple guy like me."

"Please. You are the farthest thing from simple," she says, incredulity in her tone. "And I wouldn't call myself a tough city girl. More like a spoiled-rotten city girl."

"You don't act spoiled rotten," I tell her, earning a surprised look. "I'm serious. You're pretty easygoing." I haven't seen one sign of the spoiled, rich, horrible brat that the media portrays her as. Makes me think they've got it all wrong.

"Yeah, well, I am. At least, according to my family and . . . everyone else who knows me," she mutters, shaking her head.

"Like your mom and dad? Wouldn't it be their fault, if they consider you spoiled?" I ask casually, already knowing her background. Curious to see how she answers.

"My mom died when I was little." She doesn't so much as look at me when she says that, keeping her head bent, her eyes on the ground.

"I'm sorry." Now it's my turn to feel as awkward as she probably did when I told her about my tattoo.

Lily lifts her head, a sunny smile plastered on her face. Fake as hell. "Yeah, well, that's life, right?" She's repeating my false words right back to me.

And it sucks.

"Right," I say firmly.

"What about your family?" she asks.

"What about them?" *Shit.* I don't want to do this, but she's making it so easy. She makes me want to tell her stuff, share with her intimate details, which is fucking insane. I can't give this girl any information. She could use it against me later.

When she finds out I'm working for Pilar.

"Do you have brothers or sisters? Are your parents married or divorced?" She pauses, then blurts, "I have two sisters. I'm the oldest. My dad never remarried, but he has a girlfriend none of us can stand."

I'm shocked that she'd reveal so much. "I have a brother, he's older. My parents are still together. My dad is retired military and my mom stayed at home to raise us." I hope like hell this is enough information to keep her happy so this game of sharesies is over and done with. I'm putting an end to it right now. "You doing okay there, princess? This hill is steep."

"I'm fine." She sends me a shy glance, then bends her head again. "Barely making it with the flip-flops, but I'll survive."

"Hell." I step right in her path, my back to her as she comes to an abrupt stop. "Get on my back. I'll carry you the rest of the way up."

"I couldn't. You already carried me to the waterfall. I can't expect you to carry me back to the Jeep."

"Don't fight me." I look over my shoulder and send her a meaningful glare, one that says I'm not going to let her argue. "I'll just end up carrying you anyway, so be agreeable."

"Bossy man," she mumbles as she takes a few steps back like she did last time, giving herself distance so she can hurry toward me and tackle my back.

I grasp her to me with ease, my hands curved around the

back of her knees, her slender arms wrapped lightly around my neck. She presses her cheek next to mine for the briefest moment before her mouth goes to my ear. "Thank you for humoring me."

"Carrying you is never a burden," I reassure her. More like a tricky form of torture, since I can feel her soft, tempting body wrapped all around me.

"I wasn't talking about that, though I'm thanking you for that, too." She pauses, gasping and tightening her arms around my neck when I climb a particularly steep part of the trail with no problem whatsoever. Years in the military is excellent training for this kind of hike. "I'm referring to when I asked about your tattoo. I didn't mean to make you uncomfortable."

"I didn't mean to make you uncomfortable, either. Besides, you were straight with me, so I thought I would be straight with you." And it's the truth. I couldn't keep everything from her when she was so forthcoming in regards to my question. Yeah, we're talking surface stuff here. Silly stuff. Non-important stuff, like tattoos and belly rings, but little slivers of our personal lives came out with those revelations regardless.

Not enough to do either of us any damage, but it allowed me a glimpse into the secret world of Lily, the world Lily doesn't let just anyone see. And damn it, now I want to see more.

Chapter Fifteen

Lily

We drove back to the resort with the jeep's top removed, the warm air blowing through my hair and whipping it into my face, tangling it into knots. I tried my best to work my fingers through the snarls, but it was beyond repair and I gave up. That was all I had the energy for, anyway. I sat slumped in my seat pretty much the entire way, my body weak from the two intense orgasms the man gave me in a short amount of time. After he made me come with his long, thick fingers, Max dragged me back to shore and proceeded to make me come again with his long, thick cock.

The way he looked at me, the things he said . . . a shiver steals through me just remembering. The man commands my body like no other. And I don't use the word *command* lightly, either. When he told me he was in complete control whenever he was fucking me, I swear I became light-headed. My world was spinning, all because of a few choice words uttered in the sexiest growl I've ever heard. I could have spontaneously orgasmed right there on the spot, and I've never been the type of girl to come easily. A lot of work is always required beforehand.

Max is unlike any man I've experienced before, and though at first his bossiness rubbed me the wrong way, I've come to realize I almost . . . crave it. I want more of him. I want to learn more about him. It's been fun and games for the most part, beyond the moments when he saved me—and those are important moments. I'm grateful he was there, that he never hesitated. He just jumped in and took care of the situation. Took care of me.

We spend time together, but I feel like I've only scratched the surface of who the man really is. That's why I asked him to share something with me. Something personal. I know I was asking for trouble, opening myself up to him and posing the same sort of questions that I don't want to answer, but the fact that I was willing to give it a shot said a lot about how I feel about this man.

And my feelings for him are conflicted. Confusing. One minute, I can't stand him. More and more, though, I find myself drawn to him beyond the sex stuff, though the sex stuff gives us a deeper connection that I can't deny.

I want more. I know he's from Texas, I know he served in the military and lost friends over there. Comrades. That he's sad about it but doesn't want to talk about the experience, either.

Does he have deep, dark secrets? Demons that chase him? Is that why he doesn't offer up any personal details freely? I know what that's like. I have plenty of secrets. Like who I really am and why I'm here. I couldn't even give him a firm answer if he asked; my vague *I'm from New York* answer was about as detailed as I can get. If he'd dug any further, I probably would have made up some lame lie, and knowing that makes me feel ashamed.

Shame. An emotion I don't like to think about. An emotion I'm utterly too familiar with.

Seriously, though. It's not like I can tell him I'm on the run from my father's evil girlfriend who's out to take me down no matter what the cost. And she could if she really wanted to.

Convince Daddy to freeze me out. He's done that to me before and he knows how desperate I am for his approval. For his . . . love.

She has it instead. All of it. He is a man who can't give his love freely. Forrest Fowler doesn't know how to spread it around. He's tight with his emotions. It seems he can only focus on one person at a time; otherwise, he doesn't know how to show affection. So right now, he can only give it to Pilar. Forget his three children. The only one getting his love is a conniving, two-faced, cutthroat bitch.

My God, just thinking about her and my father together makes me want to punch something. Or rip Pilar's hair out of her head. Take your pick. My life is straight out of a soap opera. Who would want to deal with that? I don't want to and it's *my* life. How can I expect such a seemingly . . . normal, overly private man to put up with my bullshit when I'm constantly running away from it?

I'm so zoned out, so inside my head, I don't even notice the sound at first. And then when realization hits, I know it's not my phone that's ringing. It's Max's. I look at him, my curiosity piqued, since this is the first contact I've seen from the real world. *His* world. He shoots me a guarded look, his gaze skittering away when he realizes I'm watching him, and uneasiness shoots down my spine. I sit up straighter in my seat, peering at him as he fumbles with the phone, staring at the screen like he wants to scream at it.

He's acting weird. Almost like he's . . . guilty. And he's letting the phone continue to ring, as if he has zero plans to answer it.

My guilt radar is on high alert.

"Aren't you going to answer it?" I ask, my voice deceptively soft. I really want to yell at him. Demand he get that call so I can hear who it is. Not that it's any of my business.

Answer it, asshole!

I clamp my lips shut so I don't blurt that out.

The ringing stops and he appears relieved, which only makes me more suspicious. He dumps his phone in the center console, where it sits between us, dividing us. Guilt on one side and suspicion on the other. "I'm sure it's nothing important. They'll leave a voicemail."

They will. No definitive he or she. I'm over-the-top suspicious now. Especially when that phone of his starts ringing again. He's grimacing as he glares at the center console for the briefest moment, his eyes immediately going back to the road. He grips the steering wheel, heaves out a harsh breath, and then with a muttered curse, he reaches down and answers it, bringing the phone up so he's holding it tightly to his ear.

I'm holding my breath, anticipation rolling through me— and not the good kind—as I wait to listen to his side of the conversation. I try my best to appear nonchalant, but I'm tense. He's tense.

This isn't going to end well.

I hear a voice. Most definitely a woman's voice, from the high-pitched, almost screechy sound of it. She's angry. I can't make out what she's saying, but I can decipher the fury in her tone and it almost sounds familiar. But I can't quite place it.

"I'm on it," Max says, his voice tight, his jaw clenched. He looks furious and he won't even glance in my direction, keeping his gaze firmly on the road. I should be thankful for that. I don't want to get in a wreck.

But I also want him to look in my direction and mouth an apology. I want him to slip his hand over my knee and offer a reassuring squeeze. Something, anything that indicates he isn't up to no good. Because I have the sense he is. That he's hiding something, doing something that I won't like.

It scares me.

"I told you I would call you—" He's cut off; I can hear her

yelling at him as he silently fumes, his nostrils flaring, his mouth drawn into a thin line. He says nothing, just takes the verbal beating, and I'm dying to know exactly who this woman is that he allows to talk to him in such a horrible manner.

I may not know much about him, but from what I've learned so far, he's not the sort to take this type of treatment. He's always in charge, always in command. And even when he's not giving directions, he has this ease about him, this quiet confidence that tells everyone he knows who he is, what he wants.

"I'm busy right now," he bites out when the woman finally stops her tirade. "I'll call you when I get back to the hotel." She starts to speak and he's the one who cuts her off this time, saying, "Yes. I will." He yanks the phone away from his ear as if it's about to bite him and he hits the red "end call" button, then throws the phone back into the console's cup holder.

Nothing is said for long, tension-filled minutes and I hesitate, unsure of how I should approach this. Afraid because I don't *want* to approach this. Any other time, any other guy, I'd be all over his shit. Ready for the fight. Accusing him of cheating, of leading me on, of tricking me, of acting shady, because hell yes, right now Max is acting 100 percent shady and I don't like it. My invisible bullshit antennae are pricked, standing on end, because I have a nose for this sort of behavior. Though this time around, Max and whoever he was speaking to were acting pretty obvious.

And maybe I'm aware of this kind of behavior because I'm always up to no good myself. A long time ago I realized I was drawn to bullshitters who are just like me. They can't tell the truth, don't want to be in a committed relationship, none of that. They just want to party and have fun all the time and . . . that describes me perfectly. At least, it describes my past behavior and patterns perfectly.

I thought this guy was different. I believed I got through to him a little bit. And I thought maybe *I* could be different, too.

Maybe I can't.

Finally I can stand the tense silence no longer. "Everything okay?" I ask.

He says nothing for a moment, and I can almost see the cogs turning in his brain as he tries to come up with an explanation for what just happened. "Yeah," he answers. "Everything's fine."

That's it. That's all he says. I stare at him, willing him to look my way, but he won't.

Guilty. He has guilt written all over him. In bold, bright red slashes, all over his skin, his face, in his eyes, in the way he fucking sits. *Damn it.* I thought I could avoid this. I'm on vacation. Sort of. This should be a casual thing. An island fling. So why am I wound up so tight?

Why do I care? Why do I want . . . more?

"Who was that?" My voice rises, is a little sharp. I sound angry. And I really don't give a crap how I sound.

"No one important." He, on the other hand, sounds disgusted. At me? Or at himself?

Fuck his dismissive answer. "She sounded pretty important to me. As in, she's really pissed off at you. What did you do?"

He flicks on the blinker and hits the brake, slowing the Jeep so he can turn onto the road that leads to the resort. "Trust me, Lily. You don't want to know."

"I'm sure I don't," I retort, my entire body going stiff when he finally looks my way. I see something in his eyes, something I don't like.

Wariness. Uncertainty. And that ever-present, shitty guilt.

"If you've got a girlfriend or you're married or whatever . . ." I pause, inhaling sharply, shocked at how much more those words, and the possible reality they suggest, hurt than I care to acknowledge. "Now is the time to admit it," I finish, crossing my arms in front of my chest, my heart thumping so hard I swear he'll be able to see it beat beneath my thin tank top.

Again he says nothing and I want to hit him. Yell and scream and carry on like the woman did on the phone. But I do none of that. Instead, all I feel is . . . hurt. Disgust.

Shame. That maybe I'm the piece on the side, the secret affair.

"I don't have a girlfriend," he says wearily, but he still won't look at me. His hands grip the steering wheel so hard his knuckles are white. "And I'm not married either, Lily. I swear. It's just . . . it's complicated."

"Complicated," I repeat, hating that word with everything I have. Life is complicated. Everything is fucking complicated. That's just the way it is. So when people use it as an excuse, a reason for why things are shitty or why they can't explain their actions, I don't find it *complicated*.

I find that single word one giant, stupid excuse. The same excuse I gave Rose when I first got to Maui.

Ugh. That word sucks.

"Yeah." He blows out a harsh breath and turns onto the hotel resort's drive. "It's work shit, nothing major."

Nothing major. He's almost . . . flippant. Acting as if I'm making a big deal out of nothing. And maybe I am, though that doesn't make me feel any better. He's behaving like a total dick and I'm acting the jealous shrew and what the hell am I doing, reacting this way? I'm a big girl. I knew what I was getting involved with. I have my own secrets.

I guess I just didn't expect him to have so many, too. "What do you do, anyway?" I ask, wanting to know. *Needing* to know.

No answer. Asshole.

He slows the Jeep as we approach the front of the hotel, maneuvering carefully so he doesn't hit one of the many eager hotel employees that hover in the drive, ever ready to assist us and meet our every need. Their over-the-top help annoys me, especially right now. I want to be left alone. I don't need some pretty boy smiling at me as he opens my car door. I don't want someone greeting me with a cheerful aloha and asking how my afternoon was. What would they do if I answered them honestly?

Well, it definitely started out amazing. Went on a scary ride through a Hawaiian jungle and laughed and screamed and got turned on by how confidently Max drove. Got in a little argument with him before he fucked me by a waterfall and gave me two orgasms. It was so good, I saw stars, damn it, and it's the middle of the day. Oh, and then asshole over here got that call from work—wink, wink, nudge, nudge—and it ruined everything.

I keep my lips clamped shut and won't even look in Max's direction. It's easier that way. No more words are spoken as he stops the vehicle and puts it into park, an employee opening my door at the same time Max gets out and says he wants the Jeep parked in valet.

My earlier high is totally gone. The euphoric, almost sleepy state the delicious orgasms put me into is long forgotten. Those little revelations we shared? Null and void. I'm mad. Irritated. I don't need this kind of shit. Some *complicated* guy entangled in too many *complicated* relationships. Whatever just happened had to deal with his work?

Yeah, right.

Without even acknowledging him, I start toward the entrance of the hotel, my back stiff, my head held high. I refuse to look back. I don't want to see Max, don't know what I would say to him even if he stopped me to talk.

"Lily." He calls out my name and I hesitate, wanting to turn to him. Wanting to run into his arms and let him whisper lies in my ear.

It'll be all right. That call was nothing. She's nothing.

You're everything.

I'm so stupid to be imagining this. Like this is some fairy tale and I just found my magical, perfect prince, when really, he's just another toad. I'm being ridiculous, but I can't help it. I like this asshole.

Probably too much.

Slowly, I turn to find him standing directly behind me, looking torn. "I gotta go make a phone call. Take care of a few work things."

I nod stiffly, lifting my chin, firming my lips. Emotions threaten, foreign ones I don't recognize that I am desperate to shove away. My lips tremble, my eyes sting, and I blink hard. I'm being rejected. Certainly not for the first time, though I usually like to beat them to the punch.

Definitely won't be the last time I'm rejected, either. I've dealt with it all my life.

Thanks, Daddy.

"Maybe I'll . . . see you later?" He says it almost hopefully, and the tone of his voice lights a flicker of hope within me as well. But then I squash it down and tell all that useless hope to go to hell.

"Maybe." I shrug, taking a few backward steps. I need to get away from him fast. Standing too close allows me to smell him, really see him. His hair is mussed from the wind and I remember how soft it is. How the short strands curl around my fingers. And the dark stubble that lines his cheeks and jaw, how rough it is, like sandpaper. How I like to feel it brush against my skin. His hands are big and they know just how to move over my body, touching me in all the right places. Places I didn't know even existed. His mouth, those soft, warm lips, that hot, insistent tongue . . . "Or maybe not."

Max frowns and I feel an odd sense of pleasure seeing it. I want him to hurt as much as I'm hurting. Or get angry. It's easier when we're angry. Then the hurt is hidden and all I can focus on is how mad I am. "Don't be like this, Lily," he says, his voice low but firm.

I stop in my tracks, irritation coursing through my veins and making me want to yell. To rage and hit and scream. "Be like what, exactly? Suspicious? Uncertain? Irritated that you claim whoever that was calling you is involved with your work, yet you won't tell me what you do?"

He takes a step closer, his hand automatically going for my arm, but I jerk away from his touch before he can reach me. "There's nothing going on. What I do for a living is . . . confidential. I just can't talk about it."

"Oh, right. You can't tell me what you do, but you can go ahead and fuck me by a waterfall in broad daylight where anyone can see us. That's just great." The sarcasm is thick and I want to smack him. Just pop him on the side of the head and tell him to go fuck himself.

"Keep your voice down," he mutters, glancing around as if he's afraid someone might hear us, but I'm too far gone for that. I couldn't care less. And this time when he makes a grab for my arm, he's successful, pulling me toward him despite my obvious reluctance. "Why are you so angry?"

"Why can't you be honest?" I throw back in his face, immediately feeling guilty. I'm one to talk. I've been lying to him the entire time we've been on this stupid island. He doesn't know who I really am or why I'm here.

His gaze darkens as he studies me and I swear, it feels like he can see right through me. See the lies and the façade that I throw up so no one can discover the real me. I have that wall up all the time but right now, in this very moment? It's twice as thick and pretty much impenetrable.

"I don't think you'd want to hear what I'd have to say if I was going to be honest with you," he says, his voice a honeyed, Southern drawl, oozing over me and making me warm despite the ugliness of his words. "I think you much prefer those pretty little lies we all tell, now don't you?"

My heart sinks at his knowing gaze. "I don't like liars," I whisper.

"I don't either. Not usually," he returns, letting go of me, pushing me away the slightest bit as if he can't get away from me fast enough. I don't like what he said, the implications behind his words.

I don't either. Not usually.

Is he referring to me? Does he know somehow that I'm lying about . . . everything? Though I was honest with him. I wanted to open up. He's the one who was so resistant.

"So is this it?"

I blink at him, confused. "Is what it?"

"This? Us? You're pissed and you don't believe me, so it's over? You're done with me?"

"I . . ." I don't know what to think, what to say. I can only gape at him like a stupid fish. He's acting like we're in some sort of relationship and he can't believe I want to end it. Talk about confusing.

"Right." His expression shutters closed and that's it. He's thrown up his own wall and it's a doozy. One I'll probably never be able to climb. "See ya around," he mumbles as he turns and walks off.

I watch him leave, desperate to call his name, ask him to come back. Ask him to stay one more night with me. It's amazing how one little thing changes the course of your day. Not even an hour ago Max had me naked by a waterfall, his mouth latched onto my nipple, his hand between my legs, his cock heavy and insistent against my thigh. I'd begged him to fill me, to fuck me, whispering his name over and over, my hands in his hair, my body undulating beneath his.

And now he's walking away from me without a backward glance. His shoulders are stiff, anger coming off him in obvious waves. I ruined it. *He* ruined it, with his stupid phone call and the angry woman and how he tried to hide information from me.

I don't need a man like that. No woman does. He's nothing but trouble.

But so am I. I don't know how to look for anything else.

Chapter Sixteen

Max

THE TIME HAS COME. I NEED TO GET MY SHIT TOGETHER AND temporarily earn back Lily's trust. Suck up to her, sweet-talk her, tell her how sorry I am, make up a few lies, get her in bed, fuck her until she passes out, and then take that fucking laptop once and for all and get the hell off this island.

That's my plan. Tonight, I'm going to put it into place.

I bought a one-way ticket to Maui since I had no idea how long this would take me, so I called the airline the moment I got back to my room yesterday and booked the earliest flight out of here I could find. I'm going to end up hanging out at LAX for way too many hours before I can get on the connecting flight home, but fuck it. I had no choice.

Pilar Vasquez destroyed my original plan.

Bitch blew it when she called me. Hell, I blew it by taking her call. Should never have answered it. I could have been inside Lily for the rest of the night, but no. I had to give in and answer my fucking phone, scared out of my mind that woman would have kept calling and calling and calling . . .

Thank Christ I never plugged her actual name in my contacts list. I gave her a fake name, Patty Villa, because it's what I always do with clients. I take extra precautions and though, yeah, my phone is password protected, that doesn't mean shit.

She gave me an ultimatum. And I hate ultimatums with every fucking thing I have. But I could tell by the tone of her voice that she meant business. She screamed at first, but then her tone dropped, became very even and low and downright menacing. The hairs on the back of my neck stood up when she made her threat.

Women don't scare me. Hell, no one really scares me. But what she said terrified me—and made me worry for Lily's safety.

I'll tell her. I'll send her a text and tell her you're there because of me. That you're trying to trick her. I'll blow your cover wide open. I can get the laptop another way. Hire someone else. Someone smarter. Someone meaner. Someone who can get the fucking job done.

That was it. I couldn't risk it. The woman has no boundaries, no remorse, no conscience. What if she sent someone after Lily who's determined to get that laptop and the information inside it, no matter what it takes? By force, if necessary?

I may be an asshole who's using her, but I would never physically *hurt* her.

Emotionally? Yeah, pretty sure I already did that. Not proud of it, either.

After I arranged my flight and made a few other necessary phone calls, I texted Pilar and let her know I would be back in New York within forty hours and would bring her what she wanted. She didn't call me back; she didn't rant at me via text, something she's an expert at. Her answer was a simple Good.

That's it. *Good.* But nothing feels good about any of this.

Nothing.

I tossed and turned most of the night, trying to figure out a way to get back in Lily's good graces, and came up empty. She was so pissed. Worse, she looked upset. Hurt. Like I'd disappointed her, which I'm sure I did. I couldn't come up with a good explanation beyond my *work is confidential* and it's *compli-*

cated. That sounds fucking lame when you're lying in bed in the middle of the night. Staring at the ceiling, full of regret.

Sleep came fitfully, and the morning sun blazing through the uncovered sliding glass door—yeah, I was a dumbass and forgot to shut the curtain—made me feel like a vampire. Hissing and squinting and cursing the light as I groaned and threw up my arm to try and block it, reminding me of Lily when she woke up yesterday morning.

Fuck. Lily. Just thinking about her hurts.

I took a shower and halfheartedly stroked my cock to relieve my morning wood but I wasn't into it, so I gave up.

My dick had a mind of its own and only wanted Lily.

I plotted and I planned through the rest of my shower. As I packed up what little shit I'd brought to Maui and set my suitcase by the front door. I went to the hotel restaurant and ate breakfast by myself, catching up on email and making a few calls, trying my best to look busy and unobtrusive because I don't want anyone to notice me.

No way do I want to be remembered.

Lily is nowhere to be found and I'm disappointed, though I should be realistic. This resort is huge, filled to the brim with singles and couples, all of them crowding around the pool or the restaurants or the bars. Walking the grounds, jogging, headed to the beach. The place is completely overrun with horny people looking to score, either with the person they brought or someone new and exotic. A stranger they can fuck during a vacation and forget about once they go back to reality.

Yet somehow, among the crowds and the chaos, in a club or on the beach, we always found each other. As if there's some sort of magnetic field between us, drawing us closer without our even realizing.

Maybe I fucked it up. Somehow broke the force field by pissing her off. I regret it. I . . . miss her. Incredibly stupid on my part because I don't even know her, and what I do know of her, I shouldn't like. She accuses me of hiding something, of lying, when she's the biggest liar out there. I'm not supposed to know she's Lily Fowler. She's probably one of the richest people currently staying at this ridiculously expensive hotel but she's not flaunting it, which goes against her normal behavior. She's famous, a nonstop party girl who likes to drink and flirt and spend too much money and cause too much trouble. A complete wreck, the press has called her more than once.

Looks like she wrecked me instead.

After I finish my late breakfast, I head out to the pool, my gaze automatically searching for Lily. It's extra crowded today for some reason and I have to go on an extensive hunt to scrounge up an empty lounger. I finally find one and throw my towel on top of it before I settle in. Two women sitting nearby watch me with unabashed interest, but I ignore them.

There's only one woman I want to see and so far, she's nowhere to be found.

A hotel staffer stops by and takes my drink order and then I settle in, my gaze razor sharp behind my sunglasses as I search the perimeter. The place is packed, mostly with men and women around my age, and there's lots of alcohol flowing. I keep an eye out for Lily, silently willing her to make an appearance, but maybe she's gone into hiding. She's probably purposely avoiding me and I can't blame her. I fucked it up. Bad. If I can't find her, talk to her, persuade her I'm not such a bad guy after all, I'm going to have to break into her room and steal that goddamn laptop. A situation that could go sideways at any given moment, and it's the last thing I want to do.

I quickly grow restless, pissed that I haven't come upon Lily yet. And I'd really like to see her in one of those skimpy bikinis she seems to prefer. The waiter shows up, setting my iced tea on the table beside my chair, and asks if I want anything else before he zooms off, ready to feed the hungry and thirsty pool guests.

"Hey, cowboy."

I jerk my head up at the familiar voice to find Lily standing in front of my lounger blocking the sun, her hands on her hips, a sly smile on her face. As if my damn imagination made her materialize in front of me, as if she isn't furious with me anymore, which is strange.

And unnerving.

"Cowboy?" I ask, lifting a brow. "Bringing that back, huh."

She shrugs those pretty, bare shoulders, which are turning a bright shade of pink. "You drove like a hell-bent cowboy yesterday so I still think it's apt, even if you disagree."

"I've never been much of a cowboy," I confirm, though I like it when she calls me that. I like it a lot.

Probably a little too much.

She stares at me for a moment and I return the look, both of us silent. I see the hesitation in her, can read it in the way she shuffles her feet, how she tucks a wild strand of hair behind her ear and glances around, looking for . . . an escape?

I make her nervous.

And she does the same to me.

"Oh, I don't know about that," she finally says, her voice deceptively nonchalant. I see a challenge in her gaze, one that tells me she's going somewhere with this. "I definitely like the way you ride me."

I regret choosing that precise moment to take a sip from my iced tea because I nearly choke on it. The liquid goes down the wrong pipe and I end up in a coughing fit that lasts maybe thirty seconds, which is thirty seconds too long.

"You okay?" she asks once I stop.

Wiping my hand across my mouth, I nod, feeling like an asshole. "Yeah. I'm fine. You just . . . shocked me."

"Bad choice of words?" She tilts her head, waiting for my answer.

"Interesting choice," I correct. "Surprising."

"How so?" Her head is still tilted as she watches me and I feel on edge. Like one wrong move . . . if I say or do the wrong thing, she'll turn and leave without a backward glance. Offer me up a spectacular view, because nothing's better than the sight of Lily's perfect ass in a barely there bikini bottom, but yeah. I don't want her to leave.

I need her to stay.

"I figured you were still pissed at me."

A casual shrug is my immediate answer as she contemplates me. "I decided it's not worth it, to hold a grudge."

"Hold a grudge." I lied to her. I was purposely withholding information. She should tell me to go to hell and hope that I choke on my iced tea and die. Instead she's saying how she shouldn't hold a grudge. And she's watching me like she wants to rub her naked body all over mine.

"Life's too short," she says, laughter tingeing her voice. "Don't you agree?"

It feels like a trick question. "I guess."

The look she sends me could probably slay me dead. "What are you saying? Are you a grudge holder, Max?"

"No." I shake my head. Most men aren't; at least the ones I know aren't. I get over shit fairly easy. Unless I'm wronged. Betrayed. I should be pissed at this woman because she's betraying me as we speak. Keeping her true identity from me even though I know it. I've always known it. Meaning I'm betraying her as well. Beating her at her own game. Aren't we a fucking pair?

More like a fucked-up pair.

"Good, because grudges get us nowhere." She smiles. "I'd like to start over if we can. *Cowboy.*" Her emphasis on the word isn't lost on me. If this is what she wants, then I will definitely deliver, because it's what I want, too.

For entirely different reasons, of course, and none that I can mention.

"Well, fancy meeting you here, darlin,'" I drawl, though

truly, I'm nothing close to a cowboy. I like the nickname, though. More like I appreciate that *she* came up with it.

I'd like to see her ride me again like a sexy cowgirl, full breasts swaying with her every move, nipples tight and tempting me to suck them deep into my mouth. Her long, wavy hair falling down her back, eyes heavy-lidded and lips parted as pleasure rocks through her . . .

Yeah. I'd like to see that real bad.

Her smile grows and she settles in the chair next to mine, which had been abandoned a few minutes ago. She's clad in another tiny scrap of a bikini, a real attention-getter in bright yellow, the top a strapless band that barely contains her breasts. The belly ring twinkles and shines in the sunlight, and I'm tempted to flick it with my tongue just before I move down and taste that delicious pussy of hers.

"What's your name, cowboy?" she asks, batting her eyelashes at me.

Seems like she's taking this starting-over game seriously. "Max," I say with a shrug. "Yours?"

"Lily." She smiles and the sight of it zaps me straight in the heart, then moves lower and settles in my cock. I will myself to remain in control. I don't need to lounge around a public pool with a boner in my swim trunks, though I wouldn't doubt there are a few boners standing at attention around here, what with all the fine-looking women wandering around.

"Nice to meet you," I say, sitting up and leaning toward her with my hand stretched out.

She stares at my hand, her eyes going wide before lifting her gaze to meet mine. "My, what big hands you have," she murmurs as she slips her hand in mine.

We shake and when she tries to let go, I clamp my fingers around hers, keeping the connection. I missed that connection. It's not even been twenty-four hours since I was last inside her and I fucking *missed* her. "The better to touch you with," I murmur, my heart thudding fast and hard when I see desire light her gaze.

I let her hand fall from mine and she turns away, keeping her head averted, like she doesn't want me to see her face—more likely her reaction to my words—which of course makes me want to see her that much more.

"Maybe you should get out of the sun," I suggest. My gaze roves over her and I see how pink her skin is. How long has she been out here, anyway? And why didn't I see her? I looked everywhere. I always found her before. Always.

But maybe those who don't want to be found remain in the shadows.

"You're probably right." Her words draw me from my thoughts and I glance up to watch as she turns to face me once more. I'm struck yet again by her beauty. The woman is flat-out gorgeous. And she doesn't have a lick of makeup on, not that I can tell, and this afternoon she's forgone jewelry, too, except for the belly ring. Just a bikini and her hair twisted into a knot on top of her head, wild tendrils curling around her face. She doesn't even have her sunglasses on. She looks like she ran out of her fancy bungalow in a big hurry.

To come find me, maybe?

Probably not. More like wishful thinking on my part.

"Got sunscreen on?" I ask. The pink hue of her skin looks like it could get painful fairly quick if she doesn't watch it, her chest especially. The Hawaiian sun is intense. Don't want all that pretty flesh burnt.

"I didn't even bring my bag with me." She bites her lower lip and I want to groan. *Damn*, she's sexy when she studies me like that. Those big, unblinking eyes, the way she looks at me like she wants to lick me up and down. "I was hiding from you, you know," she confesses softly.

No surprise. I say nothing, just study her and hope she senses I want to hear more.

"I could've stayed at my bungalow, but I didn't want to be alone." She sinks her teeth into her lower lip and I'm filled with the almost violent urge to grab hold of her and kiss her. Push her right into that lounger and let my hands roam all over her body.

"You didn't?"

She releases her lip, then licks it. The sight of her pink tongue makes me hiss in a breath. *Fuck,* being so close to her like this and not able to touch her hurts. "No. I was so pissed at you last night, Max. So fucking angry . . ." Her voice drifts and I sit up straight, shocked by her display of honesty. "But despite myself I came down here looking for you. And when I saw you, I hid. Doesn't make much sense, does it?"

"It makes perfect sense." I get it, though I'm shocked by her admission. She's a game player, one of the best from what I can tell, and I didn't expect her to tell me the truth.

"Really?" Her voice is full of hope, like she's pleased I understand her.

"Yeah, princess," I murmur. "I missed you last night. This morning."

"Is it wrong I like that you missed me?" When I open my mouth she rushes to add, "Don't answer that."

"We're drawn to each other, like we can't help it," I tell her, my voice low, my gaze locked on hers for a lingering moment before I let it sweep down her sexy-as-hell, pretty much all-on-display body. That body is mine. I own it, at least for the remainder of the time that I'm here on Maui. And this afternoon, tonight, I plan on exploring every last bit of that sexy body until I make her scream.

Again and again.

"I don't want to lay out around this pool. I was hoping that maybe we could go back to my bungalow and sit on my lanai," she suggests shyly.

Would you look at that. Lily Fowler, shy. Un-fucking-believable.

"Why do you want to sit on your lanai?" I know why I want to. Fewer people, less hassle, less everything. I figure she's the type who likes the attention, though. That she'd want to strut herself around in front of anyone who happened to look, their hungry gazes feeding her equally hungry ego.

Maybe I'm wrong.

"So I can get a tan without tan lines?" She smirks, batting her eyelashes at me, and I burst out laughing, trying my best to ignore the arousal swiftly moving beneath my skin, settling in my cock.

I sit up, scooting to the edge of my lounger so I can get closer to her. Lowering my voice, I murmur, "You thinking of lying out naked?"

Without a word she nods, the smirk disappearing. I can see the way her chest flushes deeper than the faint sunburn, the wild flutter of her pulse at the base of her neck. "At least with my top off," she admits quietly.

My gaze drops to her top. Her nipples press against the fabric, tiny and firm, and I want to put my mouth on them, on *her*, so fucking bad I can barely stand it. "I'd like to see that," I admit hoarsely, even though I've seen her breasts enough that I can close my eyes and conjure them up in my mind. Full and soft, with rosy pink nipples that taste like heaven, a perfect handful, mouthful, whatever.

I'm done playing games. I need to move this shit along, and besides, I'm dying to have my mouth and my hands on her again, for one last night. My time is limited. I need to make this happen.

"I want to show you," she whispers.

"You're not mincing words today, princess."

"I figured what's the point? Why fight it?" She stares at me, those pretty eyes never leaving mine. "I know what I want."

My skin tightens. She keeps this talk up and I really will end up making an ass out of myself, walking around the pool with a hard-on. "You do, huh? And what would that be?"

She leans in closer, her hand going to my knee. Her touch burns, awareness sizzling through me as my gaze drops to her lips, and I watch as they form one perfect word.

"You."

We stare at each other for a long, tension-filled moment like a couple of dumb kids until I decide to not waste any more time. Reaching for her hand, I stand, taking her with me. She grabs hold of my cell phone and gives it to me and I shove it in the pocket of my swim trunks.

We don't say a word as we exit the pool area, our hands still clasped together, fingers entwined. I lead her through the lobby without a word toward the bungalow area, and she practically runs to keep up with my stride.

It doesn't matter how eager I seem. She's right. Why bother hiding it? The chemistry between us is there, strong and over-whelming, and I'm not going to deny myself one last chance for us to be together and neither is she. This is the perfect excuse to get in her bedroom, get some satisfaction, give her some satisfaction, and then . . .

Take the damn laptop and disappear.

Plus, I'm just doing my damn job. I'm not scared of a hot little piece like Lily. Most people who know me think I'm a bad-ass. Unafraid, bold as hell, and doing as I please. I sound like an arrogant prick even in my own head for just thinking it, but it's the truth. Sometimes my boldness has got me into trouble—lots of times, actually—but no way could this girl ruin me.

Back up, asshole. This girl can completely ruin you. She's your target. And instead of objectively observing her before going in for that damnable laptop, you're too busy thinking with your dick and wondering how fast you can stick it in her hot, eager pussy?

Catching a glimpse of the real woman behind the façade helps my decision, too. She'd been so damn responsive. I want to experience that again. Soon.

Now.

We start to go up the front walkway of her villa but she jerks on my hand, making me stop and turn to look at her.

"I don't have my key," she admits.

I frown. "How are we going to get in? Do you need to go back to the front desk?"

She shakes her head. "We can sneak in through the sliding glass door."

I can feel my frown deepen. The woman is careless. "Any asshole can walk right in, you know."

"I'm not worried. We're at an exclusive resort. In the most exclusive *part* of the resort," she points out.

"Assholes hang out in fancy resorts, too, princess. Don't think you're so untouchable. That'll get you in trouble." I release her hand to tap my index finger against the tip of her nose.

She presses her lips together, her gaze never leaving mine. "I have a habit of that. Getting into trouble."

The grin that spreads across my face can't be contained. "Why am I not surprised?"

"People hate me for it," she admits.

My grin fades, just like that. "Who could hate you?" She drives me insane, but in a good way. In a *let's get together and fuck each other's brains out* way.

I don't *really* know her, though. What she does on a day-to-day basis. What her normal life is like. This woman in front of me is vacation Lily, not real-life Lily. For all I know she's a raging bitch who makes everyone crazy with her needy, arrogant ways.

"Lots of people hate me." She stands up taller, throwing back her shoulders. "Hopefully not you, though."

"Never me, baby girl," I say, meaning every word I say. How can I hate her when she looks at me like that, her skin shining from the sun, her body on blatant display, just for me? Grabbing her hand once again, I lead her around the house, taking the same path I did a couple of nights ago when I snuck into her room. The slider is unlocked, just as she said it would be, and she darts inside while I wait for her on the lanai, coming back out in a few minutes with a towel in one hand, sunscreen in the other, and her sunglasses firmly in place.

She drops the towel and sunscreen on the lounge chair closest to her and turns so her back is to me. "Will you unhook it?"

I stare at her back, knowing exactly what she wants me to do but wanting her to spell it out. "Unhook what?"

Lily glances at me from over her shoulder. "My top."

Reaching out, I do as she requests, my fingers brushing against her smooth skin when I ease the clear plastic hook out and the top springs apart. She sheds it with a flick of her fingers, letting it drop to the lounge chair before she turns to face me, clad in the skimpy bikini bottom and nothing else.

"Could you help me put some sunscreen on?" she asks, eyes wide, voice full of innocence.

A trap. I know what she's trying to do, but it's a trap I'm willingly walking into because hell yes, my fingers are itching to rub sunscreen all over her body. Any excuse to touch her again.

Not that I need one.

"Lie down," I order, and she grabs hold of the sunscreen bottle, handing it to me before she settles onto the lounger, lying on her stomach so all I see is the smooth skin of her back, her ass barely covered by the bikini, and those long, sexy legs tempting me.

Every bit of her tempts me and she knows it.

Her arms are folded beneath her head, her right cheek resting on her clasped fingers, as she watches me from behind her sunglasses. I nudge at her legs and she scoots them over, allowing me room to sit on the edge of the lounger as I open the bottle of sunscreen and squirt a huge dollop of liquid into the palm of my hand.

I rub my hands together and start on her shoulders, smoothing the creamy lotion all over her warm skin until the sunscreen is absorbed. A dreamy sigh escapes her, making my dick twitch, and I power on, my hands moving lower, to the base of her spine, just above her ass.

I love her skin. The way it feels beneath my hands, her intoxicating scent. I swear I feel her quiver beneath my touch when I start in on her legs, my fingers curling around her ankles and spreading her a little bit. Not obscenely, oh no, but just enough to make her think of sex.

Sex with me. Hopefully she's remembering just how good it was between us. I know I sure as hell am. I want to touch her there, between her legs. I know she'd be wet and hot and the moment I pushed my fingers deep, she'd moan.

I slide my eager fingers up, tickling the back of her knees and making her giggle. She has a sexy laugh. She has a sexy everything. When I touch her thighs, she stiffens the slightest bit, just before she starts to relax as I massage her skin, my fingers curling around the inside of her thighs, drawing closer, closer . . .

A little whimper escapes her when I hook a finger beneath her bottoms, my thumb tracing the luscious curve of her ass. She shivers and tilts her head—I can tell she's watching me from behind her sunglasses—and I keep my gaze fixed on her as I sneak my finger in farther, until I'm touching her pussy.

Fucking soaked. Just like I knew she'd be.

"Max." The whispery groan that falls from her lips makes my cock hard. I trace her slit, tease her, slip inside her with a shallow thrust, and she spreads her legs farther, giving me better access. "Please."

"Please what, princess?" I sound tense. My voice cracks and I'm sweating, and not because of the sun barreling down on us.

"More," she whispers, another moan falling from her lips when I cup her.

"More what? What do you want me to do?" She's a dirty girl. I know it. And she's not ashamed to show her wicked side, either. Lily has no problem asking for what she wants. She has a confidence I can't help but admire. Even better, she does as I demand, no questions asked.

It's almost like she was made for me. What would it be like, seeing her again once we both return to New York? What would she say if I told her I lived close to her, that we could be together again? Not just have some island fling but a real . . . relationship.

That line of thinking will only get you in trouble, asshole.

"Fuck me with your fingers," she says, her voice thin as she wiggles her butt. "Make me come."

I shake my head, getting rid of the serious thoughts. She doesn't want a relationship and neither do I. Not really. She wants hot sex. She wants me to fuck her with my fingers. That's all this is. A steamy affair. A lot of fucking with very little emotion.

Why do I feel like I'm trying to convince myself?

"Demanding today, aren't you?" I withdraw my hand from between her legs and tug at her bikini bottom, easing it down, baring that perfect, biteable ass of hers. Jesus, I want to spank her. Mark her. Bite her.

I tear the bikini off her and let it fall to the ground before I run a hand over my face. The woman makes me fucking crazy.

She makes me want things I can't have.

"I know what I want," she says, her voice wavering, belying the confidence of her words. "And I want you."

"Is that why you came looking for me, baby? Even though I

pissed you off yesterday?" I run my fingers across her ass, back and forth, warming her skin, dying to slap that perfect little butt.

"Yes," she whispers as I squeeze her ass, my palm covering one cheek, and she drops her head, whimpering. "I couldn't stop thinking about you."

"I couldn't stop thinking about you, either," I admit just before I lightly slap her ass. Her cheek jiggles. The scent of her arousal fills the air and *fuck me*, I can't stop myself.

I spank her again. Hard. So hard her skin reddens, and I don't doubt for an instant the imprint of my hand will soon appear on her skin.

"God." She jerks against the lounger, squeezing her legs together before she lifts her ass into the air, making me crazier. "More."

"You like that, don't you?" I spanked her before but never like this. Never this hard. "Fucking perfect, is what you are," I mutter, overwhelmed by the realization of how truly perfect she is for me.

Only me.

I gentle my touch, drift my fingers over her skin, watch the goose bumps rise at my caress. I'm all hard, jagged edges, but this woman makes me want to be soft. To slow down and take my time with her, show her exactly what she means to me.

What does she mean to you?

I'm not 100 percent sure.

Taking a deep breath, I refocus and devote my attention to her other ass cheek this time. I alternate between cheeks, spanking her on one side, then the other, again and again, the sharp smack of my fingers against her taut flesh driving me wild. Driving *her* wild. She squirms and bucks, her ass red as she rises up on her knees, her legs spread, offering me an unbelievable view of her pussy.

Pink. Glistening, dripping wet. The prettiest pussy I've ever seen. The only one I've ever craved. She's so aroused, I swear the inside of her thighs are drenched.

And I'm hard as a fucking rock, dying to plunge inside her and fucking come. But I don't. Not yet.

Anticipation is everything. This is the last time I'll have with her, so I need to make it extra special. I want this girl crazed for me. I want to be crazed for her. Hell, I already am.

I want to drive her and myself out of our ever-loving minds.

Chapter Seventeen

Lily

I LOVE THE WAY HE TOUCHES ME. HIS INSISTENT FINGERS HELP me forget who I am, what I've done, what a failure I've become. I don't worry about anything else when I see his eyes lock on me. All I can focus on is him. How fast can I get him alone, how quickly can I get him to put his hands on me . . .

After what happened yesterday, I let the anger and the disappointment consume me. He hurt me and I held on to it. But I also knew that I was just as much a liar as he was. Who am I to judge, to hate him, when he should hate me, too? I was lucky enough that I didn't get caught.

Yet.

Even though I told myself I wouldn't search him out, I did anyway. I hid from him, scared he would find me, even more scared that he wouldn't, and finally I gave in to my urges. It's like I can't stay away from him and that's okay. I can own up to my feelings for Max. I decided to be honest with him. Real.

And he liked it. I could tell by his body language, by the huskiness of his voice. I get near him and the air changes between us. Becomes charged with an energy I can't deny. One I don't *want* to deny. My need to tell him I want him overcame any of my fears or insecurities.

He makes me feel greedy. And I'm pretty sure he feels the same.

My ass still aches from the way he spanked me, my flesh searing hot. I like it. I want more. His big hands roam my body, the slope of my back, the curve of my ass. His touch is gentle but insistent, commanding yet reverent. He's still got his clothes on and I'm completely naked, the sun shining on my skin. Anyone could pass us by on the beach, none of the beaches are private in the state of Hawaii, but access to this particular stretch of sand is limited.

Not unattainable, though. Knowing someone could walk along and see me like this, the two of us together . . .

Excites me.

"Dripping wet, princess," Max practically growls as he sinks his fingers inside me and pumps them once, twice. I close my eyes and grip the frame of the lounger, still on my hands and knees, Max sitting right behind me. "I know you'll taste damn good, too. I've been craving your pussy since the last time I saw you."

I glance at him over my shoulder to see the tips of his fingers disappear in his mouth as he sucks them and a shuddery sigh moves through me, making my entire body sway. He's taken off his sunglasses, letting me see that handsome face clearly, those beautiful eyes full of heat and want.

All aimed directly at me.

"You want me to fuck you, don't you?" he asks.

Pressing my lips together, I nod, scared to say anything for fear I'll sound like a babbling idiot. Unsure that I'll even be able to put together words. Or worse, that I'll say something I'll regret. I feel unhinged, raw and painfully aroused, my skin so tight I'm afraid I might shatter if he so much as touches me.

And I definitely want him to touch me. I'm dying for it.

"From behind?" He runs a hand over my butt, his fingers

sliding perilously close to my pussy. I angle toward him, ready for those fingers to go exactly where I need them, but he's teasing me, his hand moving away.

"Please," I beg, not recognizing my own voice. What's come over me? I don't even know myself in this moment. My body has been on fire since our stupid argument. I crave him, want him to do everything he did to me yesterday and the night before, plus more. Anything. I'm up for anything he wants. He stuck his fingers in my ass and that was something I swore I would never let any man do to me, and now I'm this close to begging Max to do it again.

He chuckles. Doesn't seem to be affected by me whatsoever, which I find infuriating. But I'm too aroused to be anything else, let alone angry. Such a wasted energy. "However you can get me, princess?"

"Yes. Just . . ." I choke on my own words when he traces my pussy with his fingertips, his touch feather light. "Please. Fuck me."

"Such a shame that you're so impatient. Don't you want to stretch this out, baby?" He says this conversationally, as if we're talking about the weather. "Maybe I could just get you off first."

Oh, God, no. I want his cock. I want to feel him stretch me, fill me. I want to get lost in the rhythm of our bodies, the drag of his cock deep inside me, thrusting again and again . . .

I want the closeness. The skin-to-skin contact, his eyes staring into mine. I want that to take home with me so I never, ever forget him.

"Come here." He grabs hold of my hips and pulls me toward him. I go willingly, gasping when he flips me around as if I weigh nothing and settles my naked body in his lap, my legs automatically wrapping around his hips. "Lie back."

I stretch back along the lounger, watching him from beneath heavy lids as I spread my legs wide, straddling either side of the chair. He moves away from me, his gaze locked on the spot be-tween my thighs, parting his lips as he sucks in a harsh breath. My entire body is trembling, my exhales are coming in short bursts, and I curl my toes against the ground, needing release.

"You look like you're dying for it, baby. Dying for me."

I am. *Oh God,* I completely am. I'm reluctant to admit that I just don't want to get off. I want *him.* "If you won't touch me, I will," I threaten.

His eyes darken and his jaw goes tight. He doesn't like it when I try to wrestle control from him. Max much prefers to be in control.

So did I. Always with Max, I've let him take over. I'm tempted to see what he'll do if I try and wrestle the control away from him.

"Do that and you're in trouble," he murmurs, his gaze, his voice, full of dark promise.

I feel like defying him. I want to know what he'll do to me. What he'll do for me. What sort of trouble does he mean? Nothing scares me. Nothing ever has. So his threats are meaningless.

Cupping my breasts with both hands, my gaze remains locked on his as I brush my nipples with my thumbs. "What kind of trouble are you talking about?"

His gaze tracks my every move. "The kind you should be afraid of."

"You don't scare me," I taunt. Playing with my nipples only seems to hurt, so I release my grip on my breasts, let one hand trail down my quivering stomach. Everything I'm doing, feeling, wanting, centers right in the spot between my legs. My pussy aches. My clit pulses. And when I run my fingers over my slit, cupping myself, I want to scream out loud because it feels so good.

But I don't. I remain quiet. In control. The heat of Max's eyes on me sets me on fire, makes me burn, but I don't stop. Not even when I see the anger flare deeper in his gaze, not when I note the way his hands clench into fists. He's trying his best to remain in control, too, but he struggles.

Looks like I'm winning.

I tease my clit, search my folds, and I can hear how wet I am. Bringing my fingers to my mouth, I suck them, lick them, then settle them back between my legs, stroking in earnest now.

"Jesus," I hear Max mutter and I smile, whimpering when I stroke against my swollen clit extra hard. My flesh is tingling, I'm already so close to coming, and it's because Max is watching me. The orgasm hovers, tantalizing me right on the horizon's edge, and I reach for it, closing my eyes, straining my hips, throwing back my head . . .

Strong fingers clamp around my wrist, stopping my ministrations dead in their tracks. "No fucking way are you going to come like that."

My eyes fly open and I glare at Max, my hand useless, wiggling directly over my body as he holds my wrist tight. "Let go."

The smile that stretches across Max's face is almost feral. He doesn't look happy. Nor does he appear pleased. He's . . . pissed. Furious at me for defying him, and the secret thrill that races down my spine makes me shiver.

"No." He tugs on my wrist, making me sit up so his face is in mine. "I told you not to touch yourself and you did it anyway."

"What are you going to do to me?" I'm breathless with anticipation, my entire body on edge waiting to hear what he has to say.

His smile softens, causing his eyes to crinkle, and my breath leaves me for another reason. He's so handsome, so big and masculine yet rough around the edges. Stubble lines his cheeks and I have the sudden memory of those rough cheeks rubbing against my thighs . . . my pussy . . . driving me wild.

"What do you want me to do to you?" He brings my hand up to his face and inhales. "Fuck, you smell amazing."

My entire body goes weak at his words. "Make me come so many times I pass out?" I ask hopefully.

He chuckles. "That doesn't sound like punishment."

"Passing out is definitely not a good thing," I tell him, licking my lips, mimicking the way he's licking my fingers. Tasting me. *Oh God*, this man is wicked.

"Passing out from too many orgasms is a fucking awesome thing." He shakes his head. "I'm not going to tell you what I'm going to do to you."

I frown. "You're not?"

"Nope." His smile grows. "I'm going to show you. And you're going to both love it and hate it."

Wariness fills me, along with fear and excitement. "O-okay."

"Now lean back again." I start to but he gathers me, his hands on my ass, lifting me up so my pussy is directly in front of his mouth. "Watch this, baby girl," he murmurs just before he licks me.

A little scream escapes and he lifts his head away, glaring at me. "Quiet," he whispers, and I clamp my lips shut, closing my eyes when he licks me again. And stops.

"I said watch me," he commands, and my eyes fly open, excited and scared to see what he does next.

What he does is drive me out of my mind with pleasure. Just as I'm about to come he pauses, pulls away, changes the motion, rains kisses on my inner thighs. He toys with my clit with just the tip of his tongue, nudging it, flicking it, drawing it between his lips for one long, good suck, and then he's moving on. Kissing my belly, stroking my thighs.

Driving me fucking crazy.

"A bad girl like you doesn't deserve to come," he whispers against my pussy after about ten minutes of exquisite torture. "Greedy girls have to learn patience."

"What . . ." I swallow hard, my throat dry, my pussy anything but. Max's lips glisten and just the sight of that alone turns me on. I'm so worked up I'm afraid he'll breathe on my clit and I'll come. "What if I can't stop myself from coming?"

His gaze glitters like perfect sapphires. "Then you'll be in even more trouble."

He means it. He'll do something to me that I can't even fathom. And this torture he's putting me through now is beyond ridiculous. I feel like I'm having an out-of-body experience. Like I'm observing the both of us as he grips my ass with his large, flexing hands, my pussy an offering for him to feast on. His tongue touches every part of me, his lips, his teeth. I feel mindless, out of control, scared that I'll come and he'll hate me for it.

Excited that I'll come and he'll do something deliciously awful to me for disobeying him.

"You need to learn how to take orders, princess. Not give them," he murmurs against my thigh as he kisses me there yet again. "Learn how to restrain yourself and do as I say."

But it's so hard. So incredibly hard. I'm dying to grab hold of his hair and tug him close, tell him exactly where to lick and suck. I've always taken charge with the other men in my life. It was all fun and games but ultimately, I was in control. They did what I said and I loved it.

Not this man. He won't do anything that I say. He's in command and I . . .

I love it. Hate it. Want more of it.

"You want to come?" he asks, sucking my clit between his lips before he lets it go.

I nod, not saying a word. Scared he'll deny me if I say or do the wrong thing.

"I bet you're going to convulse and cry out my name," he says, his voice low. Hypnotic. He nuzzles my pussy with his nose, breathing deep, dropping sweet little kisses all over my flesh and making me shiver. "Maybe I should stick my fingers inside you so I can feel it when I finally let you come."

God, whatever he needs or wants to do, I'd let him. Gladly.

"Not going to protest, princess? Did I finally break you?" I squint at him, batting away the anger that wants to surge, and he sees it. I can tell just by the change in his expression. But why do those words make me mad? Is it the way he said it? Or is it the word *break*? Everyone seems to want to break me, have a piece of me. I'm sick of it.

Can't he just want me for me?

"You don't want me to break you, do you?" he asks, shaking his head. "Well, too damn bad. By the time I'm through with you, you'll be an obedient little girl, just how I like it."

I can't stand the thought of him being with any other women, which is crazy. Why do I care? I've been with plenty of men—not something I'm proud of, but I can't deny it since pretty much every guy I've been with is documented via social media. But you don't hear me talk about them. Don't hear me bragging about my many conquests.

God, I'm jealous. A foreign emotion I rarely feel, at least when it comes to men.

The breeze blows over me, cooling my heated flesh, and I close my eyes, popping them back open when Max's hands squeeze my butt. "I bought more condoms," he says.

I breathe out a sigh of relief. "Thank God."

He leans in close as he pulls me even closer, until I'm tumbling back into his lap and his face is in mine. "You're not mad at me, are you," he murmurs just before he claims my mouth.

I open wide for him, our tongues thrusting, the unmistakable musky taste of my pussy making me even hotter. He has no shame, this man, and neither do I. He's rough and a little mean and a lot sexy and I can't get enough. There's a connection between us I don't want to fight. I like him. I want to spend more time with him, learn more about him.

The idea scares me.

His hands clamp around my waist and pull me down so I'm grinding my naked pussy on his clothed erection. He's huge and hot, thick and long, and I rub against him shamelessly, whimpering into his mouth, increasing my pace.

"You getting off, baby?"

No need to answer because the orgasm hits me at full blast right at that very moment. I cry out, circling my arms around his neck as I cling to him, my hips working against his cock, loving the friction his swim trunks give me as I come all over him.

I can't even care if I went against his rules. I'm limp in his arms, shivering and shaking, and he's looking at me like he wants to both hug me close and shove me away.

"You disobeyed me," he whispers, reaching out to trail his fingers across my cheek.

My eyes slide closed at his gentle touch and I tip my head back. My legs are wound tight around his waist and I bury my hands in his hair. "Sorry." I don't sound remorseful because I'm not. That was absolute torture and I needed the relief.

His other hand goes to my neck and he grips my nape, forcing me to face him once more. "It's like you can't help but be a bad girl."

I smile, my heart aching at his words. "Haven't you realized that's what you're dealing with? I *am* a bad girl. I do what I want, when I want. No one can tell me what to do." Pausing, I let my gaze roam over his handsome features, seeing the familiar disappointment in his eyes. Typical. I make no one happy. "Not even you," I add in the softest whisper.

He stares at me, his gaze unwavering. There's no disappointment in his eyes; he doesn't appear upset any longer. "Aren't you tired of being alone? On your own? You against the world, always fighting, always struggling?"

I want to say no. It's easier to pretend I'm tough and I don't need anyone, definitely not a man trying to tell me what to do. But Max isn't like that, not really. He treats me like an equal. That he enjoys taking command in the bedroom doesn't bother me, not really.

I almost . . . prefer it.

"Yes," I finally whisper, my throat raw with emotion. "It's . . . hard, being alone."

"I know." He reaches out, drifts his fingers across my cheek. "I agree."

Should I say something more? Tell him we don't have to be alone as long as we have each other?

No, that's too much. Too soon. He'll freak. Or worse, make fun of me. Make a joke of it.

He would never do that and you know it.

"Let's take a step back and calm down." Max traces my jaw with his fingers, his thumb smoothing over my chin. "After all, we've got all night."

There's a finality to his statement that sends panic racing through my veins. All night isn't enough. It would never be enough. But I can't admit that.

So I don't.

Chapter Eighteen

Max

I took her to dinner, to torture myself and to give us some much-needed distance. My irrational anger at her getting herself off by humping my dick while I had my swim trunks on still simmered low in my gut, which was ridiculous. But I didn't like how she defied me, how she did what she wanted despite my telling her not to.

It was the first time she'd done that since we'd started playing this sick game and it made me mad. Made me feel out of control. I didn't like it.

At all.

I really wanted to walk out on her and never look back, but I couldn't. Not only because I flat-out can't leave her, but I have a job to do and by God, I'm going to finish it. Plus, if I left her and gave back Pilar her fucking money, that bitch would send some other dick after Lily instead and God knows what would happen. So I'm protecting her.

Yeah, keep telling yourself that, jackass.

The idea of not having this last moment with her hurts more than I care to admit. It was Lily's idea to suggest a hands-off approach for tonight and like a dumbass, I agreed.

"No sex," she'd said, her expression stony, her gaze steady.

Though I saw the slight flicker in her eyes. She was probably afraid I'd tell her no and leave her. Like I could. "We only seem to piss each other off."

Easy for her to say—she already got her orgasm for the day.

"Fine," I said, rubbing a hand over my face, ready to agree to anything so I could see her again. I almost blew it, getting so mad at her. But this is what happens when you get yourself physically and emotionally involved with someone you have no business being with.

Heavy emphasis on the word *business*.

We went to a restaurant in the resort, a place that was dark and expensive and served up intoxicating, exotically named drinks. Lily had three and I had two and she was a little giggly, a lot beautiful, helping me forget my anger, the tension that radiated through me over what I was about to do.

Steal from her. Betray her.

I've done a lot of things in my life that I didn't like or that I didn't want to do, but I always did them honestly. With integrity, though I know of others who would disagree with me, especially from my military past. Going off the mental deep end still embarrasses me when I think about it, but what's done is done. My family accepted me back into the fold, even though my brother Sam thought I was a complete dumbass at first. He served his time in the military, left after four years, and is now a cop, just like our dad. He did everything right.

I, on the other hand, did everything wrong. Guess Lily and I have more in common than I first thought.

But never have I done something so dishonest, so cruel. So fucking risky, both to me and to Lily. I can't study my subject with an objective eye. I've had her every which way I could sexually. I know the taste of her lips, the taste of her pussy, the way it feels when it clamps tight around my cock before she comes. I'm in way too fucking deep.

I like her. A lot. If I'd met her under any other circumstance, I'd pursue her relentlessly until I made her mine. Pretty much like I'm doing right now. The difference?

There's no choice. I have to walk away. And I don't want to.

The minute I pay the dinner bill I'm on my feet, offering my hand to Lily. Our conversation when we first arrived at the restaurant had been stilted. Awkward. She knew I was mad—though I was more angry at myself than at her—and it pissed her off, too, so we had a sort of standoff across the table from each other.

I gave in first. I needed an opportunity to get back to her bungalow. To spend time with her alone. Once our food came—and we were both on our second drink—the conversation flowed, the flirtation grew, and I knew I had her.

She is too damn easy. I feel like a complete asshole for thinking like that.

I passed on a third drink because I wanted to keep my wits about me, and too much alcohol would result in me falling into a deep sleep later. Something I can't do considering I need to stay awake past Lily so I can grab that fucking laptop.

"Thank you for dinner," she says after we leave the restaurant, reaching out to touch my arm as we walk side by side. Her fingers burn my skin and I almost pull away from her, but instead I stop, my fingers curling around her wrist so I can pull her in closer. She goes willingly, her eyes wide, her lips parting.

Looking sexy as hell.

Doesn't help that her hair is up, revealing her edible neck, and she's wearing a strapless bright green dress that makes her skin appear extra golden. Large, thin gold hoops dangle from her ears and a delicate long gold chain hangs from her neck to rest between her breasts.

She's not just sexy, she's also beautiful. Sweet. I want more of her. So much more . . . but I can't have it.

"I should've never agreed to the conditions you put on tonight," I mutter, running my gaze over her body, wishing it were my hands trailing all over her.

She laughs, her eyes sparkling, her cheeks the faintest pink. I made the secret dirty girl blush again? Go figure. "Are you the type who wants what you can't have?"

"Not usually." My fingers tighten around her wrist. With her, yes, a thousand times yes. "I tend to just go for it."

Lily presses her lips together, and I feel her heart rate speed up since my fingers are pressing directly against her pulse. "Like you did with me before?"

"Exactly." She's so close, I can nuzzle her hair, breathe in her sweet scent. *Damn,* the woman smells good. Fragrant and fresh, rich and decadent, a contradicting combination I want more of.

Just one more taste. One more night.

"I never go against a lady's wishes, though," I tell her, stepping away. I see the disappointment cross her face and it matches the disappointment that spreads through me. I mean what I say but I'm hoping . . . I'm fucking *praying* she'll give in and let me have her. At least one more time. "I may be an asshole, but I'm not that much of one."

"Sometimes . . ." She moistens her lips, the luscious, shiny curve of her bottom lip sending a bolt of lust straight to my dick. "The lady says things too rashly. She has a bad habit of not thinking things through."

Hope sparks within me. Stupid, idiotic hope. I squash it down. I shouldn't do this. Shouldn't want this. But I do. God, I do. "Does she, now?"

"Oh yes. All the time. Usually it ends up with her doing something she regrets. She tends to make a lot of mistakes," Lily admits softly.

I don't know what she's talking about. Past regrets? Possibly. I understand that. "Does she think what happened between us is a mistake?"

Slowly she shakes her head, taking a step toward me. Her

body brushes against mine and it's like my entire being has been lit on fire. "Maybe. I don't know. But I don't care. Some things are just too hard to fight."

I give in to my urges and touch her. Cup her cheek, tilt her head back, and I know by the way she parts her lips that she's ready, eager for me to kiss her. I love how responsive she is to me. It makes me feel like I can conquer the whole damn world. "I won't do a thing until you say the word."

Her delicate brows draw down as she stares up at me. "What word is that?"

Leaning in so close my mouth hovers above hers, I whisper, "Yes."

Her breath wafts across my lips, minty and sweet from the chocolate mint I saw her pop in her mouth as we exited the restaurant. She tilts her head back the slightest bit, aligning our mouths perfectly, and murmurs, "Take me to your room, Max."

I settle my lips on hers, not caring that we're surrounded by people as they exit and enter the restaurant. The Hawaiian music that plays fades to the background, as does all the chatter. All I can see and hear and taste is Lily, the perfect offering to placate my raging need. She tastes like heaven, her mouth opening eagerly to mine, our tongues sliding.

She draws away from me before the kiss gets too out of control and keeps her hold on my wrist, my hand still at her cheek. "So is that a yes?" I ask.

Nodding, she kisses the side of my jaw. "Yes."

UNFORTUNATELY I COULDN'T CONVINCE HER TO GO TO HER bungalow. She was adamant about seeing my room, so here we are, frustration rippling through me as I escort her down the hall toward my door. My mind is scrambling, trying to come up with a plan B, but then she looks at me, the smile on her face soft, her eyes glowing, and fuck, all plans to take what belongs to her are obliterated from my brain.

All I can think about, all I can focus on, is Lily.

Maybe I don't need to grab that laptop after all. I can destroy whatever evidence is on the damn thing and somehow prove it to Pilar. Hell, I can make a copy of everything on it and give it to her. Though that would probably not ease her mind. I don't think anything will pacify her. She's as high-strung as they come.

We're silent as Lily enters my hotel room, her gaze scanning the interior, as if she's looking for clues. Hints of what makes me tick. I'm sure she's disappointed by the cleanliness of the room, the fact that my suitcase sits on the folding stand they provide for it, zipped closed and packed, ready for my early-morning departure that she has no clue exists.

Whereas her villa was always a bit of a mess every time I was there, with clothes everywhere, jewelry scattered on the dresser, shoes kicked off by the front door, and an array of beauty products spread all over the counter in the bathroom.

The mess had been telling. A hint of chaos in her life, not a surprise. She claims she likes control but her habits, her behavior, prove otherwise.

I could be the one to control her. To calm her. Growing up, my life hadn't been mine. I'd wanted to meet my father's expectations. I'd had no choice. It was his way or no way. I'd learned that fast. When I was a teen, I hadn't understood my need for control with a girl. Not that I was an abusive asshole, but I was intense. I'm still intense.

Now I understand it, run with it. Find a woman who understands my needs, too. I can see it in them sometimes. The way they lean into me, the words they say, the look in their eyes.

I couldn't with Lily, not at first. She presented a challenge. One I pursued doggedly.

"Do you have a good view out there?" she asks as she draws closer to the sliding glass door that leads onto a balcony.

"Not as stellar as yours, princess. But it'll do," I answer, smiling at her when she glances at me from over her shoulder.

She looks nervous. Unsure. I plan on easing all that nervousness right out of her, so I'll let her look around, do what she needs to do to get comfortable. I need her comfortable, trusting, open. Then I need to exhaust her and slip out of this room while she sleeps.

Fuck, talk about doubling the risk.

Lily opens the sliding glass door and steps out onto the balcony, her voice carrying on the breeze that slips through the room. "It's beautiful out here," she calls out.

Stopping in the bathroom, I grab a condom from my travel bag that still sits by the sink and shove it into my pocket. I want to be prepared. She's so nervous, I'm afraid one wrong move and she'll run. And I can't have that.

I join her outside, the cooling air washing over my skin, carrying with it Lily's addictive scent. She's leaning against the railing, staring out at the ocean in the near distance, the palm trees that line the resort property swaying to and fro, their fronds rattling with the wind. "You like the view?" I ask. I know I'll miss it when I return home. This island is truly a paradise, and the view from my bedroom window in my apartment is the brick building across the street.

"I do. It's gorgeous. The way the moon shines on the water, it's so bright." She stiffens when I stop just behind her, as if she can sense my nearness though she never looks back. I hope I don't make her too uncomfortable. The last thing I want is her being afraid of me. "You can see everything this high up. Imagine if you were higher."

"I can't afford higher. No penthouse for me," I joke, settling my hands on her bare shoulders. They tense up as she breathes deep and I whisper close to her ear, "Relax. I'm trying to show you how sorry I am for what happened earlier."

"I'm sorry, too," she whispers as she bends her head down, offering me a tempting view of her neck. I give in, pressing my mouth against her nape, trailing light kisses to her shoulder. She softens with every touch of my lips, gooseflesh rising in my wake, a quiet sigh escaping her. I crowd in closer, my hands going to the railing as I box her in.

"What are you doing?" she asks, turning her head toward mine just as I take her mouth in a deep kiss. I don't want to talk. Talking causes problems between us and tonight I plan on finishing what I started. Her hand goes to the back of my head, fingers threading through my hair as she holds me close, and I drink from her lips.

"I just want to make you feel good," I whisper against her skin, satisfaction filling me when I feel her shiver. My cock is already hard, just being this close to her. Tasting her, feeling her, smelling her again. I break the kiss and she turns her head, facing toward the ocean once more. A couple passes by down below, holding hands as they walk along the winding sidewalk, and I slip my arms around Lily, reaching my hands up so I cup her breasts.

"Someone could see us," she whispers as she pushes her breasts into my palms. Her automatic responses to my touch build the need already roaring inside of me to a near frenzy. How can I walk away from her?

How can I let her go?

"Max," she whispers urgently, though she hasn't pushed my hands away. "I'm serious." She doesn't sound serious. No, more like she sounds keyed up. Turned on.

I smile. I think she likes the idea that someone might see us. "I doubt they'd look up." I tug on the elastic that keeps her strapless top up, pulling the fabric down so her breasts are bared. A gasp escapes her as I brush my palms over her hard nipples, kneading her abundant flesh, and she leans into me with a soft moan, her ass rubbing against the front of my pants, teasing my dick.

"What if they do?" she asks breathlessly.

"Then we'll put on a show for them," I whisper in her ear, then kiss and lick her neck. With my right hand I reach for the fabric of her skirt, gathering it, lifting it up. Leaning away from her, I watch as I pull her dress up past her perfect ass, hissing out a breath when I reveal her to my gaze.

A lacy white thong runs up the crack of her ass, all that tight flesh on display just for me, and I smooth my palm over the tantalizing curve, triumph filling me when she backs into my touch. I squeeze her ass cheek hard, leaving marks on her skin, and then I spank her, more of a light tap that makes her suck in a harsh breath.

I slip my hand down between her legs, where the lacy fabric of her panties is soaked straight through. I nudge it aside, sinking my finger into her drenched heat, and she moans my name as I start to finger-fuck her.

"Like that, princess?" I ask, my other hand busy squeezing her breasts. She nods furiously, like she's too overcome to speak, and I slide another finger inside her tight pussy. "I want to fuck you right where you stand," I growl, overcome with my base need for her. I touch her, kiss her, and all I can think about is conquering her. Making her mine.

All mine.

"Do it," she murmurs, working her hips against my fingers and sending me deeper within her. "Fuck me."

"That means I have to stop touching you and I'm not ready yet." She doesn't protest, doesn't make any sorts of demands, and I'm surprised. That's our biggest problem when we're together like this. It's a battle of wills, a show as to who's the one ultimately in control. Drives me fucking nuts and I know it makes her crazy, too.

But we're so damn good together. She's so responsive, so needy for my touch, my mouth, my cock. She's writhing against me right now, her pussy so wet, and those inner walls are clenching rhythmically. She's getting off on this, her hands gripped tight around the metal railing, her ass thrust toward me almost obscenely.

Hell, *I'm* getting off on this, on watching her, touching her, feeling her. My cock strains so hard against the front of my pants, my zipper will probably imprint on my fucking skin if I don't let it free soon. It's as if we can't resist each other.

And we can't. I don't want to resist her.

I think she feels the same.

"Please," she whispers as she strains against my hand. The need in her voice is intense and I slip my arm around her waist, my fingers still buried in her pussy.

I bend over her, resting my cheek against hers as I whisper, "Please what, baby girl?"

"Please let me come," she says, whimpering when I still my fingers.

It's the words *let me come* that gets to me. As if she's asking permission. As if she's finally realized who's the one in charge here and it's not her.

Fuck.

"You don't want to wait for my cock?" I ask her.

Now it's her turn to go completely still, though her body trembles in my embrace. "I do. I want it. But . . ."

"You want to come now," I finish for her.

She nods. "I'm sorry."

That does it. She's giving me everything I crave, saying all the right things, responding in exactly the right way. If she's purposely trying to drive me out of my fucking mind, it's working.

"No need to say sorry," I reassure her. "I'll give you what you want."

Before she can say anything, do anything, I angle my hand, slipping my thumb over her swollen clit, and press hard. A relieved sigh escapes her and she rotates her hips, grinds her pussy against my hand as she starts to pant. She's working toward her orgasm, racing toward it I bet, and I decide to help her along.

"So goddamn tight, princess," I murmur against her cheek. "You like the way my fingers fuck you? Do you like them better than my cock?"

"I—I like b-both," she stutters, and I'm impressed she can even speak.

"I'll give you both. Come with my fingers and then I'll have you coming all over my cock. Do you want that?"

"Oh God . . . yes," she moans as I feel her pussy tighten around my fingers and then she explodes, sobbing as her entire body is overcome. She shakes within my arms, my fingers coated with a fresh gush of wetness. When she sags against me, I carefully withdraw from her still shuddering body, grabbing the condom out of my pocket before I'm shoving off my pants and underwear, practically hopping out of them when they fall to my feet.

I tear into the wrapper, pulling the rubber ring out as I kick her legs open so she's spread wider for me. Stopping in my race to get inside her, I stare dumbfounded for a moment at her pussy. It's pink and glistening, on perfect display just for me, and I tear my gaze away from the fascinating view to catch her studying me from over her shoulder.

Her shoulders heave with her still ragged breaths. Her lips are parted and wet. Those big, luminous eyes watch me and I lean in, kissing her fiercely, stealing her breath and mine with the intense connection that we've woven between us in such a short amount of time.

"So fucking beautiful, princess," I tell her, my gaze never

leaving hers as I move away from her so I can slip on the condom.

Voices sound and she turns her head on a gasp, peeking down below. More people are walking by, looks like two couples this time, and they're laughing and chatting loudly, sounding a little drunk. Lily leans over the balcony railing, her hands still gripping the metal, her breasts practically dangling over the edge, and I take that moment to slip inside her, inch by inch, filling her up.

Making her sway and moan low in her throat.

The sound makes the chatter stop and we both go still, my cock throbbing inside her tight pussy. I wait, all the air trapped in my lungs, one hand smoothing over her ass, the other gripped around her waist. Slowly she starts to move and I look down at the spot where we're connected, entranced by the way her pussy glides over my dick, taking it deeper and deeper until I disappear inside her body and then moving back out till only the very tip is nestled within.

I exhale through my nose, telling myself to keep it together when all I want to do is ram inside her until we both splinter apart. She's riding my cock back and forth, in and out, her breasts swaying, her ass nudging against my front until I'm balls-deep buried in her snug heat.

"Fuck, you feel good," I tell her, urging her on. The people are gone. I didn't even hear them leave, too enraptured with the way she's taking me, fucking me. Because she is definitely the one fucking me right now. I'm letting her control the depth, the speed, because I'm fascinated with the way she moves, the shape of her ass, the eager yet controlled way she rides me.

She swings her head, the hoop earrings flaring out as she watches me from over her shoulder yet again. Her eyes are dark, her mouth parted as if she's struggling for breath. I reach for her, my hand snaking into her hair, fingers gripping the strands as I tug, bringing her to me. She lifts up, my cock still embedded in her body, her back to my front as we kiss, tongues tangling, teeth clashing, and she moans so loudly I'm afraid she'll draw attention to us up here.

Not so afraid that it'll stop us from doing this, though. There's something freeing about being up here where anyone could see us, our bodies bared and the moonlight shining on her skin, her soft moans, my harsh grunts, the breeze wafting across our connected bodies, cooling our heated skin.

"You having fun controlling our fucking?" I ask when I break the kiss first. She smiles against my mouth. "Ready for me to take over?"

"You don't like what I'm doing?" She squeezes those velvety inner walls around my cock, making me groan, and then I'm shifting her around so she bends back over, her hands on the railing once more, my hand in her hair and the other hand on her hip as I start to pound inside of her. Taking her.

Claiming her.

She doesn't miss a beat, her body moving with mine, her legs going wider and somehow sending me even deeper. I let go of her hair and grip either side of her hips, thrusting so hard my stomach slaps against her ass hard. Again. Harder. Taking her deep, my fingers embedded in her skin, my balls brushing against her pussy.

"Oh, fuck yes," she whispers just before I feel her come apart, her pussy clenching around my dick, her body quivering. I gather her up close, hold her through her orgasm, crooning a mixture of sweet and dirty words in her ear that make her shudder harder, her body melting against mine. I'm strung tight, my head spinning, my heart racing, my cock pulsating with the need to come, and when she finally quiets, that last shivery breath escaping her, I begin to move again.

"Bend over and hold on tight, princess," I tell her, and she does as I command. "I'm going to fuck you hard." It's supposed to be a warning, but I don't think she's scared.

No, not scared at all. She wags that tempting butt at me, my cock still buried deep, and I slide in farther, as far as I can go. Taking her without care, using her with every mad thrust of my hips. I'm like an animal out of control, unleashed, the familiar tingling at the base of my spine starting, spreading up, over, taking me straight over the edge until I'm the one falling completely apart.

And wondering, for once in my life, if I can ever be put back together again.

Chapter Nineteen

Max

LIKE THE DICK I AM, I WALKED HER TO HER BUNGALOW, CLAIM-ing I wanted to tuck her in.

"Can't I just stay the night in your room?" she'd whispered as she'd rubbed her hands all over my chest, her sexy body scooting closer to mine.

I'd slipped out of my bed and gathered up her clothes, thrusting her dress and panties out toward her. "Get dressed, princess." I ignored what she said, and she was still a little drunk, a little too out of it to question me further.

She let me into her bungalow—through the locked front door since she didn't keep the slider unlocked anymore, thank God—and I steered her toward the bedroom, helping her strip out of her clothes before I took her by the shoulders and gently pushed her into bed.

"Don't go." She held her arms out to me, the sheet falling to her waist, those spectacular breasts on display just for me. I see a red mark on her neck and I know that's from my lips. Pride fills me, swift and sharp, and I tell myself I'm an asshole for getting a thrill out of marking her, but that doesn't matter.

It still makes me proud. Makes me want to beat my chest, grab Lily by the hair, and proclaim to the world that she's mine.

Fucking ridiculous.

"Come here." I stretch out beside her on the bed, above the covers, because I know if I slip below them, I'll start touching her again and then I'm done for.

She snuggles into my arms, a sigh escaping her as she rests her head against my chest. I press a kiss to the top of her head and rest my chin there, willing myself to resist her despite how good she feels, how delicious she smells. I just had her not even twenty minutes ago. We had sex three times in the span of no more than ninety minutes and it was fucking amazing every single time.

But then she started to fade. Lots of yawning. A few silly giggles, her eyes falling closed, and she'd cuddled with the pillow. Too much alcohol was putting Lily under, and I knew this might be my only chance to get back to her bungalow. She was reluctant, she put up a fight, but now here she is, in my arms, soft and sweet and trusting, and I'm feeling like the biggest asshole on the planet.

I can't believe I'm going through with this. I've had ample chances and blew every one of them on purpose. I told myself I couldn't take it from her, not yet. My motives were purely selfish. Every single time I was with her, in this bungalow, when I had my chance . . . I told myself no. One more afternoon with Lily. One more night with Lily. One more kiss, one more time inside her body . . .

Why the fuck does Pilar need the damn laptop so desperately anyway? What could be on it? What did Lily discover about the woman who is dating her father? She has something on Pilar. She must. Lily's smart. But so is fucking Pilar. She's calculating, too. Mean as hell.

Dangerous.

"Tell me we'll hang out again tomorrow," she says sleepily.

My heart seizes in my chest. "We will."

Liar.

"Tell me we won't fight and say stupid stuff."

"We won't." That isn't a lie. We can't fight if we're not to-gether.

"Good." She sighs and kisses my chest, her lips damp and warm and making me shiver. "I like you, Max. I like you a lot."

I'm miserable. Why does she have to go and say something like that and worm her way into my hard-as-steel heart? Fuck this, I didn't mean to . . . fall for her. Not that I've fallen for her for real, more like I'm physically attracted to Lily and I find her hard to resist.

Admit it, you've fallen for her, you heartless bastard.

Fine. I have. But I'm not heartless. My heart is beating like crazy, pounding to a rhythm that suspiciously sounds like her name. *Li-ly. Li-ly.* It's fucking crazy. *I'm* crazy.

Crazy for her.

Sighing, I keep my gaze fixed on the window across from us, staring at it until my vision goes fuzzy and I close my eyes. Lily's body grows heavier and heavier and her breathing evens out, indicating she's fallen asleep.

A few minutes, I tell myself. I'll stay with her a few minutes and wait until she's in a deep sleep and then I'm out of here with what I came for.

Problem is, I fall asleep, too. For a couple of hours—and I dream. Horrible, shitty dreams that feel so damn real. I'm escap-ing the bungalow, the laptop clutched tight in my hands, and Lily catches me. Tears stream down her face as she yells how much she trusted me and I hurt her so bad. That she hates me. She hates me so much, she'll never talk to me again.

I beg for her forgiveness. I try and hand her back the laptop but she won't take it. She keeps refusing it and I become more insistent, shoving the damn laptop toward her, pushing it into her stomach . . .

And then she turns into Pilar and she's laughing at me. The sound is mocking, shrill, and she snatches the laptop from my grip. I clamp my hands over my ears and try to turn away so I don't have to look at her but it's as though I can't. She laughs and laughs, her mouth getting wider and wider, like a black hole, and then she's coming toward me, the laptop held over her head, as if she's going to hit me with it.

I startle awake, lifting my head, holding back the groan that wants to escape at the pain in my neck from sleeping in such a weird position. Lily is still snug against me, her head fitting perfectly between my shoulder and neck, and slowly I disentangle myself from her, slipping from beneath her inch by careful inch. She never wakes, I'm able to adjust her into position in her bed, and I tug the sheet and comforter up higher, covering her to her neck.

I stand above her for a moment, blinking hard as I try to wake myself up. She looks so beautiful, so peaceful, lying there on her side. Her lips are pursed, her hair is a wavy mess, and she's the prettiest thing I've ever seen.

I don't want to walk away. I want to keep her. I want her to be mine. We could really be something, Lily and I. I know we could. We're more alike than even I care to admit. I think we could be good for each other. Good together.

But we can't. I have to do this. It's my job. And my job—my business—is all I have. Despite how I feel about Lily, there are no guarantees. I must take that fucking laptop, despite my never wanting to do it since I got here, hating Pilar Vasquez and her shitty demands.

Closing my eyes, I tighten my hands into fists and take a deep breath. I'm being completely irrational. This woman . . . I don't know what could happen between us, but it's not real. It can't be real. I'm too caught up in this tropical location, the pretending I'm on vacation. If she finds out the truth, I'm fucked. I need to go. Just . . . grab that fucking laptop and leave. But this is the last time I'll be with her, look at her, touch her . . .

Reaching out, I streak my fingers across her cheek, lightly. She shifts and sighs, her eyelashes fluttering, and I snatch my hand back, praying she won't wake up.

She doesn't. I can't help but be relieved—and a little disappointed, too. If she woke up, I'd have no choice but to stay.

I take a deep breath and go to the closet, quietly sliding the door open. Stepping inside, I reach for the laptop, not surprised at all to find it in the exact spot that I last saw it.

Holding it close to my chest, I make my escape from the bungalow.

And never once look back.

Chapter Twenty

Lily

"Looks like Maui agreed with you." Violet greets me as I walk toward her, practically falling into her welcoming hug. I squeeze her back, closing my eyes for the briefest moment as I absorb her love and warmth, so incredibly thankful to be with her again.

"It's been a long time since I've seen you in person," I tell her before I withdraw, though I don't let her go—my hands still clasp her shoulders and she's holding on to my arms.

"I know." Violet's smiling at me, looking gorgeous with all that dark hair falling down her back in luxurious waves, her dark eyes sparkling as bright as the giant diamond on her finger. I don't know if I've ever seen Violet look so genuinely happy.

I could almost get choked up, having her here in front of me. I didn't realize I missed my sister so much until now. "Skype just doesn't cut it, you know," I say, my voice rough as I clear my throat past the emotional bubble clogging it.

Violet rolls her eyes and smiles. "I totally agree. But guess what? You're stuck with me now. No more going back to London for us except to visit."

I'm so grateful for her warm acceptance of me that I can feel the tight knot in my chest slowly unravel. I was scared to death this morning as I prepared to come into Fleur. Seeing Daddy,

Grandma, Rose, and Violet . . . and worst of all, that evil witch Pilar . . . I wasn't looking forward to it, and that's the understatement of the year.

I was petrified really, afraid of what any of them might say. I'd rather pretend the fact that I ran away to Maui to escape my problems—especially a problem that neither I nor Pilar wants made public knowledge, I'm sure—was swept under the rug.

I don't even want to talk about Maui and what happened there. The man I met. The man who somehow, some way, double-crossed me. Stole from me . . .

I have my suspicions about why Max did what he did. Nothing confirmed yet, but come on. I had jewelry in my suitcase—expensive jewelry. Cash in my wallet and stashed away in my travel bag. Yet he took my laptop and that's it. The fucker *stole* from me.

Why?

Could he be working for Pilar?

No. It couldn't be possible, just some weird coincidence. Maybe he *didn't* steal from me. Maybe one of the hotel employees snagged my Mac. I hadn't checked on it in days. For all I know, it could have been missing since the day I stashed it up on the shelf in my closet.

That's the problem. I don't know what happened, when it was stolen or why. I can suspect Max all I want. It makes sense in a way. He held me close until I fell asleep and when I woke up in the morning, groggy and hungover, he was gone. Disappeared like he'd never existed in the first place. He didn't even leave a note. I searched for him everywhere. By the pool, in the lobby, down by the beach, in the hotel restaurants, but he wasn't there.

I went to his hotel room only to find the door cracked open and the maids inside, cleaning. His stuff was gone. The maids let me know he'd checked out that morning.

He didn't even bother saying goodbye.

It hurts that he didn't believe me worthy of a goodbye. Worse, he lied to me. Said that we would see each other again and then ditched me. I don't get it.

What did I do wrong? That last night, when we had sex, I gave him everything I thought he wanted. I wanted to please him, wanted to be the submissive woman, not only to make him happy, but because it made me feel . . . good. I liked handing over the control to Max so I could get lost in the pleasure. It aroused me, his controlling ways, the words he said, the demands he made on my body. I wanted more. I wanted all of him . . .

And he didn't want me at all.

Coming home set me on edge. Just booking the return flight nearly sent me into a panic attack. I'd taken a Xanax on the flight home to help me relax and I ended up sleeping through practically the entire trip. Went home and crashed into bed only to wake up at three in the morning, wide-eyed and petrified. Deciding to give in to my alert state rather than fight it, I got up, picked out my outfit, took a long, hot shower, went over what I would say to everyone again and again in my head while I blew dry my hair, and hoped like hell I didn't make a complete idiot of myself.

Violet is my first obstacle and so far, so good.

"I thought you were serious about staying in London indefinitely," I tell her as she goes around her desk and settles into her chair as if she's never been gone from the Manhattan headquarters of Fleur. They kept her office intact and for good reason. She's such an integral part of the company and will most likely be running it one day. And I'm sure Daddy realized quickly that she couldn't stay away for too long.

I settle in the chair opposite her desk, amused by the exaggerated grimace on her face. "We didn't want to deal with Pilar—that's why we stayed away for so long. Ryder and I both thought it was for the best. But then grumbling started happening around here. Lots of rumors of how people weren't happy with the direction she was taking the company in. And then Father started finalizing the marketing and release plans with our perfumes, telling me constantly he needed me here. Even Grandma called me, asking me to come back."

I go tense at first mention of Pilar's name. I always forget that Pilar and Ryder used to be a thing, which I shouldn't because, *hello,* that's huge. And weird. Though I don't fault Ryder, since Violet told me about his background and what a shitty life he had growing up.

"There's grumbling about the direction Pilar is taking the company? What are you talking about? What sort of control does she have, anyway?" I ask, curious. If Pilar had her way, she'd bump all of us and take over completely. Not that I'm a threat per se since I don't even work at Fleur, but I still own a percentage of the company and I know that drives her crazy.

I know all three of us make her crazy. That's why she's plotting and scheming, coming up with ways to take us out—and Violet's her biggest target.

I should tell my sister my suspicions, that I believe Pilar is trying to sell trade secrets to Fleur's competition, but how? How can I break it to her without completely freaking her out and sending Ryder on a murderous rampage? I can't risk it.

So I keep my mouth shut. I have my own plans. Now that I'm back, it's time for me to set a few things in motion.

"There's lots of talk about expansion in the works and no one is pleased, least of all me and Ryder." Violet smiles every time she mentions her fiancé's name. I wonder if she's even aware of it. "She wants to grow too fast and that could harm the infrastructure of the company. Her grandiose plans were getting out of control and I couldn't stand hearing about it another minute. Neither could Ryder. That's the real reason we're back, to put a stop to her before she ruins Fleur for good."

I raise a brow. "So you're back to undermine Pilar's plans?" Pilar has to know this. And that's why she's being such a bitch, pulling out all her weapons and lining them up in a nice, neat row.

Violet smirks. "As best we can. We can't have her ruining our legacy, can we?" She pauses, her eyes dancing with mischief. "I've heard, too, that there's trouble in paradise."

"Do tell." I lean forward, eager for gossip about Daddy and Pilar. Any information I can glean I'll store for later purposes. As in using said information against Pilar.

Violet glances at the closed door with a little nod of approval. Heaven forbid she get caught gossiping about the company, even if it is with just me. "She's pushing for marriage soon and he's not agreeable. Yes, he gave her an engagement ring, but it was more to shut her up than to do anything else. She's getting restless," she says, her voice low, as if there are microphones in the room catching our every word. "Grandma told me he came to her complaining. He's not ready to get married."

"Really?" I'm surprised he would confess something like that to his mother, our grandmother. Our father loves nothing more than putting on airs about how perfect everything in his life is. He gave Pilar that ring not only to please her, but because it looked good, the two of them working together, a beautiful, younger woman on his arm. A partner in crime who's savvy and headstrong, and who's more than ready to take Fleur to the next level. Forget his daughters who are willing to do the same thing.

Well, *daughter.* I have no interest in running Fleur and I'm starting to think Rose has lost interest as well.

Of course, heaven forbid we girls cause him any trouble— hello, I was born to give him trouble—or a scandal. Rose's new husband with the slightly shady past and her out-of-the-blue pregnancy didn't make him happy. Violet's quick dumping of her ex Zachary and rushing into a relationship with Ryder McKay didn't please him at first, either.

We won't even get into how often I displease him. Almost on a daily basis.

"Yes. Really. I don't know how much longer they'll be together, but it's not looking so good. And I think Pilar's aware of it," she admits. "I'm not protesting, though. You know how I feel about her."

I put on an innocent look. "You think she's awesome?"

"Ha." Violet makes a face. "I hate her." And Violet hates no one.

"I think we all do," I say.

Violet waves a hand. "Enough about Pilar. Tell me about your vacation. How was Maui? Did you have a good time?"

Vacation. That's what I finally told her when I texted her the morning I left Maui. What else could I say to Violet?

I'm on the run from Pilar because she's about to get her revenge on you and possibly destroy our family legacy?

Yeah, that wouldn't work. I keep my mouth shut because I don't have 100 percent confirmation. It's one thing to accuse Pilar of having relationships with other men besides my father—I have proof of that via emails. But my suspicions of her selling company secrets to one of Fleur's competitors? That's all I have.

Suspicions. No proof.

"It was nice. Relaxing." Lies. I feel more stressed out than ever. And I definitely don't want to divulge any information about my entanglement with Max. A man whose last name I don't even know. I don't really know what he does for a living beyond that it's a secret and he's ex-military, or whether he lied to me about being single—nothing. For all I know he's married with kids and is living this crazy, double life.

What I do know is that he kissed like a dream, I fell apart every time he so much as looked at me and when he fucked me, he took complete command of my body.

And I liked it.

Memories of that last night with him assail me, one after the other. Letting him take such total control over me, I'd slipped over an edge I'd never experienced before. I felt lost, deliciously, wonderfully lost in the absolute best way. My mind had emptied completely when he touched me, shoved my skirt up to my waist, and then proceeded to give me not just one but two orgasms in a matter of minutes. All while we stood on the balcony of his hotel room where anyone could see us.

The hottest experience of my life, hands down.

All of it ruined by his leaving me. Stealing from me.

God, how could I be so gullible?

"Nice? That's all you're going to give me?" She props her elbow on the edge of her desk, resting her chin on her curled fist as she studies me. "I suggested we go to Hawaii for our honeymoon, but Ryder would rather go to the Caribbean. You'll have to fill me in on the resort so I can report back to him and convince him to change his mind."

"But the Caribbean is nice, too," I tell her, grateful for the minor change of subject. And no way am I going to suggest she go to the resort I was at. That Vice club would shock the hell out of her.

"I'd rather do Hawaii. I'm sure I can convince him it's the better place to honeymoon." She grins. "So what did you do while you were in Maui? Check out the sights? Go to the beach? Did you meet anyone? I've never gone on a vacation by myself before. I'm not sure I'd know what to do with myself."

"Um . . ." I scramble for what to say. Fucked around with a strange man? That wouldn't go over too well. "It was super relaxing. I laid out by the pool a lot." I don't bother mentioning my injury from the first day. My palm is healed and there's no reason to bring it up. Then I'd have to mention Max and the story would spiral out of control.

"I can tell from your tan." She lifts her head, her gaze darting toward the windowed walls of her office. "Oh, there's Rose." She waves to her, the door opening moments later, and in walks our pregnant baby sister.

I leap up from my chair as Violet shoots from behind her

desk, and we're both fighting over who gets to hug Rose first. She laughs and wraps her arms around our shoulders, bringing us in so we're all hugging each other, and I'm so overwhelmed with love for them I almost choke up. Again.

But then Rose shoves us away with a laugh, and my overwhelming emotions fade when I catch sight of her growing belly.

"Rosie!" I drop a hand to her tummy and give it a gentle rub. "Look at you. You're so . . ."

"I know, I'm so *fat*," she moans, though she's smiling. Glowing, really. I've never seen her look prettier, and Rose is already flat-out gorgeous.

"You're not fat," Violet reassures her as she rests her hand on the other side of Rose's belly. "You're full of child."

The smile on Rose's face is nothing short of dreamy. "Trust me. I feel fat. Like I don't know how to move with this belly. I've become awkward and clumsy, which is totally embarrassing. Though Caden says I look sexy with his baby growing inside me. And my sex drive has been off the charts lately—my God. He comes home from work and all I want to do is attack him the minute he walks through the door."

"Ugh, gross. Don't take us there," Violet says, sounding like she's thirteen, and making all three of us crack up.

"You look good, Lily," Rose says, turning her attention to me as we all sit around Violet's desk. "Maui definitely suited you, hmm?"

I brush my hair back from my face, thankful I wore a dress like my sisters. I look like I might actually work here, though no way would I ever want to. Rose is here because she's sitting in on an afternoon meeting.

I'm here because I knew they would both be here and we're all going out to lunch.

"She's being terribly vague," Violet tells Rose, the two of them settling their skeptical gazes right on me. I feel pinned in place by the way they examine me. How could I forget that my sisters are so nosy? "Makes me wonder if something else happened while she was on Maui."

"I stayed out of trouble, just like I promised," I say, throwing up my hand in a Girl Scout pledge. "Didn't really drink much. No partying, either." That was sort of true, so I don't feel like a complete liar.

"Well, the media certainly quieted down once you disappeared. I think they've moved on to the next troublemaker," Rose reassures me, her expression solemn. "That's a good thing, I suppose."

"Definitely," I say. Relief floods me. Arriving at JFK yesterday, I'd disguised myself as best I could. Hair up in a sloppy topknot, giant sunglasses on, boring, everyday clothes, as in matching black sweats and a hoodie I picked up from Victoria's Secret's PINK line. I wanted to fit in and look like every other woman my age on that plane and I succeeded. There were no paparazzi waiting, no cameras flashing in my face.

"I don't think they realize I'm back," I say.

"And you should keep it that way," Violet says firmly. "You don't want to make Daddy angry or give us any bad publicity. He was mad that you just disappeared, you know. He was worried, too. Though I think he's over it, now that he knows you're safe."

"In my dreams he's over it," I mutter, making them both laugh. But I can certainly hope that's the case. "Are you guys ready to go to lunch? I'm starved."

Both Violet and Rose frown at my abrupt change of subject. "You are coming back with us to the meeting after we have lunch though, right?" Rose asks with a puzzled frown.

"No way. I don't belong there." I shake my head. I don't want any sort of confrontation with Pilar, especially on her turf. I may own a piece of this company, but she's worked here for years and feels like Fleur is hers. She'd tear me apart.

"We're talking about the perfumes and testing the sample

scents, and you're an integral part of that, Lily," Violet explains. "Ryder is sitting in on the meeting since this was his idea from the get-go. Pilar's not involved, so she won't be there. This is *our* project. Ryder and I were both up front from the beginning that Pilar plays no part in this project ever. Father understands how important it is to us and no one else." Violet smiles softly. "So don't worry about her."

"Ugh. So glad that bitch isn't involved. I wouldn't go to the meeting either if she were there." Leave it to plainspoken Rose to lay it all out. "God, I hate her so much."

She's insidious, Pilar. Like a bad disease that lies in wait inside your body, poised to attack. Or a weed that grows in a lush garden, taking over and choking the beautiful flowers out until all that remains is the nasty, ugly weed that no one wants.

The phone on Violet's desk rings and she goes to answer it, giving a few noncommittal replies until she ends the conversation with a clipped, "We'll discuss it during the meeting," before she hangs up and turns toward us. "Father asked if you were attending, Lily. He wants you there. I think it's in your best interest that you show up. Though I must warn you, everything we discuss this afternoon is top secret. No one knows about the project and Father doesn't want anything to leak."

Dread consumes me and I stand, smoothing the skirt of my dress with trembling hands. "I don't want to go to the meeting," I blurt out, wanting them to know. Needing their support.

Rose turns to me, surprise written all over her face. "Why? It's no big deal, Lily. We're just offering our opinion on the scents. How hard can it be?"

"But Daddy will be there. Having to face him . . . makes me nervous." Tears prick the corners of my eyes and I will them away. I refuse to fall apart. Not now, not before I see him and he can pick at my weaknesses.

I'm vulnerable enough, after what happened with Max. I've never felt so unloved, so unwanted, as I do at this very moment.

Which is so incredibly stupid, because I'm surrounded by love and support in the form of the two most important people in my world.

My sisters.

"He'll get over it." Violet grabs hold of my hand and squeezes it. "Just go in there and be yourself. The real you, Lily. Not the party girl who doesn't care what anyone thinks as long as she's having a good time."

Her words make the air stall in my throat. Leave it to my sister to see right through me.

"You've got it in you," Violet continues. "You're smart. You know fashion and cosmetics and you're always on trend. You'll know exactly how to pick out the perfect scent that'll represent your name. I believe in you. We all believe in you. You just need to learn how to believe in yourself." She gives my hand a little shake before she lets go.

"Yeah. Don't worry." Rose comes to stand on the other side of me. "If Daddy gives you any trouble I'll just tell him to fuck off."

We all start to laugh. "Definitely don't do that," Violet says, pointing a stern finger at Rose.

"Thanks, you two," I say, grabbing their hands and pulling them close to me. "I needed the pep talk. I'm not as comfortable here at Fleur as you are."

"Fleur is as much a part of you as it is me," Violet says. "And Rose. We're all equals here. Don't ever forget, Lily."

I'll try my best to take her advice.

Chapter Twenty-one

Max

"WE'RE RUNNING OUT OF TIME." I SETTLE INTO THE CHAIR BE-side my friend—and computer expert—Levi Cates. He's hunched over Lily's laptop, his own laptop hooked up to it, endless streams of code filling the screen. "Got anything yet?"

"Quite a bit, actually. I've been saving it up so I can dump it on you all at once," Levi says, leaning back in his chair and crossing his arms behind his head. He's a big motherfucker. I met him when we served in the army together and now he assists me on the complex computer jobs. I know plenty about code and getting into a system and I discovered a few things, but there were encrypted sections deep inside Lily's laptop that were impenetrable. That's when I called in Levi.

"Like what?" I crack open the water bottle I brought with me and take a few swallows, trying to calm my nerves. My forty-eight hours are up, as Pilar so kindly let me know via a nasty voicemail message she left a few hours ago. She plans on dropping by my office by the end of the day.

I never let her know I had the laptop, just informed her that the job was done. I wanted to find out what the hell was on that computer before I just handed it over.

"First, the owner of this laptop is an expert at infiltrating other people's systems. As in, she's a well-trained hacker," Levi says as he continues to tap the keyboard, his gaze never leaving the laptop's screen.

"I figured that out already." And the realization shocked the hell out of me. I had no idea Lily had the skills in her. Though I'm sure I'm not the first person to underestimate the woman.

"Uh-huh." Levi hits the enter key a few times and then turns to look at me, his dark brown eyes laser sharp behind his glasses. "She broke into multiple email accounts of one Pilar Vasquez."

"Right. My client." I nod, glad I didn't give Levi any information before he started digging. That's how it usually goes. I want him to find out the info on his own unless he asks me about it. "Wait a minute. Multiple accounts? I only saw one."

"So Pilar Vasquez is your client? Interesting." Levi returns his attention to the laptop. He hits a few more keys and brings up an in-box. "She works for Fleur, right? That's the in-box you found? Not much to note on the surface—a few flirtatious emails between her and Forrest Fowler, who I looked up. He's the CEO of Fleur."

"Yeah, and he's involved with Pilar," I add.

"Got that from the tone of their correspondence. But here's what's interesting." Levi skims his index finger across the track pad, opening a folder entitled *Home Design*. Most of the emails that pop up are older, but there are a couple of recent ones, including an email from a few weeks ago. "She's been chatting up a Zachary Lawrence, who from what it looks like travels all over Europe for work—he's also a Fleur employee—but his current home base is in France. And he's engaging in rather explicit emails with Pilar."

"You gotta be kidding me." I grab my phone out of my pocket and bring up one of my old web searches, one that involves Violet Fowler. Just as I thought. "That's Violet's ex-boyfriend." I feel like a complete idiot for ignoring the folders saved within Pilar's in-box, figuring they weren't anything important. And I was in a hurry to find out any details I could to help Lily. I should have dug deeper.

"And that is . . . one of Forrest's daughters." Levi cocks a brow.

"The daughter who's set to run Fleur one day," I tell him.

"Yeah, well she's not with this Zachary guy anymore, right? Because he's chatting up your client every chance he gets, describing in lurid detail exactly what he's going to do to her naked body the minute he gets near it. Here's an example." He clicks open one of the emails.

I miss the taste of your skin, the way your nipples feel between my lips, the way you scream my name and pull my hair when I make you squirt in my mouth.

Squirt? Shit. That's not sexy. "Uh, I didn't really need to see that," I say with a grimace.

Levi closes out the email. "Yeah, well I thought since I had to suffer through it, you should, too. Considering you didn't find it in the first place."

Way to make me feel like a loser. I can beat my own self up, thank you very much. "Great. Appreciate it," I mutter. "I'm sure her old man, Fowler, would be pissed to discover this interesting bit of information."

"Well, this is just the tip of the iceberg." Levi practically bounces in his chair he's so excited. He lives for this sort of thing. Closing out of the Fleur in-box, he clicks on a few links, taps a couple of keys, and another in-box appears. "This is Pilar's personal Gmail account. And let me tell you, this one is full of the goods."

"Like what?" I lean in closer, peering at the screen, reading the endless list of emails that clutter up the in-box. "Doesn't she ever clean this thing out?"

"From what I can tell, no, and that's what makes it such a gold mine of information. I'm sure your little hacker had a field day when she discovered it."

"And how do you know I took it from a woman?" I ask, turning to glare at Levi.

He laughs. "Give me a break. I know for a fact this laptop belongs to Lily Fowler, asshole. Forrest Fowler's oldest daughter."

"That obvious, huh?" We've run into computers in the past where Levi was never able to figure out exactly who owned it, they were that good at hiding their personal information. There are a lot of paranoid people out there.

Looks like Lily Fowler isn't one of them.

"Yeah, there was no hiding for this chick. She's as bold as she pleases." Levi's description of Lily is apt, making me miss her. It's more than that. My entire body aches for her, and not just because of the sex, though it's so damn good between us, I can't deny it.

I just flat-out miss her. The sound of her voice, her sweet and sexy laugh. The way she looked at me, the things she said. How she so easily trusted me. And I screwed her over like a callous asshole.

An asshole who's halfway in love with her, truth be told. I barely know her, but I know enough. I care for her, making what I did to her that much worse.

I felt like a shit the entire flight home, that laptop in the new backpack I purchased at the airport before the plane left sitting right at my feet. Mocking me, making me feel like the world's biggest asshole.

I tried to sleep on that long-ass flight but I couldn't. Was too wracked with guilt over what I did to Lily. Leaving her in her bed alone was one of the hardest things I've ever done. Taking the fucking laptop from her scored right up there as well.

She must hate me. And I can't blame her. I wronged her. Stole from her.

She *should* hate me. I hate myself for what I did. But did I really steal from her? Or do her a damn favor?

"And there's no hiding for Pilar Vasquez, either." Levi shakes his head, a faint smile curling his lips—a rare sight. The dude is beyond intense, serious all the time. "I was blown away reading a lot of this shit, and you know me. I don't get embarrassed easily."

The stuff Levi has stumbled upon while thoroughly investigating someone's hard drive has shocked even me, but he's usually as cool as they come. Completely unruffled and always composed—that's why I enjoy working with him so much. He gets the job done and he knows how to handle himself.

"Nasty shit or what, bro?" I ask, curiosity filling me.

"More like evil stuff. She's mean as fuck. Like, *makes me feel uneasy and afraid she's lurking around the corner ready to jump me* type shit." Levi runs a hand through his dark hair, mussing it up further. The guy looks like he hasn't slept or shaved for days and he probably hasn't. He's been too intent working on this case for me. I handed the laptop to him within a few hours of arriving back in New York after my search became stalled and he hasn't let up since. "I'll tell you this. I wouldn't fuck with this chick. Lily Fowler's got balls."

Hell, and I'm seriously considering fucking with this chick. But I got balls, too. "So break it down for me. I need details." We're talking all around it and I need to know exactly what Lily did to Pilar—and what Pilar, in turn, did to Lily.

"All right, this is what I've come up with so far. Let's focus on Fleur." Levi holds out his splayed hand and starts counting down. "Let's call your client PV. PV is a management employee at Fleur. She also happens to be fucking the CEO of Fleur. Looks to me like she has another Fleur employee on the side, but he's in another country, so I don't know if he really counts."

"She used to be involved with yet another Fleur employee," I point out, needing Levi to know this bit of information as well. "Ryder McKay. Violet Fowler's current fiancé."

"Well, hot shit. PV definitely gets around. Okay, so that adds an interesting twist. Explains a few things." Levi strokes his stubble-covered chin, like he's some sort of old-world professor. "She hates the Fowler sisters, that much is clear. Specifically Violet, and now I understand why. She's with Ryder, who used to be with PV."

"Soap opera shit, right?" I ask, shaking my head.

"Definitely twisted. Okay, here's where it gets . . . bad. Besides PV messing around via email with Violet's ex, who seems like a real slime ball from the communication I read between them, and probably having a hate-on for Violet because she's with PV's ex . . . there's another element to the story." Levi pauses, returning his attention to the laptop and opening up another email. "Pilar has become recent friends with one Felicity Winston, who is president of Jayne Cosmetics, which is a company similar to Fleur. The company was named after Felicity's mother, Jayne, who died many years ago of breast cancer. Her aunt Laura Winston recently retired and handed over the reins. Felicity has a younger sister and brother, and they both work at Jayne Cosmetics, too." Impatience rolls through me, making me feel twitchy. Levi's giving me a bunch of information as if he's leading to the buildup, when I want him to just get to the point.

"So?" I ask. "Friendly competition is normal, right?" I'm acquaintances with plenty of guys who run private investigation companies in the city. So is Levi.

"This goes beyond that," Levi tells me. "It starts out innocent enough. Read this email."

You are such a doll. Thank you again for inviting me to your party last Saturday night. It was such a delight to spend more time with you and your sister. I loved talking shop. Perhaps we can get together again soon.
Kisses,
Pilar

"This is the first email she sent to Felicity after she went to Felicity's party, dated four months ago. They continued to chat each other up via email, nothing serious. Casual gossipy correspondence that's boring as shit. But then about two months ago, things got interesting," Levi explains.

I hate it there so much. Forrest is so cloying and tries to control my every move and he's so fixated on Violet's opinion on everything, it's like I can't make a decision on my own. Ever. Dahlia totters in on occasion and pontificates as if what she has to say matters, the old hag. I'm sick of it. Forrest is undermining my authority, as is Violet, and she's in London for fuck's sake! I know you have no openings at the moment for someone of my expertise but the second you know of something, please let me know.
xoxo
P

The venom in that one short email is telling. She wants out of Fleur. And she blames Violet for all of her problems.

"Pilar's emails to Felicity go on in a similar vein for a few weeks, until everything changes," Levi continues, his mouth settling in a grim line.

"What do you mean, everything changes?" I ask. "So she

was trying to get the hell out of Fleur. So what? Wouldn't Lily want that to happen?"

"I don't know if Lily read the remaining emails. I can tell what was opened and what wasn't; there's a history that's left behind and if you're smart like me, you can figure it out." Levi grins and I shove his shoulder, muttering under my breath. Show-off. "Lily stopped reading emails at the one you just read. No others were opened until me."

"And what did those emails say?"

"It's this one in particular that you need to read. It's probably what's pushing Pilar to get this laptop from Lily so damn bad," Levi explains as he opens another email.

Felicity,
I understand you're nervous, but trust me. I swear no one will find out about this. Please confirm you received the information I sent you, as promised.
xoxo
P

"Attached to this email is information about Fleur's new line. The colors of the cosmetics, the names, the new perfumes named after the sisters. Everything," Levi says.

Jesus. I take a drink of water, then run a hand over my face, my throat immediately going dry again. Pilar blames Lily for causing family turmoil and is giving away Fleur corporate secrets to their direct competition on the side, all while having an affair with Zachary Lawrence, Violet's ex-boyfriend.

This is some seriously fucked-up shit.

"She must really hate Violet," I say, blowing out a harsh breath. "All of the Fowlers, really."

"No shit, Sherlock." Levi snickers. "Though this isn't funny, not at all. Your client PV? She is one conniving bitch."

A conniving bitch I need to keep away from Lily. I should call her. Text her, though she probably won't answer me. Would she? I doubt it. She'd probably tell me to go to hell and not believe a word I said, not that I can blame her.

"The Fowlers need to know about this, stat. Felicity Winston never responded to Pilar's email and that went down a few weeks ago. Pilar's probably freaking the fuck out, especially since she thinks Lily knows all and Felicity is ignoring her. Shit is about to hit the fan my, friend," Levi continues.

"I need to talk to Lily first," I mutter, rubbing my hand over my mouth, along my jaw, my mind spinning with all the possibilities. I want to tell her. I need to see her. But how do I approach her? She must be furious with me.

Levi turns in his chair to look at me, shaking his head. "This is a mess, bro. You're working for the wrong person, you know."

I sigh and lean forward, propping my elbows on the edge of the desk, and bend my head so I can run my hands through my hair. "I know. But how can I get out of it now? Pilar is going to be here any minute. She'll want the laptop." I narrow my eyes, trying to think of an alternative.

"Don't give it to her."

He makes it sound so easy. As if I can just tell Pilar to fuck off. It's not even the laptop that Pilar should be concerned about. It's the fact that Lily dug into her private information and knows what she's done in the last couple of years, including some damning details. All the bullshit, all the lies, all the conniving and plotting and planning to fuck the entire company over by giving away information in the hopes of getting get a new position.

Taking that laptop will not solve all of Pilar's problems. Ruining Lily is what's going to give her any sort of satisfaction.

"What else is on it?" At Levi's questioning glance, I continue. "The laptop. Anything . . . incriminating?"

"Nothing much else, with the exception of one thing." Levi

sighs. "Hey, I know Lily Fowler is a public figure. I've seen her on that TMZ TV show or whatever. I don't get why everyone's fascinated with her. I mean, she's hot. But what does she do? I lump her in with the Kardashians and the Hiltons, useless celebrities who look pretty and cause trouble."

I press my lips together to keep from blurting out that there's so much more to Lily than looking good and causing trouble. She's sweet and easygoing. She never acted like she wanted a lick of attention from anyone but me. When I was with her, she was nothing like the party-girl persona I saw in the media. But he doesn't know that I actually spent time with her, got to know her, got naked with her.

It's best that he doesn't know. He's my friend, but I don't want to look like a complete failure in his eyes.

And fucking around with the person I'm supposed to be trailing after? That's definitely failing.

"What's that got to do with anything?" I ask, keeping my voice even, trying my damnedest to appear neutral. That Lily doesn't matter to me.

"You wanted to know if there's anything incriminating on this laptop? Well, there is—against its owner. I found other encrypted files, ones that Lily put on the laptop over a year ago. I broke into them." Levi studies me, his gaze narrowed. "What exactly *did* she do when she was in Maui, anyway? 'Cause she sure wasn't trying to gather up evidence against Pilar. She totally missed those last emails between her and Felicity, which blows my mind. But maybe that was enough for her? Before the actual dirty dealing started to happen, Felicity would hint that she wanted to know the latest happenings with the Fleur product lines, but Pilar always blew her off. It read like they were circling around each other, trying to see who'd cave in first and offer up the goods."

"Lily spent a lot of time outside," I lie. More like she spent a lot of time with me.

"Huh." Levi rubs his chin again. "There's naked pictures on it."

"*What?*" The word blasts out of me like a shot. "Of Lily?"

Levi nods. "Lots of them. Topless shots, ass pics, and one full nude—the girl is crazy for leaving them on her laptop, but they're there. Some of them I can tell were transferred from an old cell phone. Most of them are old. I thought they might all be on her cloud storage, but I think she only saved them to her Time Capsule at home. No one else would be able to access them unless she has another computer in her apartment that has access to the Time Capsule."

Ah, Lily. Keeping naked photos on her laptop? What the hell is wrong with her? At least they're not in the cloud, like all those other celebrity photos that were recently exposed. "Pilar would love to have them."

"She'd probably blast them all over the internet," Levi says.

"I can't let her have this laptop." I exhale loudly and hang my head.

"Nope, you absolutely cannot," Levi agrees cheerfully.

Chapter Twenty-two

Lily

"God," I groan, slumping over the tiny desk in my bedroom, blearily staring at the giant screen of my iMac. I was so tired, so freaking depressed and angry after I came back from Maui, I fell into bed the minute I got home and slept for hours. More like a day. I managed to make myself presentable and went to see Rose and Violet at Fleur—which was supposed to only be lunch but turned into an all-afternoon adventure with lunch and then the meeting . . .

That, surprisingly, went well. Daddy was pleasant. Grandma wasn't there, so I didn't have to deal with her. I love my grandma, but she knows how to lay on the guilt.

In an extremely thick layer that suffocates me.

I came home from the meeting only to crash again, sleeping through the entire night. Woke up in the morning, brewed myself a pot of coffee, and finally started to make an attempt to open the hard drive that's included in my router so I can figure out exactly what's stored on my stolen laptop.

And I'm starting to freak out.

My hand on the mouse, I open up the folder I forgot I'd created, the one entitled *Naughty*, and I click through the endless photos of me . . . naked. Cringing, I squint at the screen, shuf-

fling through the pictures, my stomach slowly twisting and turning. They're mostly of me topless, with a few butt photos mixed
in. A series in particular featuring me standing naked with my
back to the camera, hands on hips and sassy smile fixed in place
as I look coyly over my shoulder.

I remember exactly who I took those photos for. A guy
named John. Ten years older than me and richer than my daddy,
he made me feel like I was special. He spoiled me rotten, took
me shopping, bought me sexy shoes, sexy lingerie . . .

He was also a total pervert who loved to look at me naked—
particularly my butt. Claimed he could stare at it all day.

Being the generous semi-girlfriend that I was, because we
weren't necessarily a couple but we were together one Valentine's Day, I decided to send these photos to him via text.

Too bad his actual girlfriend found them. The one I didn't
know existed. The one who didn't know I existed, either. Thank
God John deleted all of those photos before she could do any
major damage.

Did I learn from that lesson? Um, no, doesn't look like I did.
Not when the last photo appears, the image filling my screen in
vivid detail. Of me sitting in the center of my bed, my head tilted
to the side so my hair spills over my shoulder, covering one of
my breasts, my nipple peeking through. A sultry smile curves my
lips and my legs are spread wide, knees bent and feet planted
firmly on the mattress, all my goods on blatant display . . .

I cover my face with my hands and make an inarticulate
noise, trying to tell myself it's all going to be okay. Despite the
laptop being gone, these photos won't show up anywhere. At
least I didn't save them to my cloud storage. I don't trust the
cloud, and for good reason. But hey, I'll be fine. Absolutely, perfectly fine.

Inhaling sharply, I hold my breath then let it out, trying to
calm my racing heart. But it's no use. Whoever has my laptop—
fucking Max, motherfucker—has access to those photos.

Those horrible, reputation-ruining, there's-absolutely-no-mistaking-it's-me photos.

My family is going to shit their pants if they're ever made public. Daddy will disown me, Grandma will probably have a heart attack, and disappointing Violet and Rose . . . I don't know if I can handle it.

And I have no one to blame but myself.

I scream into my palms as loud as I can but I don't feel any better. My head is pounding, my hands are shaking, and if Max appeared in front of me right at this very instant, I would probably kick him in the face before I rammed my knee into his balls.

The violent thought doesn't satisfy me one bit.

My cell phone rings, startling me, and I drop my hands to check the screen to see who's calling.

Rose.

Dread churning in my stomach, I answer with a tentative hello, praying the shit hasn't already hit the fan. Could it happen that fast? With the speed of information these days, yeah, it probably could. My naked ass could be up on a Times Square billboard for all I know.

"What are you doing?" Rose asks cheerily, like nothing's wrong.

Which means nothing *is* wrong, right?

"Nothing much," I say, my voice tentative. "Just . . . messing around on my computer."

"Not changing anyone's grades up, huh?" Rose laughs. She knows what I used to do; she's heard all the old stories. "You don't do that sort of thing anymore, right?"

"Actually . . ." I swallow hard, not sure how much I should confess. Or if I should confess anything in the first place.

"Lily, you're not up to any trouble, are you?" Rose's voice changes in an instant, full of worry and concern.

"No," I say quickly—too quickly. "Why? Is something going on?" My entire body goes stiff waiting for her reply.

"No, I just . . . I don't know." Rose's voice lowers, as if she's telling me a deep, dark secret. "Caden says I've been jumping to conclusions lately and that's unlike me. He feels like he's always on the defensive when we talk, even about stuff like the weather. I told him I have no idea what he's referring to."

Now it's my turn to worry. What if Rose's handsome, charming devil of a husband is up to no good? "Is he acting suspicious?"

"No, no, no. He's like, perfect. Almost too overprotective, but I have no business complaining about that, right? He loves me." Rose sighs. "That's the weird thing. It's all me. I'm the one who's acting freaky. I know exactly what Caden's talking about, but half the time I pretend I don't have a clue."

My sister is making little sense. "Are you okay, Rosie? Seriously. You're not acting right."

"I know, tell me all about it. I blame the baby. The little monster is making me crazy," Rose whispers. "I love my future little booger, but listen to me! I sound like I'm insane."

She does. I can't explain it, but I feel like she's talking in circles and I can't keep up. Though I'm thankful for the conversation because it takes the heat off me and focuses on crazy, pregnant Rose.

"The real reason I called is I wanted to go out to breakfast." Rose pauses. "And I want you to go with me."

"Okay." I draw the word out, feeling unsettled. "When?"

"Now? Are you dressed? I'm already in a cab, headed toward your building."

I glance down at myself. I'm wearing skimpy little sleep shorts and a tank top. My hair is a mess and I'd bet I have raccoon eyes since I slept in my makeup from yesterday.

If Grandma knew, she would have an absolute fit.

"I'll need a few minutes," I tell her. "Do you want to meet somewhere?"

"Yes, that little bakery down the street from your building." Rose sighs. "They have the best cupcakes."

"Are you talking about Piece of Cake?" They have good coffee at least. "And a cupcake for breakfast? Gross."

"I'm craving frosting. Don't judge."

Double gross. Being pregnant is making my sister weird. "Give me twenty minutes."

"Perfect, see you there."

"Oh. my. god." rose sinks her teeth into the biggest cupcake I've ever seen, topped with a thick layer of pink frosting. She's chewing slowly, like she's savoring every bite, and she closes her eyes, a little moan falling from her lips that makes me vaguely uncomfortable.

As if she's finding some sort of weird erotic pleasure from eating the cupcake.

"That good, huh?" I squirm in my seat, look anywhere but at my dreamy-eyed sister as she licks her fingers and then wipes them with a napkin.

"Thank God you showed up when you did. I was about to buy a dozen of these suckers to go and head back home." Rose stares at her cupcake like she's going to attack it. I seriously hope she reconsiders. "How's your muffin?"

I bought a blueberry muffin but I'm not hungry. I pick at it, pinch a crumble off the top and then let it drop on my plate. "I'm not that hungry."

"Hmm." She eyes my plate hungrily, then returns her attention to hers, swooping her finger into the frosting. "What's bugging you, Lily?"

"Nothing." I give her a wan smile and take a sip of my coffee, pausing mid-sip when I see the way Rose is watching me.

Like she can see right through my lie.

"Tell me," she says, her voice low, her fingers curled around the edge of the round table as she leans over it. Not that she can lean much, considering her growing belly gets in the way. "You haven't been acting right since you came home from Maui. And I still don't get why you went there in the first place."

"Vacation," I say, wincing at the dirty look she shoots me.

"You made me lie and act like I had no idea where you were when I did know the entire time!" Rose bangs the edge of the table, making the plates rattle, and she reaches out, grabbing hold of her cupcake as if she's going to lose it. "Tell me why you went there."

"I can't," I whisper, but Rose shakes her head, clearly not accepting my answer.

"Not good enough. Tell me."

I try another tactic. "Aren't I the big sister here? Isn't it my job to be the bossy one?"

"Not when I'm the only pregnant, married one of the bunch. I trump both you and Violet." Her voice lowers almost to a hiss. "Tell me."

Glancing around, I make sure no one is nearby before I start in with a vague retelling of why I ended up in Maui, who I met in Maui . . . and what I think he stole from me before I left. In all, it takes fifteen minutes for me to tell my sad tale and by the time I'm finished, Rose has devoured every crumb and speck of frosting and she's staring at me with her mouth hanging open.

"Are you freaking serious?" she finally manages to say.

I nod, chugging a huge swallow of coffee before I set my cup on the table. "I haven't even told you the worst of it."

"How much worse can it be?" She shakes her head and stares off into space, blinking hard before she looks at me. "What were you going to do, blackmail Pilar? I mean, she's talking to Felicity Winston. She's the freaking *enemy*, Lily."

"I thought I'd blackmail Pilar, yeah, but then she got so weird on me. Her voice during that phone call was chilling. She scared the crap out of me, so I just . . . ran. I know it was a mistake, my leaving, but I panicked." I cross my arms in front of my chest and heave a big sigh. "She's still fucking that asshole Zachary. Daddy would flip if he knew that."

"Are you going to tell him? You need to tell him," Rose says sternly.

"He probably wouldn't believe me," I say miserably. I've lied before, lots of times. Daddy wouldn't believe me, especially since I'm ratting out Pilar. He won't *want* to believe me. "And I don't have the laptop, so it's not like I have any proof."

She nods, not bothering to deny what I say is possibly true. She knows Daddy wouldn't believe me. She knows my past, how I've lied before just to try and get in our father's good graces. My lies always backfired. Now I want to tell the truth and no one will believe me. "But how can it get any worse?"

My voice lowers to an almost inaudible whisper. "There's naked photos of me on that laptop."

Rose's face falls. "Oh, Lily."

"I know, I know." I wave my hand, dismissing whatever lecture she's about to give me. "It was stupid. I should've never taken photos like that, but most of them are old. Like from a few years ago old. Remember John?"

She shrugs, then shakes her head.

"Yeah, well, I took them for a guy, as a Valentine's Day present. Then promptly forgot to delete them."

"How could you do that? Why keep them on your computer?" Rose shakes her head, makes a little face. "I let Caden take a few photos of me on his phone a while ago but I made him delete everything. Then I made him go on the stupid cloud or whatever and delete them from there, too. Freaking cloud saves everything."

"I keep nothing on my cloud, thank God. But they were on my Time Capsule hard drive, which means they were on the laptop," I say miserably. "Once something has been done, it's really hard to undo it. Not like the old days, when you could tear up a photo and destroy the negative."

"Everything lives forever on the internet," Rose singsongs.

"Exactly. It sucks."

"So Pilar is scheming with Fleur's enemy, sending graphic emails to Zachary and . . . what else? She's not trying to do anything to me, is she?" Rose rests her hand against her chest.

"No, you're not on her radar. It's always been Violet she's after. I think she wants Violet's position at Fleur. And when she didn't get that, she decided to go after the competition with promises of inside information."

"Do you have proof she gave information to Felicity Winston?" Rose asks.

"No." I shake my head and stare at the table. "They sort of flirted around the subject, but that's it. I was about to go back into Pilar's in-box when you called." Truthfully, I became too distracted by the naked photos. I need to go back home and search what's on my stolen laptop. See if Pilar actually offered information to Felicity. I want to believe that she didn't, but we know who I'm dealing with.

Pilar doesn't give a shit about anyone. She will do whatever it takes to get what she wants.

I glance up to find my sister staring at me, her expression serious, her entire body still. "You need to go home and see if there's anything else in Pilar's emails," Rose says gravely, her gaze locked with mine. "And then you need to talk to Daddy and Violet."

I wince. "They're going to be furious."

"Not at you. Never at you," Rose says in a rush. "All of their anger will be channeled toward Pilar, and it's justified. What that bitch is doing . . ."

"I know. She deserves every bit of their anger. Every bit of *our* anger. But . . ." I pause, chewing on my lower lip as I contemplate what I'm going to say next. "I don't want to tell them yet. I need to confirm first that she's being shady."

"Right. Confirm away. But the minute you confirm, you need to tell them. Hell, this could blow up in our faces, Lily. Jayne Cosmetics could run with this information and make Fleur look terrible. They could release the colors before we do, with the same names and everything, and make Fleur look like they copied them. This could get bad. Really, really bad." Rose leans back in her chair and rubs a hand over her belly. "The faster you tell them, the faster we can put a stop to all of this."

"I need to talk to Pilar." That is the last thing I want to do, but I must. I need to tell her she has to resign from Fleur and get out of our lives before I tell my father what she's doing. That might make her think twice before she launches into another one of her schemes.

"That will be a complete waste of your time and you know it." Rose sits up straighter, her eyes going wide. "What if that guy you met in Maui . . . what if he's working for Pilar? Maybe he grabbed the laptop for her. Did you ever consider that?"

Yes . . . no. Fine, yes. I so considered it. "I don't know what to think about him." I hate him. If he were to walk into this bakery right now I'd probably body slam him to the ground and kick him in the nuts.

I seem to be rather bloodthirsty for his nuts.

"You've only told me a little bit, but from what I see, your meeting him, his taking the laptop from you before he disappeared . . . it doesn't feel random." Rose studies me. "You liked this guy, didn't you? I can see it your eyes."

"I did. He was different." *He made me feel, made me want . . . too much.* I clear my throat, feeling like the world's biggest fool. "But he betrayed me. If he was working for Pilar . . . there's no way I could ever forgive him."

Ever.

Chapter Twenty-three

Max

I WAIT INSIDE LILY'S APARTMENT, PACING THE LENGTH OF HER bedroom, which is impressive. I keep one ear cocked toward the front door, waiting for the sound of her key in the lock. She won't see me back here and I'll wait for her, try to gently surprise her so she doesn't try and kick my ass the second she sees me.

Not that I can blame her, after what I did. She's going to be furious with me for breaking into her apartment, too, but I couldn't risk approaching her outside, in public. God knows what she'd do. Make a scene, chew me out, call the cops. I didn't want her to run in the opposite direction when she spots me for the first time.

I'm taking a risk by being here, but it's one I need to take. She could call the cops on me here, too, but I think I can convince her otherwise.

Hell, I hope I can.

Stuffing my hands in the pockets of my sweatshirt, I glance around, noting the giant iMac on her desk. I go to it and wiggle the mouse, the screen coming to life with no password protection log-in appearing.

Nope, instead I'm looking right at Lily sitting on her bed, gloriously, beautifully naked. Her legs are spread, her pussy on blatant display and a seductive smile curling her lips. Seeing her like this makes my blood burn. Knowing she took these photos for another guy makes me want to kill him.

No one can look at her like this but me.

Growling low in my throat, I tear my gaze away from the monitor, catching my reflection in the giant mirror above her dresser. I look like hell. I'm wearing old jeans and a black sweatshirt, and I haven't shaved in days. My eyes are bleary and my mood is for shit.

Dealing with Pilar yesterday afternoon had been nothing short of exhausting. Like a chicken shit, I'd made Levi stay at my office so I wouldn't have to face her alone. Not that I'm particularly scared of the woman—though Levi reaffirmed after she stormed out that she was indeed mean as hell—I wanted a witness to the madness that was Pilar Vasquez.

When I told her I didn't have the laptop after all, she'd ranted, she'd threatened me, she waved her fist in my face, and she tried to grab hold of my shirt. That's where I drew the line, telling her she'd better keep her hands off me because though I didn't hit women, she was pushing her luck.

My threat barely fazed her. The woman is out-and-out nuts. And hell-bent on taking all of her rage out on Lily.

I didn't reveal I knew what was on that laptop, the incriminating evidence. I kept my lips shut about that and told her I'd grabbed Lily's bag, mistakenly thinking the laptop was inside. I only discovered the laptop was missing once I was mid-flight.

The skeptical look she gave me called a silent bullshit and she accused me of being a total moron. Wanted her money back, so I told her I would credit her fees immediately. I'd rather take the loss than be responsible for whatever trauma she inflicts on the Fowler family.

I yank my cell out of my sweatshirt pocket and check the time. Almost eleven. Where the hell is Lily? I saw her leave earlier, practically running out of the building with her hair wet and up in a bun on top of her head, wearing jeans and an oversized black sweater, a giant purse hanging off her arm.

My mouth went dry at first sight of her.

I've seen her in a skimpy bikini, in a sexy dress, in shorts and a tank top, naked . . . many, many times naked, but nothing beats seeing Lily for the first time after not seeing her for days. I felt like a starving man who just caught sight of his first meal. I didn't realize how much I missed her until she passed right by me, not paying attention to her surroundings, the sound of her heeled boots as she went striding by loud on the sidewalk.

It was easy to fall into step behind her. The sidewalks were crowded, and she was so intent on getting to her destination she never looked back once. Never seemed to feel my presence, which left me strangely disappointed.

Stupid but true.

She entered a bakery a few blocks away from her building, a pregnant woman who had similar features hugging her close when she walked inside.

Her sister. Rose.

They sat a table in the front of the bakery, right by a window. Dangerous as hell. What if Pilar already had someone on the case, spying on her? She was a sitting target, and I yearned to go inside and protect her.

I didn't. I didn't move from my spot. Oddly fascinated with watching her talk to her sister, though the usual spark that lit Lily from within was gone. Rose devoured a cupcake while Lily picked at her muffin. My girl looked sad, distracted, worried, upset. My heart ached to go to her and offer her comfort.

But I'd guess she'd rather smash my face in than let me near her.

The sisters remained in the bakery for more than an hour, until the place was pretty much empty save for the occasional person walking in for a cup of coffee to go or picking up a bag of pastries. I loitered outside the entire time, pacing back and forth, going across the street, trying my best to be unobtrusive. I didn't want Lily to notice me.

Yet.

I decided to hightail my ass back to her building when I saw them gather up their trash. It was time for me to talk to Lily but from within the confines of her apartment, no matter how apprehensive I was over how she'd handle seeing me again. Does she realize I stole her laptop? She has to. And will she listen to me when I want to talk to her?

Probably not. But I have to at least give it a shot. I need to tell her she's in danger.

I need to tell her that I'm sorry. That I miss her. That I hate myself for what I did. I need to beg for her forgiveness and ask for another chance. I want to tell her that I need her in my life, that I can't give up on her, on us, though I know she probably hates me.

Closing my eyes, I shake my head and breathe deep, her scent invading my senses and making my head spin. I hope to God she listens to me. Don't know what I'll do if she doesn't.

Within minutes I hear the key in the lock turning and then the door opens, her boots clicking on the smooth wood floor. She closes the door and locks it, and I'm thankful. My need to take care of her, watch over her, grows every time I so much as catch a glimpse of her. If she hadn't locked the door right then and there, I might have blown my cover.

I hear the clank of her keys landing on a table or in a dish, I can't tell which, and she sighs as she yanks off her boots. I hear them land on the floor with a plop. I glance around her bedroom and peek into her closet, thinking I could hide inside it, rearing back when I see the interior.

It's fucking huge. Majestic. As big as my living room and

kitchen combined in my tiny apartment, maybe even bigger. Clothes and shoes everywhere, and there are shelves for her purses, scarves, jewelry . . .

Holy hell, this woman has a lot of stuff.

I shut the closet door, deciding it's best I wait for her in her bedroom, out in the open. I don't want to scare her. But I don't want her to throw something when she first sees me, either.

She's moving about the apartment; I can hear her. I wait for her to come to her bedroom and then she's here, inside her room. Standing in front of her dresser and taking off her hoop earrings, setting them carefully in a small dish.

Now is my time. Slowly I push away from the wall and murmur her name.

"Lily."

Her head comes up on a gasp, her gaze snagging on mine in the mirror. I stand a few feet behind her, our gazes locked. Her eyes are wide, her chest heaving, her mouth dropping open in shock, and then she's whirling on me, headed straight toward me like a tornado, her hands clenched into fists as she bombards me with an endless string of curse words and hits, her knuckles sharp against my chest.

"Calm down." I manage to grab one of her wrists, but she wiggles out of my hold. "Lily, please."

She steps back and stretches out her arms, hands wide as she shoves at my chest. I let her make contact, a grunt leaving me. *Damn,* the girl is stronger than she appears. "Please? You have the nerve to ask *please*? Fuck you!"

I grab her, holding her wrists, my fingers loose, my thumbs sweeping across her skin at first contact like they can't help themselves. *Christ,* she's soft. So soft and warm, her entire body vibrating with righteous anger, hatred blazing in her eyes as she glares up at me. Like that old saying goes, if looks could kill.

I would be a dead man, slashed to ribbons by the hate in Lily's gaze.

"Get your hands off of me," she says through gritted teeth, her arms stiff as she tries to break free from my hold.

"I need you to listen to me. It's about Pilar," I tell her, not letting her go. If I do, she's gone. She'll run out of this apartment without looking back, and no doubt call the cops.

"Listen to what? More lies?" Disgust laces her voice, making me feel like shit. But I still won't let go of her. "Fine, you want to talk? Let me ask you one thing."

"Anything," I agree, hopeful that she'll be reasonable and listen to my explanations. Once she does that, we can put a plan into motion and figure out how we're going to expose Pilar for the vengeful person that she is. I've already got Levi on board. His technological expertise will come in handy.

"Were you working for Pilar the entire time we were in Maui? Is that why you stole my laptop? Was it for her?" She stops fighting me, her arms slack in my grip, and I keep hold of her, my entire body going still at her words, the air stalling in my lungs.

Fuck. I shouldn't be surprised. She's damn smart. Smarter than just about anyone gives her credit for, including me.

I have to be truthful with her. No more lies. If I want to get her back, I need to be honest. It's all or nothing now.

"Yes," I say, my voice so low I almost can't hear myself.

She starts to struggle once more, even harder this time, and she dislodges one of my hands from her wrist. "I *knew* it! Asshole! Let me go! Fuck you, let me *go!*"

I yank her in my arms and wrap her close, my mouth at her ear. "Stop trying to fight me, damn it. I need to talk to you. There are things you need to know, princess."

"What else do I need to know? You work for the enemy. I can't believe you tricked me! God, I'm so stupid. So incredibly . . . dumb." Her voice cracks and she slumps against me for the tiniest second. Just enough for me to remember exactly what she feels like in my arms, the scent of her hair filling my nostrils, making me weak. Making me want her.

"I didn't give her the laptop," I whisper, drifting my hand down her back, wanting to offer her comfort. Knowing she'll refuse any sort of help I want to give her because she's stubborn like that. "I still have it."

Lily lifts her head—*ah, fuck me,* her eyes shimmering with unshed tears. I can't stand the sight, the thought that I'm the one responsible for making her cry. "You here to bribe me then? Break into my apartment and demand money for the laptop or whatever? Well, fuck you, I don't want it. Go ahead and give it to Pilar. Let her try and ruin me. Hurt my family."

"Jesus, I don't want your money, Lily. I want . . ." I blow out a harsh breath, pulling her even closer to me. She doesn't try and fight it, doesn't do anything but stare at me with disappointment and sadness filling her damp eyes. Leaving one arm clamped tight around her waist, I reach up and touch her face, let my fingers drift across her cheek. She visibly flinches, as if my touch disgusts her, and I let my hand drop, fighting the disappointment that wants to engulf me.

I have no right to be disappointed. I brought this on myself. I ruined this.

Us.

"What do you want?" she asks warily.

"I want your trust."

She laughs, an ugly, mocking sound. "You lost that. And you're never going to get it back."

I will. Eventually. I have to. "Can I tell you what I discovered on your laptop?"

"Not here. I don't want to talk about anything with you here." She shakes her head, as if she can't stand the thought of me being anywhere near her private sanctuary.

"Let's go to a restaurant, then. Somewhere quiet, where we won't be interrupted much. I have—there's a lot I need to tell you." My fingers ache to touch her again but I don't. *God,* she feels good in my arms. Her body molds to mine perfectly. Does she see it? Feel it?

Or did I fuck that up completely?

"I don't want to talk to you. You need to leave," she says. "There's nothing left to say."

"There's plenty to say. I need to tell you why." Her glare shuts me up for a second and I push past my worry. I need to come clean. It's the only way we'll get another chance. "And I need to tell you what I found."

Her eyes flicker with worry. "I know what you found. It's my laptop, asshole." She drops her head and talks to the ground. "The photos of me. Is that what you're talking about? They were taken a long time ago."

"I don't care about the photos of you." I give her a little shake and she lifts her head once again. "We found Pilar's in-boxes. The ones you broke into. We know what Pilar is planning to do."

"We? Who's 'we'?" She looks confused. And she's right—we should go somewhere public and talk. For all I know, Pilar's hired someone else to keep tabs on Lily and find that laptop I supposedly didn't take. Her life could be in danger.

I can't risk it. I can't risk her.

"Come with me. Let's get a cab and . . . go somewhere. Somewhere safe where I can tell you everything." I pause and stare into her eyes, wanting her to see the truth inside of me. I will do anything to help her, to keep her safe. I could tell her that, but she won't believe me. I need her to know it, to sense it. "Please, Lily."

She returns my stare, her eyes wide, her fingers resting on my chest, curling into my sweatshirt. Her touch burns, even through the thick fabric, and I will the sexual response away. I want her. I always want her. But we don't have time to deal with that now. "You look terrible," she finally says. "Like a thug."

I chuckle. I can't help it. She called me a thug. "It's been a rough couple of days."

"For me, too," she admits, her voice as soft as her eyes. "We're only talking. That's it," she says, her voice going stern. Tough. "I'm pissed that you broke into my apartment, Max. That's fucked up."

"Agreed." I nod. "And I know. I'm . . . sorry."

"I want you to tell me everything," she continues.

"I will," I say as I steer her out of her bedroom. We start down the short hall toward the entryway where she left her boots. "Did you notice anyone outside of your building? Anyone look suspicious? Like they're maybe . . . watching you?"

She gasps. "Watching? What are you talking about?"

"I'm not working for Pilar anymore, so I wouldn't doubt if she's put someone else on the case," I explain, reaching for her boots on the floor. I grab them and hand them to her.

"What case?"

I release my hold on her, watching as she slips her boots back on her feet. "You, Lily. She's after you."

Chapter Twenty-four

Lily

THE CAB MOVES SLOWLY THROUGH THE CITY, THE STREETS clogged with traffic, horns honking, brakes squealing. We've been in this car for over twenty minutes and I assume we're still nowhere close to our destination. I didn't choose it, Max giving the driver an unfamiliar address before he settled his large frame right beside me. There's a narrow strip of space between us but not enough. Though the Grand Canyon could be dividing us and I'd still feel his presence, smell his intoxicating scent, the warmth that radiates from his big, strong body.

I'd also want to reach out and touch him, despite knowing how wrong that is. I hate him for what he did to me. I want to do violent, graphic things to his body that involve pain and blood. Bruises and scrapes and maybe a broken bone or two. I want him to hurt and suffer as much as I did, because I can't stand him. He wronged me in the absolute worst way possible.

That's what I keep telling myself, my hands clenched into fists and resting on my knees, my teeth gritted, my breath coming in ragged exhales.

For most of the ride, I've kept my head averted, my gaze locked on the window, but I don't see anything outside as we pass. My thoughts are as hazy as my vision, everything within me total chaos. It's hard for me to wrap my brain around what just happened.

Max is beside me. The man who double-crossed me, who worked for fucking Pilar, is sitting next to me and wants to tell me . . . something. Lots of somethings. After the initial shock of seeing him in such a different environment, in my freaking bedroom like some sort of criminal breaking and entering, I couldn't help but be worried at his appearance.

Wan complexion, thick stubble covering his cheeks and jaw, hollow eyes, dark sweatshirt and jeans, he looked like a criminal. My first instinct was to ask him if he was all right.

So. Stupid.

Then I got good and angry. That's what I focused on for all of about two minutes, my anger. The fight seemed to go out of me in an instant and I practically collapsed in his arms, feeling like a complete failure.

And so incredibly weak.

The tension seems to thicken between us as every minute passes, and I chance a glance at him out of the corner of my eye to find him watching me. He's leaning into the corner of the seat, his legs sprawled wide, his right arm propped on the window ledge of the door. His other arm is stretched out along the back of the seat, his hand disturbingly close to me, and I scoot closer to my side of the car until I'm practically crammed into the corner.

He lets out a sigh, his broad chest lifting with the movement, drawing my attention. For that brief, shining moment when I rested my head against his chest, I had felt . . . safe. I wanted all the lies and the deceit to be forgotten so I could rely on this man. He'd rescued me countless times already.

But why? When he was working for Pilar . . . he should have left me to fend for myself. He didn't.

I don't get why. That's the theme running through my head. The same word, over and over again.

Why, why, why, why?

"I hate that you hate me so much," he says, his deep voice rumbling over me, making me turn and look at him.

"I don't see why you care," I toss, hating how shaky my voice is. I clear my throat, curling my arms around myself.

Pain flickers in his eyes. "I care more than you know."

We stare at each other in silence and I'm dying to ask why. But I don't. Right now, he'll say anything to get in my good graces once more. I think of everything we shared while on Maui and wonder how much of it was a lie.

All of it?

Probably.

We say nothing else for the remainder of the drive and I'm relieved to escape the car when we arrive at the restaurant Max chose. It's more like a pub, the exterior a dark, rich wood, the interior much of the same, with rough-hewn brick walls and dim gold lighting. He speaks to the man who greets us as if he's an old friend and the gentleman escorts us to a table tucked away in a back corner of the restaurant, pulling out my chair before he hands each of us a single-sided menu.

"Our lunch menu is rather simple, but I hope you find something you like, miss," the man tells me, his gaze twinkling before he turns his attention to Max, giving him a look of—approval?—before he leaves us alone.

"You know him," I state flatly once the man is gone.

"I knew his son," he clarifies. "We served together in Afghanistan."

"Oh." I drop my gaze to the menu, uncomfortable with talking about his past. So he must have been telling the truth when he told me about his tattoo. "You said . . . knew."

"Yeah." Max keeps his eyes fixed on his menu as well. "He died in combat."

That nice, friendly man has suffered the loss of his son. I can't imagine what that must be like. And he's so cheerful, so upbeat. "I assume the food is good?" I ask to change the subject.

"The best," Max confirms. "Their hamburgers especially, though you probably wouldn't eat one."

"I would love one." My stomach growls and I realize I'm starving. I never really ate that muffin from earlier and a breakfast of coffee isn't filling. I set my menu onto the table. "With cheese. And fries."

He lifts his surprised gaze to mine. "Their onion rings are amazing."

But then I'd have onion breath . . . not that I'm going to kiss Max. I still think he's an asshole. At least somewhat of an asshole. "I love onion rings," I say with a smile.

"Me too." He sets his menu onto the table, too, and studies me. I feel like we're having some sort of standoff and it's weird. "Burgers and onion rings it is."

"And a Coke. With lots of ice," I add, getting warmed up.

"Diet?"

"No. Full-tilt." I doubt I need all that sugar coursing through my frenzied veins but I don't care. I'm feeling like I need to prove something to Max—what, I'm not sure, but here I am, all bravado and cheeseburgers, onion rings and sorrow over what I could have had with this man.

Sorrow for the man who lost his friend in battle, for the man who lost his son. Sadness for what I lost, too.

Myself.

Max's mouth curves into a faint smile. "I missed you, Lily."

His words remind me of what he's done and I sit up straighter, all the bravery and sadness fleeing me, replaced by anger. "What did you want to discuss, Max?"

The owner reappears and takes our orders, his mood jovial, even when Max asks him for privacy. He promises to bring our drinks but, otherwise, won't return until our lunch is ready.

The moment he's gone I shoot Max a look, my eyebrows raised. I'm done with the bullshit and I definitely don't want to take a stroll down memory lane. It'll hurt too much.

"Where do you want me to start?" he asks, as if he can read my mind.

"At the beginning. When did Pilar come to you?" I want all the dirty details. So I can hate him even more? Possibly.

He blows out a harsh breath, smiling up at our new waiter who materializes out of nowhere, delivering our drinks before he vanishes as quickly as he appeared. "A couple of weeks ago. She said that she wanted me to tail someone, someone who took something from her. And she wanted it back."

"So you thought the laptop belonged to her."

"I'm not that stupid." He sends me a look. "I figured out pretty quick that what she wanted didn't belong to her. I started investigating, doing my research as I usually do, and then Pilar called me, letting me know you'd left. She wanted me to follow you to Maui, so I did."

She hired Max within days, if not hours, after I sent her that email. The one from her own Fleur in-box to her personal account, when I taunted her that I knew what she'd done.

Closing my eyes, I grip the edge of the table, remembering what a fool I'd been. How arrogant. What did I think she'd do once she saw that email? Cave in and let me tell Daddy what exactly she's been up to these last few months?

I'd only been referring to her dalliance with Zachary. The seemingly harmless email conversations with Felicity Winston from Jayne Cosmetics.

She called me, threatening me with bodily harm, accusing me of being a meddling, home-wrecking little slut. And that's when I ran like a coward.

Opening my eyes, I stare unseeingly at Max as he talks and gestures. I release the edge of the table, reaching for my drink so

I can take a calming sip. The ice-cold, sweet soda hits my tongue and I swallow hard, trying my best to listen to what Max is saying, but it's as if my ears are stuffed with cotton.

"What is it that you do exactly, anyway?" I ask, interrupting him.

He stops talking and tilts his head, studying me in that coolly assessing way of his. It makes me uncomfortable and I want to squirm in my chair. "Are you all right?"

I shrug, trying to play it off. But my head is spinning and I swear to God, I'm seeing spots. Gripping the edge of the table once more, I tell him, "I'm fine. Could you answer my question?"

He doesn't even protest. I think he wants to stay on my good side. "I'm, ah, a private investigator. I run my own company, do investigative work for a variety of clients."

"Like Pilar," I add.

"Yeah. Though truly, she's unlike anyone I've ever met." He shakes his head, his lips quirked into a weird little smile. I like those lips. Especially when they're kissing me . . .

No. I can't think like that. Remembering the way he kisses me is the path straight back to danger.

"How so?" I ask, taking another drink of my Coke. It feels like the sugar is swimming in my veins and my head is still woozy. I blow out a calming breath, trying my best to steady . . . everything, but it's not working.

I feel like I'm walking on a rocking ship and we're headed for even choppier waters.

Max schools his expression. "Lily, let's be real. She's bat-shit crazy. And if you want my opinion—I'm afraid for your safety. And Violet's. Hell, your entire family is at risk when it comes to that woman."

My heart falls, and my expression must reflect it because he's quick to correct himself.

"I know Violet's safe because she has Ryder McKay by her side. And Rose is married, so she has her husband. But you." He takes a deep breath, his gaze never leaving mine. "I don't want you alone. Not until this—thing is wrapped up."

"Why not?" I whisper, everything inside of me aching at the possibilities that aren't being said. I'm scared. I've been running scared, but was I ever truly frightened of Pilar? Of what might happen to me? Of what she could do to me?

Like an idiot, that would be a no.

"Near the end, right before I left Maui, Pilar threatened that she would . . . hire someone else to get the laptop if I couldn't get the job done."

"But you *did* get the job done," I stress. "You took the laptop. Didn't you?"

He looks cornered. Trapped. I know the feeling. "I did. But I didn't give it to her. Not after what Levi and I discovered."

I frown. "Who?"

"He works for me. Computer expert, probably as good as you are." His pause is weighted with about a hundred unasked questions. "I had no idea about your technological skills."

"You never asked." It's not something I'm comfortable talking about, especially with him . . . a guy I met and fucked around with a little.

He's more than that and you know it.

Max lets the subject drop. "You played with fire when you challenged Pilar, Lily. And now she's an inferno, ready to burn you up. She's dying to burn me, too. I crossed her and she's not going to let me forget it."

"How did you cross her?"

"I told you. I didn't give her the laptop."

"So you do have it."

He nods. "It's in a safe in my apartment."

I'm dying to see his apartment, even though I shouldn't care. I should hate him forever for what he did to me. Yet I can't help but want a glimpse into the personal haven of Max . . . I don't even know his last name. "Why did you keep it?"

"Lily." His voice is soft, his expression incredulous. "I couldn't hand your laptop over to her, not after what I discovered on there."

"You mean the photos?" I'm embarrassed that he saw them, but he's seen me naked up close and personal, so it shouldn't be a big deal.

But it *is* a big deal. I'm humiliated. I feel so . . . silly, knowing those photos are there. They're old—they feel like they're from a past life, that it's another woman in those photos, not me.

His cheeks turn ruddy, like he's embarrassed. "I saw them. So did Levi."

Oh, God. Someone saw them besides Max? Could I be more humiliated? "Great," I say, letting out a shaky breath.

"Don't worry. Levi is the most serious, stand-up guy I know. He won't tell anyone, he wouldn't copy them—nothing like that. If he were to ever meet you—and I want you two to meet—he won't acknowledge those photos, Lily. I swear. He's got integrity."

After what Max did to me, I believed he had no integrity whatsoever. He stole from me, for a job he was paid to do. How ethical can he be?

Reminds me of Rose and her husband, the former professional thief. He almost stole a very valuable diamond necklace from her but in the end, he couldn't do it, because he was in love with her.

Not that I expect Max to fall in love with me after spending a few days together in Maui, but didn't I matter to him at all? Did he have any remorse for what he did? Regret?

That he has the laptop shows that maybe he did.

"I believe you." I draw my finger across my glass, through the condensation that's formed there. "I took those photos a long time ago, for a stupid guy . . . a couple of stupid guys."

He's quiet, and I finally look up at him to find he's watching me. "Say something," I tell him when he remains silent.

"You looked beautiful in those photos," he says softly.

Okay. That was the last thing I expected him to say. I should not be pleased by his compliment. Absolutely no way should his words make me happy. But they do. "Thank you," I murmur, feeling awkward.

"I know you're scared," he continues. "And I know you hate me. You have every reason to feel that way toward me, but I swear to you, Lily, I'm not going to leave your side until this . . . problem—with Pilar is over and done with. You need to go to your sisters and father and tell them what's going on. We discovered more information on there. More than you know."

It's the right thing to do, I know it is, but I'm scared. Scared that they won't believe me. "What did you discover?"

"You didn't finish reading the emails between Pilar and Felicity Winston. Pilar sent her information. Confidential information in regards to Fleur's product line," Max says grimly.

My mouth drops open. "What?" I whisper.

He nods. "Pilar did it in the hopes she'd get a job offer. After she received the information, Felicity ceased all correspondence with her."

The dots are back, spotting my vision, and my head spins. "Shit. *Shit, shit, shit.*" I close my eyes hard, then blink them open. "I should've never left. I need to tell my dad."

"I have the laptop with the proof, Lily," he says, his voice calm. I need that right now. I feel like I'm about to leap out of my skin, I'm so freaked out. "Plus, Levi took a series of screenshots of the in-boxes, the emails. They're all located in a Dropbox account, plus on an external hard drive."

I gape at him, unable to find the words to thank him for what he'd done, and that he did it all for me. That was my biggest fear once the laptop disappeared. How would Daddy believe me if the evidence was gone? Though now I realize I could have obtained the information off my iMac, too. I handled everything wrong. All of it.

Thank God for Max gathering up all the evidence. I can now show everyone in my family what Pilar was plotting. They'll have no choice but to believe me.

I'll break my father's heart. He'll probably get mad at me. I'll enrage both Violet and Ryder, probably Rose and Grandma, too, but at least everyone will be aware of what's going on.

Plus, I'll be free of Pilar's hold once and for all. She can threaten me all she wants, but I have everything I need right here in front of me.

And I owe it all to Max.

Chapter Twenty-five

Max

"YOU SON OF A BITCH, I SAW YOU WITH HER."

I grip my phone close to my ear and sneak into the bathroom off my bedroom, quietly closing the door. *Fucking Pilar.* I don't want to talk to her. I'd hang up on her normally. After all, our business is finished. I failed her. Gave her back every dime she paid for my services, and I'm done.

But I want to hear what she has to say. Plus, I have an app on my phone where I can record this entire conversation. That's called evidence.

"What are you talking about?" I ask innocently as I lean against the counter.

"Stop being such a moron. You know exactly who I mean." She pauses, clearly for dramatic effect. "*Lily.* How stupid can you be? Why are you with her? Are you trying to get in her pants or what? Or are you still trying to get that damn laptop? Because if you are, I will pay you handsomely for it."

"I thought we were done." I don't even acknowledge the "get in Lily's pants" comment.

"So did I. In fact, I hired another investigator to finish up the job you were too incompetent to complete." I ignore her jab, though my teeth are on fucking edge. "He reported back that she spent the afternoon with a certain gentleman and his de-scription sounded eerily like you. Then he sent me photos, and what a shock. It *was* you." Another pause. "What the fuck do you think you're doing?"

"What does it matter? I don't work for you any longer," I say, emphasizing the last couple of words.

"But if you are trying to get that laptop . . ." Her voice drifts.

"What the hell is so important on that laptop, anyway? Does she have something on you or what?" I decide to play dumb. She likes it that way, I think. Makes her feel superior.

"Of course she does. But if she thinks she can double-cross me? Lily Fowler has another think coming." She laughs, making me wince. The woman is fucking loud.

And fucking annoying.

"What exactly does she have on you?"

"None of your business," she snaps, all humor gone. "So tell me. Are you going after that laptop or not?"

"I'm sick and fucking tired of talking about this laptop, that's for damn sure," I mutter as I rub a hand across the back of my neck. Just listening to this woman stresses me out.

"You were supposed to do your job," she says. "And you didn't. It's your own damn fault."

"If I get it to you, what will you give me?" I ask, an idea forming in my head.

"Double the original fee we agreed upon," she says promptly.

"Done." I end the call before she can say anything else.

Perfect.

Slipping my phone back into my pocket, I exit the bathroom and go out to the living room, where Lily sits perched on the edge of my sofa, her cell phone cradled in her hand. She's bent over the lit screen, apparently scrolling through messages, and when she hears me enter the room she looks up, her gaze full of wariness.

She doesn't trust me and I can't blame her, but it still hurts. I really messed this up. That she's in my apartment, willing to listen to what I have to say, is like a miracle.

"Everything okay?" she asks.

"Pilar just called." It's my intent to be completely honest with her from now on. Full disclosure. I don't want to hide anything from her.

Lily makes a face. "Why? I thought you refunded her the money and you're through with her."

"I did. She's hired someone else." I start pacing back and forth, my usual mode when I'm trying to puzzle something out. "That someone else is already following you and saw the two of us together earlier this afternoon. Sent her photos of us, too."

"What?" Lily leaps to her feet, her expression full of fury. "You're kidding me! That no-good, scheming bitch . . ."

"What's done is done—no need to get in a tizzy over it." I continue to pace, mentally skimming through the possibilities. I can feel her glaring at me and I probably shouldn't have used the word *tizzy*, but I'm too wrapped up in planning our next move to worry about it. "I'm going to give her your laptop."

Her face falls and she blinks up at me. "What?" she rasps out. "I thought . . ."

I stop directly in front of her and grab her shoulders, giving her a little shake. "I'm going to clean it up first. Or load a fake one with different information. I haven't quite figured it out yet. I need to call Levi."

She stares up at me, sadness in her eyes. She looks . . . lost. I want to console her so damn bad but I can't. I'm lucky she agreed to come to my place after we finished lunch. I said I wanted her here so we could discuss how we're going to approach her family with the bad news.

The truth? I just want her close to me. I want to watch over her and know she's safe. Leaving her alone is not an option, especially after Pilar just confirmed my worst fear: that she's hired someone else to keep tabs on Lily.

Who knows what that guy will do to get what Pilar wants.

"Why are you helping me so much?" Lily asks. "I don't understand."

Yet again, time to be completely honest. "I—care for you, princess. I don't want to see you get hurt. I don't want your family to get hurt, either, not at the hands of some crazy bitch like Pilar."

Lily blinks up at me as if she didn't hear me correctly, but she doesn't say a word. I feel the need to fill the silence.

"Now that she has someone else following you, we need to move. And I . . . I can't leave you alone, princess. I know you're pissed at me, I know I fucked this all up, but you're not safe. I plan on keeping watch over you."

When she continues to gape at me, I can't stand it. "What?"

She blinks again and shakes her head. "You called me 'princess.' Twice."

A smile tugs at my lips. "Sorry, habit."

"I—I like it. No need to apologize." She tears her gaze from mine and the moment is broken. "And you said you care for me."

"I do," I confirm softly. She turns to face me once more. "I meant every word I said."

"We barely know each other."

"I know enough. And I'm not going to let someone destroy you because that person was caught in her own dubious game." I squeeze Lily's shoulders, smooth my thumbs over them, and I feel the muscles loosen beneath my touch. "I won't let anyone hurt you. I swear. I'm on your side."

She's quiet again and these long silences are gonna kill me, swear to God. I continue to massage her shoulders, wishing I could touch bare skin, but I'm pushing her limits already. I'm surprised she hasn't shoved me away yet.

"No one's ever really been on my side before," she admits, breaking what I thought was my unbreakable heart.

"You have your sisters, don't you?" When she nods I continue. "They love you. Look at the lengths you've gone to protect them."

"Right," she snorts. "I ran away when Pilar threatened me. I should've stayed here and gone to Violet. I should've told her what Pilar was planning and instead like the total coward that I am, I ran. That's how I always handle my problems. I run away and hope they disappear on their own, you know?" Tears fill her eyes and she blinks against them, sending them streaming down her cheeks.

The sight of those fucking tears shreds my heart into ribbons and I pull her into me, burying her face in my chest as I slip my arms around her waist. "You don't have to run any longer, baby. Like I said, I'm by your side. I'll help you."

She doesn't reply, but I feel her shoulders shake and my T-shirt is getting wet from her tears. I run my hand over her silky, soft hair, thankful she took the band out earlier. Her hair is still damp and I thread my fingers through it, tuck a few strands behind her ear. "Why do you do it?"

"Do what?" she asks with a loud sniff.

"Run?"

Lily pulls away slightly to look up at me. "I don't know. It's easier. Everyone abandons me when I'm in trouble, so I figure it's best to run away from the trouble I cause rather than face it."

"Are you afraid of disappointing them?"

"Who?"

"Your family. Your friends. Whoever you've wronged."

"I don't want anyone to be mad at me," she admits.

"Lily . . ."

"My mom would get mad at me when I caused trouble. But I only did it because I was so jealous of my sisters taking up all of her time, especially Rose." Lily looks down, her voice small. "But she was just a baby. I didn't realize the pressure my mom was under, how unhappy she was, how sick she was over . . .

everything. I acted out because I wanted her attention, and bad attention is better than none at all, right?"

Christ, my heart feels like it's splitting in fucking two for this woman.

"And then she killed herself. For a long time, I thought it was because of me. Of what I did to her," she admits, her voice soft, her words hollow.

"How old were you?"

"Six."

I tug her back against my chest before she can say another word and hold her close. As close as I can get her. I press my mouth to her forehead, breathe in the delicious scent of her hair, her skin. "It wasn't your fault. You do realize this, right?"

"Uh-huh." She doesn't sound very convincing. "She was having an affair, too. Rose discovered that recently, after reading our mom's old diaries. She didn't love our dad. She didn't want to be a part of our family anymore."

"I'm not going to abandon you," I tell her vehemently, and I mean it. I fucking mean it. I want this girl—I care for her. Most likely I'm falling in love with her, too—as freaky as that is to think about; I can't focus on my twisted views on love and relationships right now, though.

I need to take care of her, this woman who is still like a broken little girl deep down inside. I hate that. I want to fix her. I want to reassure her that everything's going to be okay. That I'm going to be here for her no matter what.

It's crazy, how fast I've fallen for her, but I'm done denying it. Full disclosure, I promised myself. That's how I plan on treating Lily from now on. She deserves the truth, no matter what.

She says nothing and I worry that she thinks my words are meaningless. That she's heard this all before and still ended up hurt and alone. Not only do I need to tell her these things and make these promises, but I also need to show her that I mean it.

"You ready to go back home?" I ask, my voice muffled against her hair.

Lily doesn't say a word, but she does slowly wrap her arms around my waist and I close my eyes, letting the mixture of satisfaction and relief roll through me.

"Thank you," she whispers. "For helping me."

I pull away slightly and slip my hand under her chin, tilting her head up so her gaze meets mine. "I will do anything for you, princess. Anything. I want you to know that."

She nods and presses her lips together. I want to kiss her, but . . . not now. Not like this. She's upset. Mad at me. I push myself on her and she could use it against me later. And I couldn't handle that. I need to approach her just right. Prove to her that I will do right by her. Whatever it takes, I will prove to Lily that we should be together.

"Anything," I whisper again, tucking her hair behind her ear, drifting my finger across her cheek. Her skin is soft and warm, her eyelids flutter, and it takes everything within me not to haul her in close and kiss her.

"Max," she murmurs but says nothing else. Just closes her eyes as my hand falls away from her cheek. She leans her head against my chest, tucks her face in close, and I hold her. Savor the feeling of her in my arms.

This is what I need, what I've been missing for what feels like my entire life. I had no idea she would come to me as the wild-and-crazy party-girl heiress Lily Fowler, but I'm not complaining.

She is the woman for me.

Chapter Twenty-six

Lily

I KNOW ON THE DOOR AND TAKE A STEP BACK, DROPPING MY head so I can study the floor, my shoes. Reaching up, I tuck my hair behind my ear, note my trembling fingers, my fidgety behavior. My heart is racing like I just ran a marathon and I swear my throat is so dry, I probably won't be able to squeak out a word.

"You'll be fine." Max settles a large, warm hand on my shoulder and gives me a reassuring squeeze. He's standing just behind me, like my own personal shadow, and I want to turn to him and say thank you. Hug and kiss him as a show of my gratitude.

But I remain fixed in place, waiting for the door to open.

I hear the sound of footfalls coming from inside and then the door swings wide open, my sister standing there holding the handle, an inviting smile on her face. "Lily! You're early."

"I couldn't wait any longer," I tell her. Violet shoots Max a questioning look. "Violet, this is my . . . friend, Max Coleman." At least I know his last name now.

"Hello." She holds her hand out to him and he takes it, giving it a polite shake. My sister has always had impeccable manners. I admire that about her. I admire lots of things about Violet. Rose, too. Have I ever told them? No.

I need to rectify that.

"Nice to meet you," Max says, his voice gruff, his hand-shake firm. I see the assessing way Violet studies him and I wonder what she sees. I've never introduced a man to my sisters before, though Violet doesn't know exactly what happened between Max and me. Rose, on the other hand, knows most of it. Does Violet believe me when I call him my friend? Or does she think I'm bringing some random dude that I bang to her apartment?

Not that I'm banging him anymore . . . another thing I'd like to rectify.

Don't be stupid. He burned you once . . .

I really don't think he'll burn me again. At least, I hope he won't.

"Come inside," Violet invites and we follow her into the apartment, Max shutting and locking the door behind him, al-ways cautious, always safe. I'm starting to appreciate that about him more and more. "You want anything to drink? Water? Cof-fee? Wine?" Violet asks.

"I'll take a glass of wine," I say, hopeful that it will calm my agitated nerves.

"You sure that's a good idea?" Max asks, his voice low.

I stop and turn to look at him. "I'll only have one glass," I say, annoyed.

"I only ask because I don't want you to give your father any ammunition," he explains. "I'm trying to watch out for you."

Nodding, I say nothing else and follow Violet into the kitchen, grateful to see she's already got a bottle out, and she's now reaching into the cabinets and pulling out two glasses.

I want to ask Max why he's being so nice to me. There's got to be a motive behind all of this. He claims he cares for me, but does he really? It's hard for me to believe him. It's hard for me to believe anyone when they say that I matter. I've never felt like I mattered.

"Where's Ryder?" I ask Violet as I stop to stand beside her.

She fills a glass halfway with wine before handing it to me. "In the shower still. Like I said, you're a little early."

"Sorry," I say after I take a sip. The wine is cold and smooth, going down my throat easily. "I hope you don't mind."

"Never." Violet smiles. "This way we can talk before Father gets here."

My stomach drops. I'm so nervous to face him I'm nauseous.

Max walks past the kitchen and enters the living room, going straight to the giant windows that overlook the city. He stands in front of them, his back to us, surveying the land below I guess. I watch him, as does Violet, and she steps closer to me, her voice lowering to almost a whisper.

"Who is he exactly? Why did you bring him? And what did you want to talk about?"

"He's a . . . friend. Someone I met in Maui."

Violet gasps and socks my shoulder with a gentle fist. "Shut. Up. You met a man while on vacation and brought him back here? Hmm. He's not your usual type, but then again, I wouldn't really know your usual type since you never bring any of them around to meet us."

"None of them were worthy enough," I say with a shrug.

"And this one is?"

"Yes." I don't even hesitate with my answer. "And I didn't bring him home with me. He lives here. Well, he lives in Brooklyn."

"Really." Violet takes a drink, still contemplating Max over the rim of her glass. "I need more details."

"It's . . . complicated." For once, that's not an excuse. My history with Max really *is* complicated.

"Someday you're going to have to tell me everything. Does Rose know?"

"Does Rose know what?"

"About Max?"

"Sort of," I admit, hating that I can't tell Violet everything yet. She's going to be so angry when she discovers what Pilar did. Giving away business secrets, including our perfume line. That's personal. When Max showed me the other emails between Felicity and Pilar last night, I about burst a blood vessel, I was so angry. I've calmed down some, but I know talking about it once more is going to rile me up all over again.

Max was right. I probably shouldn't be drinking wine.

"Sure, you tell her everything but not me? Whatever." She's teasing, but I can tell Violet's a little hurt.

I turn to face her, grabbing her arm. "I would've told you sooner, but everything's happened so fast and . . . I'm sorry."

Violet frowns, covering my hand with her own. "I was just teasing you, Lily. Are you okay?"

"Not really," I whisper, shaking my head when she opens her mouth to say something else. I can't answer questions right now. But she needs to know I'm here for her. "But it'll get better soon, once I tell you everything that's going on."

There's a knock at the door and I hope it's Rose. I'm not quite ready to face Daddy yet, and I'd prefer to have Max by my side when he enters the apartment. Luckily enough, I hear Rose's voice greet Violet and I grip the edge of the kitchen counter, taking a big gulp of my wine before I set the glass down.

My nerves still aren't steady.

"Hey." I turn to find Max standing there, studying me with a concerned look on his handsome face. He shaved after he took a shower, so his cheeks and jaw are smooth. He's wearing a dark blue button-down shirt and jeans, and he looks . . . edible.

I should not be thinking like this. It's as if I can't help it.

"Hi." I offer him a smile and he steps closer to me.

"You all right?"

"No." I take a deep breath. "But I will be when this is over. Hopefully."

He touches my shoulder again, his fingers moving to shift my hair away from my neck, and they brush my skin. A shiver steals through me and I close my eyes on an exhale and lick my lips, wishing he would kiss me. We've been constantly together for the last twenty-four hours. I spent the night at his apartment, for the love of God, because he wouldn't let me go home. He didn't want me alone, too concerned over who could be waiting for me, watching me. He slept on the couch while I slept in his bed and I could smell him on his sheets.

Needless to say, I didn't get much sleep.

"Lily." I turn to see Rose standing in the kitchen doorway, her gaze lingering on the wineglass on the counter. "Wow, that looks good, but I can't drink." She rubs a hand over her belly.

I go to her and give her a hug. "How are you?"

"The real question is how are you? And is that hunk shaking my husband's hand your Max?" she whispers close to my ear.

"Yes." I give her an extra squeeze. "There's more to this story than what I told you."

"I can see that, considering the last time you saw Max he was in Maui and stealing your laptop." Rose withdraws from me and turns to Max, who's making small talk with Caden. "I'm Rose, Lily's nosy youngest sister."

He cracks a smile that takes my breath away and takes her hand. "Max. Nice to meet you."

She doesn't let go of his hand. "You're not here to steal anything from us, are you?"

Oh, God. Why did she go and say that? Even Caden looks uncomfortable, but *hello,* he's a former thief, so anytime the word *steal* pops up, he squirms.

Max's smile fades, his expression turning sincere. "No. I plan on doing right by Lily from now on."

Rose studies him, her eyes getting squinty as she finally releases Max's hand. Pregnancy has really done a number on my baby sister. "Good. Because I'll rip your balls off if you hurt her again."

"Rose," Caden says, his voice stern. I can say nothing because I'm mortified beyond belief.

"Well, it's true," Rose says with a shrug as she sends me a look. I don't think she regrets telling Max that whatsoever.

"I appreciate how protective you are over your sister," Max says. "And if I did something to betray her again, I'd deserve to get my balls ripped off."

Rose starts to laugh and pats Max's chest. "I like you."

Another knock sounds at the door and we all pause, looking at each other. Ryder suddenly appears, his dark hair damp, his gaze zeroing in on Max before he turns to Violet. "Everything okay?"

"Sounds like Father's here," Violet says, her voice soft, her head tipping toward Ryder when he slips his arm around her waist and holds her close.

"I'll answer it," Ryder says, pressing a kiss to Violet's forehead before he releases her and goes to the door.

"Let the good times begin," Rose says, her voice loaded with false cheer.

"I DON'T—" DADDY SWALLOWS AND LEANS FORWARD, STUDYING Max with an intensity I've dealt with before. The same kind of intensity that would make me squirm in my seat and eventually confess all my sins. "I don't want to believe any of this."

Max doesn't even flinch, making me admire him all the more. He hands over his iPad to my father. "I understand, sir, but I need you to look at this. There's your proof."

The rest of us remain quiet as Daddy reads over the emails from Pilar to Zachary Lawrence, to Felicity Winston from Jayne Cosmetics. Violet is also reading over the emails on her own iPad, after Max just sent her a link to the Dropbox account. I look over at her and see the way Ryder has his arm around her shoulders in a protective gesture, his face full of barely contained rage as he reads over her shoulder.

"Why would she give up such confidential information so easily?" Violet asks, lifting her head to study all of us, her gaze snagging on Max. I've let him talk the entire time, an offer he made on our way over to Violet's that I took him up on. Yes, it makes me feel like a chicken yet again, that I can't be the one to explain what happened with Pilar. But I knew I wouldn't be able to explain myself thoroughly enough. I'd get too emotional and Daddy would probably yell at me. Everyone would take sides and it would turn into a huge, ugly mess.

Daddy hasn't yelled at Max once, and I'm sure that's because he's explained everything so thoroughly, so objectively. He told of how he was hired by Pilar, how he followed me to Maui, got to know me, got closer to me, and then stole the laptop. He then proceeded to tell them what happened next, the information he and Levi discovered, how he lied and told Pilar he didn't have the laptop after all.

And now he's sharing with everyone exactly what he found in Pilar's in-boxes. The same information I stumbled upon but didn't look at closely enough. The plan to sabotage Fleur and leave the company in the dust. I still can't believe she had the balls to do such a thing.

Well, I *can* believe it. This *is* Pilar we're talking about.

"Once Felicity received the information, she never contacted Pilar again. At least via email," Max explains. "I don't know why she gave up the goods so quickly, but it looks like her impulsive actions bit her in the ass."

Violet—ladylike, perfect Violet—snorts. "Finally the bitch gets what she deserves. At our expense, though."

"Exactly, and that's what pisses me off. She ran and blabbed her mouth so easily to the fucking competition. You'd think she'd know better than to fuck with me," Ryder says, his eyes glimmering with repressed fury.

Unease slithers down my spine. I know I sure as hell wouldn't mess with Ryder.

Daddy lifts his head, staring at Violet like she's lost her mind. "She's been filling my head with your incompetence lately."

"Who? Pilar?" Violet asks incredulously, and I almost roll my eyes. She's upset, though, and obviously not thinking clearly.

He makes a noise, resumes his reading on the iPad. "She claims she's worried about your supposed lack of focus. Thinks you're too wrapped up in wedding plans."

"Bitch," Ryder mutters, shaking his head.

"How dare she," Violet breathes.

Rose speaks up like she can't stand it any longer. "You need to fire her, Daddy. Break it off with her and let her go, personally and professionally. She's trying to ruin us. For all you know, she already has. God knows what Jayne Cosmetics has planned now that they know about our future product line."

"And the perfume line," Violet adds.

He says nothing and we all seem to look at each other, silently communicating that we're in agreement with Rose.

"Violet, I believe if you went to Felicity Winston and told her you know exactly what she received from Pilar, you can get her to back off whatever plans they might have to steal your ideas," Max suggests.

"Maybe." Violet clears her throat, her eyes so sad. I feel terrible that I didn't realize what Pilar had done sooner. We could have stopped all this a couple of weeks ago. "I know Felicity personally but I wouldn't call her a friend. There's always been friendly competition between us, but I would've never thought she'd do something so low."

"She may have agreed to take the information, but it was Pilar who offered it up so easily," Ryder points out. "Don't forget that."

"He's right. I say you approach her carefully, maybe even send her a veiled threat. Nothing too outrageous—we'll leave that up to Pilar. But you need to let Felicity know you're onto her plan," Max says. "If you need any help with offering Felicity proof with the email correspondence between them, I can do that."

Pride makes my chest fill with emotion. He's so smart, so competent, so incredibly strong and kind. Look at how easily he wants to help my sister, my entire family. Me.

He's a good guy. The first *real* good guy I've ever been with.

I don't want to let him go.

"I would like that, thank you," Violet says softly.

"What do you want me to do about this?" Daddy asks as he sets the iPad on the coffee table in front of him. He remains leaning forward and rests his elbows on his knees, running his hands through his hair over and over again.

I don't remember ever seeing him look so distraught. I knew what we had to tell him would end up breaking his heart, but I didn't think it would break my heart as well. Despite our volatile history, I hate seeing him so upset. I'm tempted to go to him and wrap my arms around his shoulders, reassure him that everything's going to be all right eventually.

Would he want me to? Or would he tell me to go to hell? I am, after all, the bearer of bad news. I always have been.

"I don't know if confronting her would be the right approach," Max starts.

"Why not?" Rose asks, sounding annoyed. "Bitch would deserve it. She knows what she did. That's why she's so hell-bent on bugging Lily to death for that stupid laptop."

"I thought about giving her a dummy laptop loaded with false information, plus screenshots of her in-boxes," Max explains. "But now I'm thinking that would be pointless."

"Why?" Rose asks again. "I like the idea of her being tricked."

"Retaliation might not be worth the risk," Ryder says. I look over at him, our gazes meeting. Here is a man who speaks from ample experience. "When she thinks she's been wronged, she can become . . . unhinged. I don't want her to do anything that might harm any one of you." His gaze falls on Max. "Even you."

"Thanks," Max says wryly.

"I'll talk to her," my father says quietly. "It's the only way. I'll call her into my office and calmly confront her with the information you've given me, Max. She won't make a scene at Fleur, not after what I have to say. I'll let her know it's in her best interest that she give her notice and leave Fleur for good. I'll even give her a recommendation."

"Why?" Rose explodes for the third time, leaping to her feet, causing Caden to stand as well and try to calm her down. She shrugs off his hands and strides right up to where our father sits. She's the epitome of righteous, indignant fury, resting her hands on her hips as she stares down at him. "A *recommendation?* Are you serious? Why the hell would you even consider that! She gave away company secrets! Confidential information to our direct competition! Giving her a recommendation would be like a reward for all the shitty things she's done. I can't let you do that, Daddy. I say we go after her and give her a dose of her own medicine. I'm sick of the way she's fucked with our lives. She would deserve every single awful thing that might happen to her!"

"Calm down, baby," Caden says, slipping his arm around Rose's waist and steering her closer to him. "I don't like seeing you so worked up."

She drops her hands from her hips and takes a deep breath, nodding. My heart is beating triple time. I'm just as upset as Rose is and I tell myself to calm down, wishing that Max would wrap me up in his arms and never let me go.

His being here by my side and helping me, helping my entire

family, is proof that he cares. That he wants to do right by me. I can't deny that I'm still hurt over his betrayal but in the end, he kept my laptop and came to me. I can forgive him.

But I want him to ask for that forgiveness. I want him to . . . grovel a bit. Does my wanting him to grovel make me a bad person? Probably.

"He's right," Ryder says grimly. "She's not worth you getting upset over, Rose. Let your father take care of this by taking away the thing she wants the most."

"And what's that?" Max asks as he turns to him.

Ryder smiles, the sight of it almost feral. "Her job."

Chapter Twenty-seven

Max

"I'M EXHAUSTED," LILY SAYS AS SHE ENTERS MY APARTMENT.

I flick on the switch near the door, illuminating the darkening living room. The sun's almost down. We were at Violet's place for hours and I have to agree with Lily—I'm exhausted, too.

I didn't mind taking over for Lily and explaining everything Pilar did. I knew Lily wouldn't be able to get it all out, and I had a feeling her father or her sisters would shut her down anyway. Not that they would mean to—well, her father might mean to, because that guy doesn't have the best relationship with Lily— it's all a part of family dynamics. Everyone has their roles.

Lily is the fucked-up, messy one.

"Want something to drink?" I ask once I lock the door and turn on another lamp.

"No, thanks. I'm all drunk out." She smiles and I join her on the couch, not sitting too close, though I'm dying to.

Being close to her and not really touching her the way I want . . . is freaking torture, especially when she's wearing that beautiful dress that fits her like a dream. She packed a bag at her place yesterday before I brought her to my apartment and when she came out of the bedroom after taking a shower, dressed and ready to go to Violet's, I almost swallowed my tongue.

She's so damn beautiful it hurts. Feisty, defiant Lily turns me on like no other woman I've ever met, but vulnerable, soft Lily is another thing entirely. She brings out all of my protective instincts. All I want to do is fight for her, take care of her, make her realize that she needs me.

She's mad at me and she has every right to be. I wronged her and I hate myself for it. What's done is done. I can only hope my actions from the last couple of days prove that I am here for her, no matter what.

"I wanted to thank you for helping me and my family," she says, her voice soft as she stares at her clutched hands resting in her lap. "What you did today . . . it means a lot to me."

"You're welcome." I pause. Should I tell her how I feel? *Fuck it,* I'm going all in. "I'd do anything for you, Lily. I hope you know that."

A little smile curves her lips but she still won't look at me. "I don't get why. We barely know each other . . ."

I reach out and clasp her knee, my fingers tingling at first contact with her bare skin. "I know enough. I feel a connection to you that I've never experienced with another woman before."

She's quiet for a moment, but at least she doesn't pull out of my reach. "I'm not big on relationships."

"Me either."

"As in, I've never really had one. Not for a long period of time, at least," she admits, her teeth sinking into her lower lip.

"Same." I squeeze her knee and move my hand upward so it's resting on her lower thigh, on top of the skirt of her dress. She still doesn't stop me and I swear, I'm not breathing, for fear she'll tell me to fuck off and run away.

"My sisters have found love and, most of the time, I think they're crazy for tying themselves down. But Rose is so happy, married and about to have a baby, and she and Caden are madly in love." She sighs. "Then there's Violet and Ryder. I would've never picked him for my sister, but what do I know? She's going to take over Fleur someday, and Ryder will be right by her side, running the company with her."

"And what about you?" I ask. She sounds wistful, almost jealous, though I know that's not the right word. More like envious. Like she wishes she could have even a piece of what her sisters do.

"I always believed something like that isn't in the cards for me." She lifts her head, her gaze meeting mine. "You know what my motto used to be?"

"What?" I'm almost afraid to hear it.

"Live fast, die young." She pauses, gauging my reaction, and I try to keep my expression neutral but, damn, that's a shitty motto. "My mother was the most beautiful person I ever knew and she died young."

Right, because she killed herself. That's the sort of model she looks up to? I know she loves and misses her mom, but she shouldn't want to emulate her in that way. "That's a terrible motto to have." More like fucking awful.

"I know, but I can't live like this forever. I'm bound to fuck up. It's like I want to fuck up and I can't stop myself. My dad calls it a waste." She looks away, as though she doesn't want to see my reaction.

Anger fills me and I try to tamp it down. "Your dad called you a *waste*?" I thought *I* was the asshole. I wasn't much impressed after meeting him, but at least he believed what we said about Pilar, not that he had any choice. He gave Lily a hug before he left and thanked her for telling him, then shook my hand and thanked me as well.

Despite the hug from her father, Lily looked sad. I didn't ask her about it because I didn't want to upset her further. That's a relationship that's still going to need some work before all the old resentments and anger are resolved.

"No, he didn't call me a waste, though I wouldn't be surprised if he does feel that way sometimes. He's referring to what I do. He always tells me I'm wasting my life when I should be doing something with purpose. But I tell him hey, at least I'm living."

"Are you, though? Are you really?"

Those pretty, sad eyes meet mine once more. "I was, for a brief moment. When we were together in Maui. That was the first time since I don't know when that I felt . . . real. I may have kept things from you, Max, and you definitely kept things from me. But that was the real me when we were together. That girl you were alone with was me."

Her confession stirs something deep, makes me remember all that we shared, the struggles and the frustration and the triumph. She is a woman who was made to submit yet is scared to give up control.

I see the struggle right now, playing out before me. Her expression, her words, everything about her is so raw and open, especially after the day she just had. I'm filled with the need to coax the real Lily to make an appearance once more. She needs me.

And I need her.

It was liberating, our time together on Maui, for both of us. I needed that and so did she. She challenged me and I challenged her and, together, we have the potential to make a good team.

Does she see it? Does she realize what we can have?

She must.

I move closer to her and slip my arm around the back of the couch, reaching for her with my other hand. I touch her cheek, drift my fingers across her skin, and she licks her lips, blinking up at me with wide, scared eyes.

Fuck. She is my every weakness, and the realization both exhilarates and scares the shit out of me.

"I want you," I whisper, keeping my voice even, not wanting to startle her and make her run. "I know I've fucked things up and I'm so sorry, you don't even know. I have a lot to make up to you and I will, but I want you so bad, baby."

She blows out a harsh breath. "I just . . . I don't know, Max."

"I understand. But I swear to God, I won't fuck this up."

"I'm scared," she admits, licking her lips again. She keeps doing that and I'm going to kiss her whether she likes it or not, I'm that desperate to taste her.

"Why?" I lean into her, my mouth at her ear, my nose close to her fragrant hair. I breathe deep, then whisper, "Tell me how I can make this right. Tell me what I need to say to convince you to willingly come to bed with me."

It's not just about taking her to my bed, either. I want her, I can't deny that, but I also care about her. I want to take care of her and learn what makes her happy. And then I want to keep making her happy for as long as she'll let me.

Fuck, just thinking that makes me realize I'm scared, too. Scared of Lily, scared of what we could have between us. But my need for Lily overrides the fear. I don't want to be apart from her, ever. I've been contemplating asking her to work with me, work for my company. Her tech skills could come in handy. She would be an incredible asset. But would she want to?

I haven't a clue. And right now isn't the time to ask her. I'm already asking for too much.

She studies me, her expression solemn. "I want to trust you."

"I want to earn your trust," I agree readily.

"I don't like being nervous around you. Feeling unsure." She bites her lip and I finally give in, swooping toward her and pressing my mouth to hers in a too-short kiss. The brief taste of her plump lips isn't close to being enough.

"What was that for?" she asks when I pull away.

"Because I can't resist you." I shake my head, praying I don't mess this up. "I've tried. I told myself we wouldn't work. I half convinced myself you were just a job, but really, I never believed it. I liked you too damn much. I swear it's like I'm fucking addicted to you."

Her eyes flare with arousal but she says nothing.

"Fate's thrown us together," I continue. "There's a reason for that, princess."

She cracks a smile. "I didn't take you for a believer in fate, cowboy."

I chuckle, pleased that she used her nickname for me. "I'm usually not, but when it comes to you, I can change my ways."

Her smile fades and her eyes light with heat. "Take me to bed, Max."

Chapter Twenty-eight

Lily

MAYBE I SHOULDN'T HAVE ASKED MAX TO TAKE ME TO BED, BUT I couldn't help myself. Especially when he said I was worth changing his ways for. Everything within me melted at his words, at the look in his eyes, at the quick kiss he stole while we sat on his couch, as though he couldn't resist me.

And he said he couldn't resist me. I can relate. I feel the same way. Having him in front of me, looking good enough to eat, saying all the right things, his expression open and honest, I realized I'd rather enjoy the fall than worry about the risk.

That's my usual mode of operation, but not when it comes to love. I'll fling myself off a cliff for just about anything but a relationship with a man. My heart is fragile. My spirit . . . broken.

But with Max, I want to fly and damn the consequences of where I land. After what he did for me today, for the last few days, he's all I want.

All I need.

He stands, offers me his hand, and I take it, neither of us saying a word. We leave the living room, start to walk down the short hallway toward his bedroom, but then he's yanking me into his arms, his mouth at my neck, his hand sliding over my ass and pulling me into him. I can feel his arousal, thick and insistent beneath the zipper of his pants, and I want to touch him there, but I don't. With a sigh I sink against him, looping my arms around his neck, my hands buried in his hair as he licks and nips at my throat. I lean against the wall and toss my head back with a moan, enjoying the way his mouth travels all over my skin, his breath hot, his hands insistent.

"I've thought of you like this since we came back from Hawaii," he admits in this low, rumbly whisper that sets my nerve endings on fire.

"Same," I confess, my brain so scrambled by his touch I can hardly speak. Despite everything he did to me and how angry I was, he always lingered in the back of my mind. Driving me crazy with wanting him and frustrated because I was supposed to hate him.

"At night I'd lie in bed alone and jerk off to thoughts of you. Those memories we made in Maui." A shiver steals over me at his admission. His mouth is level with mine, and he's murmuring against my lips as he stares deep into my eyes. "The way you sucked my cock so hard I came in your mouth. The taste of your pussy, how easy I could make you come, make you scream. How good it felt, my cock buried inside you, fucking you."

I shudder at his words. *God*, he says the best things. So blunt, so dirty. I love it. "Aren't we wasting time talking when we could be in your bed doing?" I ask.

He smiles, the sight of it stealing my breath, hurting my heart. He's so gorgeous, so sexy, and all mine. I disentangle myself from his grip and start for his bedroom but not before he crowds in behind me, his hands on my waist, his mouth at my neck. "Max," I chastise and I feel him smile against my neck, his arms sliding around me completely so he squeezes me close.

"What, princess? Am I too much of a distraction?" He splays his hands across my stomach, his fingers brushing my breasts, and I bite back the moan that wants to escape.

His touch feels so good, but God, I'm still so unsure . . .

"You make me nervous," I admit.

"Why?" He pushes my hair away from my nape to rain kisses there, making me shiver harder. "I won't hurt you."

"Maybe not physically," I say, wincing the moment the words pass my lips.

Damn it. That was something I didn't necessarily want to admit, though he has to know how I feel, how afraid I am to let him get close.

Max freezes for a moment, his mouth still pressed against my neck, his hands spanning my stomach. I stiffen as well, afraid of what he might say, worried that he'll walk away from me and never once look back.

I'm laying everything on the line here tonight and so is he. I'm normally a risk taker. Not too long ago I would take chances with my life every single day. Acting like a fool with various men, drinking, partying, traveling the world, never caring who I hurt, how my actions might affect another person. I was careless. Stupid. Yet this moment, this night with Max, feels like the biggest risk of all.

And if he pushes me away, I'll be devastated.

Slowly he turns me within his embrace so my back is pressed against the wall, his hands resting at my waist. I stare up at him, shifting my position so my hips thrust out and I brush against his front. I can feel his erection beneath his pants and I want to touch him. Stroke him there.

But I wait for him to make the first move.

"Princess." He removes one hand from my waist and rests it on the wall beside my head, caging me in. "I'm stepping into uncharted territory here, but I'm going to do my damnedest to keep you safe. Especially that pretty little body of yours." He squeezes my waist with his other hand and I smile at him, pleased at his words. Somewhat.

His expression remains serious as he stares at me and I realize he has more to say. "And your heart. I promise to keep that as safe as I can, too," he whispers just before he presses the gentlest, sweetest kiss to my lips I've ever experienced.

So sweet, I almost want to cry. It takes everything within me not to fall completely apart and I let my lips linger on his, not wanting to break the tentative connection we're sharing at this very moment.

It feels so . . . fragile.

So real.

I can't speak. I don't know what to say and it sounds like he's having a conversation with just himself, though I think he knows what I'm feeling, what I want to say.

"Now get your sweet ass in my bed, baby," he murmurs against my lips, and I start to laugh.

"Let me go so I can," I urge him and he does so, his hand loosening about my waist so I can break free. He releases me and I enter his bedroom, about to lean down and turn on the lamp on the bedside table.

But then he's on me, hands everywhere again, mouth locked with mine, tongue thrusting deep. He devours me, consumes me with his mouth and tongue and teeth, his hands, his entire body engulfing me. I moan and clutch him close, hating how restrictive the skirt of my dress is, wishing I could wrap my legs around his hips and hang on. Grind against him shamelessly, making the throbbing between my legs grow even more, until I'm overcome, obsessed with claiming my orgasm.

Because I am obsessed. The man turns me into a freak, a needy, unmanageable, uncontrollable little freak that wants nothing more than to get off. And the only who can satisfy my needs is him.

Max.

My cheeks, my neck, my everything goes hot at the realization and he breaks the kiss, withdrawing slightly to study me, as if sensing my change in temperature, in mood, in whatever. I crack open my eyes and stare up at him, yet again unsure of what to say, what to do. This man still makes me so nervous and usually I hate that sort of thing. I don't want anyone to ever have the upper hand, especially in the bedroom.

Yet with Max, I want him to take over. Take ownership. I want to surrender and let him do whatever he wants. Command me and order me around. I love the feeling of being at his mercy.

I crave it.

"I want you to trust me," he whispers when I don't say anything. He skims his thumb across my bottom lip, the rough pad snagging on my skin, and I purse my lips around it, desperate to suck him into my mouth. He lets me play and I swipe my tongue against his finger, earning a smile from him as he withdraws his hand. "I'm sorry for everything I've done. If I could take it all back, I would," he murmurs, his words making my heart swell.

"I want to trust you, too, but . . . it's hard," I admit, looking down.

He slips his fingers beneath my chin and tilts my head up so I'm forced to meet his gaze. "I will do anything to regain your trust. Anything."

"I need you to be patient," I whisper.

"Done." He runs his thumb along my jaw. "Whatever you need, I'm here for you."

"I want you to make love to me," I admit, my voice whisper soft. I have never asked a man to make love to me in my life. It's always sex, fucking, hooking up . . . whatever. Never meaningful, always empty.

But with Max it was more—and it can be so much more.

"Lily," he starts and I place my finger over his lips, silencing whatever else he was about to say.

"I like it when you say my name." He rarely does so. I'm either "princess" or "baby girl" or just "baby"—and I like those nicknames; they're fun. They're sexy.

But the best word to fall from his beautiful mouth is my name. I wish he would say it more often.

"I like it when you say my name, too." He smiles wickedly and I drop my finger. "Especially when you're shouting it right when I make you come."

Ah, there's my cocky, bossy man. "Are you going to make me come right now?"

He pushes his hand into my hair at the side of my head, his fingers threading through the strands. His touch feels so good, so right, and I love the way he's looking at me. Like he's never seen anything better. "I'm going to make love to you all night, baby. Until you're so exhausted you'll be begging me to stop."

A whimper escapes me when he presses his mouth to my throat, leaving a path of sucking, damp kisses all over my skin.

"You love it when I talk to you like that, don't you?" he murmurs against my neck.

I nod, unable to form words.

His hand slips down to my butt and gives me a squeeze. "You like it when I touch you like this, too."

"I do," I whisper, my body seeming to catch fire when he palms my ass.

Max reaches for my wrists and pins them behind my back, holding me captive as he lifts his head and stares directly into my eyes. "You like it when I take charge?"

"Yes." My voice trembles, my entire body quakes with need.

"The way you look at me, the way your skin feels beneath my hand, sometimes I wonder if you were made just for me," he murmurs, his low voice touching me deep. "You're always so responsive. I can tell you're turned on right now. Your eyes are almost black and I can feel you shaking."

A shuddery breath leaves me, my only reply.

He tilts his head, his mouth at my ear, his breath hot and damp, and I close my eyes when he begins to speak. "I bet if I touched your pussy you'd be drenched."

A gush of wetness coats my panties at his words and a whimper escapes me. I don't need to offer him confirmation. I almost hope he thrusts his hand between my legs to test me.

"I'm going to let go of you, princess, and when I do, I want you to hike up that skirt for me. Show me what you've got on under that dress," he demands, letting go of my wrists. I step away, my hands immediately going to the hem of my skirt, pulling the fabric up slowly, giving him a show, wanting him to see.

The dress is tight and when I have the skirt pushed up to my waist he orders me to stop, his hot gaze locked on my lower half, so intense I feel as if he can penetrate the lace of my black panties. "Do you . . ." I clear my throat, unsure how to go about this. The last time we were together, we were both too overcome to do much talking. But he likes talking. And so do I. "Do you approve?"

"Black lace covering the most fuckable pussy I've ever had? Hell yes, I approve," he growls, his gaze lifting to mine briefly before dropping once more to my panties. "Take them off."

I blink, surprised he doesn't want the honor himself. I wonder if I should be offended that he called my pussy fuckable, but the shiver that stole over my body at his words tells me otherwise. Without hesitation I curl my fingers around the band of my panties and slowly pull them down my legs, again giving him a show. I let the black lace linger around my knees before they fall to my feet in a delicate heap, getting tangled around the black stiletto heels I'm wearing.

"Kick them off, baby," he says, his voice low. "But keep the shoes on."

The panties are kicked aside but otherwise I remain still, waiting for his next request. My knees are like jelly and I probably look stupid with my skirt bunched around my waist, the expensive dress crushed by my ill treatment. But I don't care.

I asked him to make love to me but he knew what I really wanted, what I needed. This is what I crave, his complete and utter control of me. Because up until Max, all I'd ever felt was out of control. I love the way he takes over my thoughts, my wants, my needs.

I love it.

Waiting breathlessly, my heart leaps to my throat when he nonchalantly unbuttons his shirt until it's left hanging open, exposing the white T-shirt he's wearing underneath it. I'm poised and anxious, hopeful he'll remove more of his clothing, but instead he flicks his chin at me, telling me without a word to remove the dress.

Reaching to my right side, I pull the hidden zipper down, feeling the fabric part beneath my arm. When it's loose enough, I shrug out of it, pulling it over my head and tossing it so it lands on a nearby chair. I spent so much money on that dress. Why I chose to wear it to this meeting with my family today, I don't know. And with any other man, I probably would have hung the dress back up in my closet so it wouldn't wrinkle.

Tonight, with Max, I don't care. I could throw it away with no regrets. As long as I get to be with him, feel his hands on my body, feel his cock thrust inside of me, hear him whisper all those dirty, wickedly wonderful words he loves to say in my ear, I'll be fine.

I'll be perfect.

"That bra is fucking indecent," he says as he comes toward me, reaching out a hand to cup my breast. "I can see everything." His thumb flicks over my nipple once. Twice. Then he brings his index finger and thumb together and pinches so tight, I gasp, sinking my teeth into my lower lip as the sting continues to burn. When he releases me, I heave out a breath, secretly hoping he'll deliver the same treatment to my other nipple.

And I think he knows it.

"So beautiful," he whispers, staring reverently at my chest. He cups my breasts, his thumbs sweeping over my nipples. My entire body quakes with anticipation, I'm so keyed up. I'm afraid

I could come just from him playing with my nipples. I want him that much.

"That feels so good," I tell him, unable to hold back.

"I know. I can tell. Your face is flushed and so is your chest. You always get this rosy glow when I touch you. Like my hands light you up from within," he says, his gaze never leaving mine. "You want me to fuck you hard and make you scream. You want me to eat your pussy until you're coming all over my face and squirming like you do. You want it all because no one else makes you feel like I do. No one."

I swallow hard. Everything he says is true. Will I ever get tired of hearing him say such gloriously filthy things?

No, I don't think so.

"Get on the bed, princess." He reaches around me and slaps my bare ass, the hard smack like a jolt to my system. I jerk forward and on shaky legs walk to his massive bed, crawling onto the mattress on all fours and earning a low whistle from Max for my efforts.

"What a fucking view," he says, and I glance over my shoulder to find him staring directly at my exposed butt.

Figures.

I turn and collapse onto the bed on my back, my arms bent at the elbow so I'm propped up and can see what he's doing. He stands at the foot of the bed, still completely clothed while I'm practically undressed, in only a bra and heels, my hair a mess, my makeup most likely smeared or worn off, and my pussy is throbbing so bad I squeeze my thighs together to try and find some relief.

It doesn't help. In fact, he notices the subtle move and his gaze darkens, his jaw tightens. "What are you doing?"

I don't know how to answer him or what to say, so I stare at him helplessly.

"Did you squeeze your thighs together? Are you close to coming?"

"Y-yes," I admit, loving the dangerous light that fills his eyes. Oh, my admission just made him so angry and I . . .

I fucking love it.

"You're not allowed until I say so." The finality to his words tells me I will be in deep, deep trouble if I come before he says I can. Which only makes me want to come quicker, sooner, harder, now.

"Do you understand what I'm telling you, princess?" he asks when I don't say anything.

"Yes." I nod.

"Good." He smiles, but it's dark. The rush that comes from the sight of his smile, the words that he says to me, are heady and strong. A realization about myself and about Max. This is exactly what I craved but never knew. His complete command over me, my total surrender to him.

My entire life, I was so used to getting whatever I wanted, and always fighting to be in control at all times for fear someone would see the real me.

Always hiding, always afraid. I never knew exactly what it was I hid but now, I've discovered myself. I'm only the real me when I'm with this man, in his arms, at his command.

And I love it.

"Tell me what you want," he says, earning my attention. "And you'd better not say an orgasm."

That's exactly what I want. He's a total mind reader. "What will happen if I do?"

He cocks a brow. "Do you really want to test me on that one?"

God, yes. But I pretend I don't. "No."

His expression relaxes. He knows he has me where he wants me. I'm not going anywhere and I know neither is he. "So tell me. Don't be afraid, Lily. Tell me what you want."

"I want you naked," I admit softly, trying my best not to

tighten my thighs and make him think I'm squirming and squeezing toward an orgasm.

He shrugs his shirt off without hesitation, his gaze never leaving me. No, it wanders all over me, from my face to my chest to my stomach to my legs. I feel his eyes on me as if he's physically touching me and it's driving me crazy with need.

"Spread your legs," he commands gruffly as he tugs off his T-shirt, revealing his magnificent chest and abs. I stare unabashedly as I bend my knees and plant my shoes on the mattress, my heels sinking in as I swing my legs open.

"You're not allowed to come until I say so," he murmurs, his gaze dropping to between my thighs, remaining there, smoldering, almost predatory, as if he wants to wreck me.

And God help me, I want to be wrecked. I'm desperate for him to destroy me in the way only he can, so he can put me back together again. I want to feel his body next to mine; I want to be connected with him and only him. I want Max to tease me and push me to the brink until I shatter completely apart when he finally allows me the orgasm I so desperately need.

I also want to clamp my legs shut and deprive him of the view. I want to yell at him and demand that he touch me so I can find some sort of relief.

But I do none of that. I merely wait.

And slowly, quietly, burn for him.

Chapter Twenty-nine

Max

MY TIGHTLY REINED-IN CONTROL IS HANGING BY A THREAD. Having Lily on such blatant display, sprawled on my bed, her long, golden-brown hair spread across the pillow, her breasts encased in black lace, legs obscenely wide open and showing me every inch of her glistening pink pussy, all that runs through my head is one single word. A word I never thought about in regards to a woman until this one.

Mine.

Mine, mine, mine.

Jesus, I feel greedy with wanting her. She wants to come, I can tell. I see her clit protruding from the folds between her legs, can see the creamy white drops clinging to her skin, coating the inside of her thighs. She's so turned on I can smell her, the scent of her arousal thick in the room, making my nostrils flare. My cock threatens to burst out of my fucking jeans at any moment and I take a deep, hissing breath, closing my eyes for the briefest moment as I tell myself I can do this. I can get through this for a few more minutes.

I want to break her. Completely break her and then put her back together again so she knows that she's mine and no one else's. My dormant possessive nature has come roaring to life, and my overpowering need to take her and make her understand her place in life—by my side, beneath me, over me—is making it hard for me to focus.

Her soft whimper gets me and without thought I unbuckle my belt, undo my jeans, and take them off, pulling my boxer briefs with them, kicking off my shoes. Until I'm naked and my cock is so hard it fucking hurts. I'm aching for her; my entire body is strung tight with my need for Lily.

I go to her, not missing how she watches me with those big, luminous eyes, and she doesn't say a word as I crawl onto the bed until I'm hovering above her, my hands braced on either side of her head and sinking into the pillow, my hips nestled between her spread legs, her lace-covered breasts in front of my face and tempting me.

Dipping my head, I press my mouth to the valley between her breasts, breathing deep her fragrance, kissing her there. Licking her. She arches against me on a blissful sigh, her hands going to my hair, holding my head in place, and I let her. I may prefer control but I let her guide me, show me what feels good.

That's all I want to do, make her feel good, make her feel safe. I'm here for her always. Her giving up control to me completely is one way she can know that no matter what, I will take care of her. And I will. Better than anyone else has ever in her life. This girl was made for me. I want her to know it.

I rain kisses across the tops of her breasts, licking at her nipples, sucking one deep into my mouth, lace and all. She lurches and tries to pull away when I nibble at her flesh but I hold her still, gripping her with my hands, wanting her to take my gentle assault. She moans my name, tugs my hair tighter, and I bite her harder, needing to remind her who's really in charge here. She cries out, lifting her hips, my cock brushing against her belly, and I can tell she's close to losing it.

"Fuck me, fuck me," she chants and I lift my head, studying her. She's so beautiful, her cheeks tinged pink, her eyes closed, her lips falling open. "Please, Max, please."

Realization hits and I feel like the world's biggest asshole. "Lily." Her eyes snap open when I say her name and she studies me, her gaze cloudy, her delicate brows lowered. "Do you have condoms? In your purse or . . ."

She snaps her eyes shut on a grimace. "No," she wails, sounding positively in pain. "Oh my God, no. Tell me you have one in your wallet."

"I don't." I don't usually pack condoms in my wallet. Safety first and all that shit, but hell, carrying them around makes me feel like I'm on the make, like I expect to get laid. "But I'm clean."

Those eyes open again, full of confusion and hope. "So am I," she admits softly. "I'm on the pill, too, so . . ."

"I've never been with another woman without a condom," I tell her, because it's the damn truth.

"I've never been with another man without a condom, either." A shuddery breath escapes her and I swear I see the shimmer of tears in her eyes. "I've been with a lot of men, Max. Not as many as the media likes to portray, but I'm no saint."

I hate thinking of her being with any man, but I'm not an idiot. I can't expect her to live the life of a saint while waiting for me, for Christ's sake. That's completely unbelievable and wrong of me to even consider. Those men aren't important, though. The only one who matters in her life now is . . . me. "I'm not a saint either, baby. You know this."

"I just don't want you to . . . judge me. Or think I'm a slut." She presses her lips together and squeezes her eyes shut, but I see the tears clinging to her thick lashes.

"You're a woman." I press my mouth to her forehead in a tender kiss, wishing I could reassure her, make her feel better. Her tears tug at my heart, pierce my made-of-steel soul, and I kiss her temple, her cheek, kiss away the few tears that escaped. "You've done things, lived your life. I can't expect anything less."

She parts her lips, ready to say something else, but I kiss her, silencing her. I tangle my tongue with hers, drink from her mouth slowly, earning a low, sexy moan that comes from deep in her chest. Christ, I can't get enough. My cock is insistent, ready to take her, fuck her hard until we're both screaming with our release. I'm desperate to take my time, treat her right, give her body all the attention and love it deserves, but I can't.

I won't last long, I want her so bad. And I'll probably be a disappointment to her after the long wait, but the thought of being inside her without a condom . . . so I can feel everything, every clench and release and burn . . . oh yeah. I'm ready to move this to the next step.

"I want to fuck you bare," I tell her, thrusting my hips against hers, nice and slow. "I want to feel it when you come on my cock."

"Yes." She closes her eyes and arches her neck, her breasts brushing my chest. The girl is on fire for me and I'm eager to quench her need. "Please."

"You want this?" I lift up so I'm on my knees, straddling her hips, and I take my cock in hand, giving it a stroke. Then another.

She opens her eyes to stare at me, her gaze dropping to where I'm touching myself. "Tease me with it," she demands, her voice low and sexy as fuck.

I do as she asks, dragging the head of my cock in her drenched folds, back and forth across her clit, driving her wild. Her long, agonized moans only fuel me further and I continue my torment, circling her clit, teasing her flexing entrance, sliding my cock in, just the tip. Driving myself fucking crazy with wanting her. I'm not going to last much longer if I keep this up.

"More," she demands, keening when I slip back inside her. "Please, Max. I'm begging you."

I love it that I've made her beg. She needs me. Can't get enough of me. And that's exactly what I wanted, what I needed.

To see her complete and total submission, but there's one more thing I want from her.

"Lily." I reach out, touch her cheek gently with a soft drift of my fingers. "Tell me who you belong to."

"You. Only you."

"Is this my pussy?" I tease her again, slipping inside her one inch at a time, then withdrawing just as slowly, the pace torturous both to her and to me.

"Yes." She wraps her legs around my hips, anchoring herself and sending me farther. "Is this my cock?" She reaches for my dick, her fingers skimming my length, teasing at her pussy and making me shiver.

"Fuck yes, baby. All yours. Just like you're all mine," I tell her just before I sink deep, all the way inside her body until my balls brush against her ass and it feels like I'm touching the very deepest part of her.

I fuck her mindlessly, my sole focus on giving her the desperately needed orgasm she's craved since we ended up in my bedroom. She claws at my back, her legs clamped tight around my hips, her mouth hanging open and pressing against my neck. I feel her hot breath, her damp lips, her tongue and teeth sinking into my skin. She's as caught up as I am, lost to the sensation of our connected bodies, my cock sinking into her depths, striving toward my orgasm and hers.

Reaching between us, I stroke her clit, circling it, and she gasps, the clench of her pussy at my touch making my vision go hazy. I don't want to come. Not yet. I need to make sure she comes first. My girl is desperate to get off and I don't want to disappoint.

"Max." She whispers my name against my neck, sending shivers all over my skin. "I'm so close."

"Me too, baby," I tell her as I increase my pace. She's so wet it's easy to sink deep and I pump inside her with long, even strokes. Heat rushes over me, making me falter, and my mind goes blank. I'm close. So damn close and I shut my eyes tight, my hips pumping, my cock full of come and ready to explode . . .

"Can I . . ." A strangled sob escapes her when I press my thumb against her clit. "Can I come, Max? Will you let me?"

I go completely still, lifting my torso away from her so I can stare down at her face. She's asking for permission. *Hell,* I forgot I told her she couldn't come unless I said so.

She drags her eyes open and she looks so damn beautiful my heart cracks. Her mouth is puffy from my kisses. Her lids are heavy, her cheeks flushed, her hair a wild tangle about her head. Her skin is covered with the lightest sheen of sweat and she looks completely undone. Nothing like the woman I saw in Maui, not even close to the woman I saw in the numerous photos on the internet. And nothing like the quiet, angry woman I've been with the last few days.

Right now, like this, she looks like mine. Like she belongs to me and no one else. That she's asking me for permission tears me up inside. Makes me feel like a fucking king.

I gentle my touch on her swollen clit, flicking it this way and that, toying with it, toying with her. Her inner walls clutch me tight, strangling my dick, and I exhale loudly through my nose, my gaze meeting hers as I continue to touch her. "I want to feel you come around my cock," I murmur, studying her, wanting to see her reaction.

She lifts her hips, her gaze never straying from mine. "I need permission first."

"I'm giving it to you." I start to move, slipping my cock inside her, still teasing her clit. "Come for me, Lily. Let me feel you. Let me see you."

Her breath catches and she starts to close her eyes but I pinch her clit hard, making her gasp. Those eyes fly open wide, frustration swimming in their depths, and I ease my fingers away from her clit. Remove my hand completely. "Grind yourself on my cock, baby," I command as I haul her in close, our connected bodies brushing against each other. "Fuck me as hard as I'm going to fuck you."

She rubs against me unashamedly, using my body for her pleasure, and I let her. Hell, I revel in her. Her head is tossed back though she still watches me and I don't look away. I know she's close, I can feel her entire body start to tremble, can recognize the signs that her orgasm is imminent. Her breaths come in short, hitching gasps and I urge her on with filthy words, wanting to see her fall apart, wanting to witness this moment.

"Max . . ." She drags my name out, her eyes still on mine, and then her body is consumed with shudders, her hips jerking against mine. Her pussy milks my cock as her orgasm sweeps over her. I cup her cheek, bring her mouth to mine and kiss her, our eyes staying open as we stare at each other. Her orgasm goes on and on as she shivers and shakes, cries out incoherent sounds. Her pussy is so fucking wet as she comes on my cock and when she whispers my name again, that's it. That's all it takes.

I push her into the mattress and fuck her like a savage. I'm grunting with every shove into her pussy. Again and again and again. I fuck and fuck and fuck until I'm shouting, my come blasting inside her body, filling her up, dribbling out, coating her pussy, and she clings to me. Never lets me go. Never tries once to break free.

Proving once and for all that she's mine. We belong together.

And now that I've found her again, I'm never going to let her go.

"I GUESS THAT WASN'T ANYTHING CLOSE TO WHAT YOU CON-sider making love, huh," I say casually, though inside I'm worried how she might answer. She's lying in my arms, her head tucked between my neck and my shoulder, her hair tickling the side of my face.

I'm exhausted from the day, from the explosive sex Lily and

I just shared. Remembering how she asked me to make love to her and instead, I fucked her like a beast and commanded her to do whatever I said.

How can she even stand me?

"It was perfect," she murmurs as she drifts her fingers across my chest. "You gave me what I needed versus what I thought I wanted."

Relief filters through me, strong enough to relax muscles I didn't realize I was holding so stiffly. "And what was that?"

"You." She lifts up, resting her hand on my chest so she can look me directly in the eyes. "I like the way you take complete control over me. I never . . . I never believed I could be into anything like that but with you, it's all I want."

I'm quiet for a moment as I absorb her words. "I feel like you were made for me, Lily. That we were made for each other."

She smiles. "I feel the same way."

I cup the back of her head and bring her down so I can kiss her. "I don't want you to ever leave my side."

"You'll eventually have to go to work, Max," she teases.

"Mmm, princess, I'll just bring you with me." I deepen the kiss, sliding my tongue against hers, making her moan. "That's a damn good idea, you know," I say when she breaks away from me first.

"What do you mean?" She moves away from me, but not too far since my hand is still curved around her head. "I can't go to work with you."

"Why not? Levi and I have been talking about going into partnership together but neither of us has made the move. We can put together a more detailed tech side to the business and you can be a part of it." I'm tense, waiting for her answer after finally getting up the nerve to ask her. Why would she ever need to work? She has all the money in the world. She doesn't have to lift a finger for the rest of her life and she'd be fine. More than fine.

She actually blushes and shakes her head. "I'm not good enough. Your friend will probably think I'm some amateur playing at computers."

"You're good enough." I tighten my fingers in her hair and give her head a little shake. "Don't ever say that you're not. When Levi infiltrated your computer, he was impressed with your skills."

"He was?" she asks breathlessly.

"Yeah. And I think you being an eventual partner in my business could benefit all of us." I bring her head down to mine once more, kissing her hard. "Plus, that means you'll never leave my side."

Her smile is slow. Tentative. "Do you mean it?"

"I fucking mean it with my whole heart, Lily." I made sure and said her name so she'd get just how serious I am.

"You want me to work for you."

"*With* me," I correct.

"And be a part of your tech team, where you'll pay me for the skills I learned by doing . . . illegal things," she continues.

I laugh. "Yeah. How do you think Levi got his start?"

Her eyes widen. "Seriously?"

"Of course. Most expert hackers start out doing things they're not supposed to. That's how they became expert *hackers*." I kiss her again because I can't stop myself. I'm addicted to her lips. I'm addicted to everything about her. "Say yes, baby girl. Be my partner in everything. Please."

She smiles and drops another soft, lingering kiss on my mouth before whispering, "Yes."

Chapter Thirty

Lily

I WAIT ANXIOUSLY IN VIOLET'S OFFICE, WRINGING MY HANDS IN my lap, gnawing on my lip so hard Violet finally hands over a Fleur lip balm without saying a word. I slather on the balm, my eyebrows going up at how it soothes my lips instantly, and I hand it back to her.

She shakes her head. "Keep it. I have a bunch of them in my desk."

"It works." I toss the lip balm in my purse.

"I know." Violet smiles. "It's good stuff."

Glancing around, I lean in closer to Violet's desk and lower my voice. "Is she here?" I know she should be here; the meeting was scheduled for two and it's a quarter past now. I arrived a few minutes ago. I wanted to be at Fleur when the firing went down.

Guess I want to watch Pilar make the walk of shame out of the building.

Violet sighs. "She's in Father's office right now. Ryder is sitting in the meeting with him. I'm sure she loves that."

"I'm sure that pisses her off," I mutter, wanting to laugh but I don't. This is serious business, what Pilar tried to do.

"I'm sure, but I really don't care." The smile Violet offers me is nothing short of glorious. She's thrilled that Pilar is finally getting what she deserves. So am I. "She's not my problem any-more."

No, she's not, thank goodness. "I still feel bad that I didn't tell you what she was doing sooner." I have tremendous guilt over it, though everyone—and I mean *everyone,* right down to my grandma and my father—has reassured me that it's all right. It doesn't feel all right, though. I'm just lucky we caught her.

And I have Max, and Levi, to thank for that.

Violet waves a hand, making a dismissive noise. "Stop beating yourself up. It's over. Your Max saved the day."

I smile. "He did, didn't he?"

Turns out Felicity Winston had a case of the guilts herself after Pilar sent her the Fleur product info and she didn't do any-thing with it. Yes, she looked everything over and knows all of the company's future plans, but she told no one, not even any of the execs at Jayne Cosmetics. Fleur lucked out. Violet didn't have to make any veiled threats, but lawyers were involved, con-fidentiality agreements were drawn up, and Felicity had to sign them.

Pilar will have a confidentiality agreement to sign as well, once her ass gets canned.

It gives me greatly ridiculous pleasure to think that, let alone say it out loud.

"How is Max, by the way?" Violet asks not so innocently.

"He's . . . great." My voice softens and I know I probably look like a dreamy, lovesick loser but I feel like a dreamy, love-sick loser, so that's okay. We've been together constantly the last few days and I can't wait to go home to see him. Now that he's in my life, I can't imagine being without him.

"Looks like you got struck, too," Violet says, amusement lacing her voice.

I frown. "What do you mean?"

"Struck by the love bug or whatever. Rose has it. So do I. And now, so do you."

Funny, how I'd been so envious of my sisters' relationships, though I told myself I never wanted one. What a lie. I can't believe how easy it is with Max, how fast it's happened. But I guess when you know, you know.

And I know Max is the one for me.

"We haven't talked about love or anything like that," I start, but she interrupts me.

"Oh, you will. Soon, I'm sure. He seems just as smitten with you as you are with him." Her knowing smile is downright cocky and I open my mouth, ready to protest—for what reason, I'm not exactly sure—when I hear a commotion just outside Violet's office door.

We both swing our heads to see Pilar standing in the hallway, our father glaring at her as she faces him, her finger poking his chest as she yells at him.

"You think I'm just going to walk out of here without saying a word, you've got another think coming." She pokes Daddy in the chest again and he doesn't try to grab her, doesn't say a word, but his face is a stone mask, his mouth drawn so tight his lips disappear.

"You called security?" Daddy asks when Ryder strides into view.

"They're on their way," Ryder says curtly, his gaze cutting to the glass window wall of Violet's office. He sees us sitting there and his expression softens, his eyes never leaving Violet.

Pilar notices and focuses her attention on us. Her gaze is narrowed, her face pale save for two high spots of color on her cheeks. I swear she's so angry I can see her entire body vibrating from where I sit.

"Stupid, smug whores!" she yells as she storms for the open doorway of Violet's office. "I hate you both! Do you two really think you can *ruin* me?"

Ryder grabs Pilar's arm before she can enter Violet's office, effectively stopping her in her tracks. "You say one more word against my fiancée and you'll regret it," I hear him murmur, his deep voice full of barely contained rage.

She sends him a look over her shoulder and then returns all of her attention to us. "You may have won this battle, but you haven't won the war. Not by a long shot."

Violet and I say nothing. What can we say? I wish she'd just go away. I'm sure Violet feels the same.

Pilar jerks her arm out of Ryder's hold and sends us a withering stare before she stands tall and starts to stride down the hall, Daddy following after her. I hear him speak to someone else—I can only assume it's the security that Ryder just summoned—and Ryder enters Violet's office, going straight to her as she leaps from her chair and practically falls into his arms.

"It's done," Ryder says as he runs his hand up and down Violet's back, as if he's trying to soothe her. "She said nothing when we presented the emails between her and Felicity Winston. She really started to protest when the Zachary emails appeared, though. That's when I called security. They'll escort her out of the building."

"Did she sign the confidentiality agreement?" Violet asks as she looks up at him.

Ryder nods. "We made sure she did that before the Zachary emails came up. Your father handled it all beautifully. Never even broke a sweat."

I'm strangely proud to hear it. "What about you, Ryder? Did you break a sweat?"

"Nah, though I did want to wring her neck with my bare hands." He smiles, then drops a kiss on Violet's lips. "It's over, baby. She's out of our lives for good."

"Hopefully," Violet adds.

"No hopefully. What's done is done. Her career in the cosmetics industry is most likely over, but I'm sure she'll reinvent herself. Or somehow convince someone she's worth the trouble," Ryder says with a shake of his head. "She did a lot for me . . ." His voice drifts and he almost looks guilty.

My sister snaps him back to reality. "But she also held you back," Violet points out as she slowly withdraws from his arms, turning to face me. "Maybe you should start working at Fleur, Lily. With Rose gone and now Pilar, too, we need someone. And I'd like to keep it in the family."

I blink in surprise. I can't believe my sister is suggesting I come to work at Fleur. "I appreciate your faith in me, but I have plans of my own."

Violet frowns. "What are you talking about?"

"I think I'm going to work with Max. Put my hacking skills to good use," I admit, feeling embarrassed. I hope she doesn't think that's a stupid idea. It's been fun, discussing plans for the future with Max. Not just fun, but exciting. I've never been one to think far ahead but with Max, it's all I want to do.

Violet's frown turns into a small smile, her eyes lighting up. "That's . . . amazing. I love the idea. Father will be so proud."

"You think so?" I'm pleased at the idea that I could truly make my father proud. I don't think he's been proud of anything I've ever done.

Ever.

"I know so. We'd love to have you at Fleur but completely understand that you'd rather work with Max. That sounds more like your calling, so I get it." Violet smiles and steps closer to me, holding out her arms. I go to her and we embrace, clutching each other tight. "Go where it feels right, Lily," she murmurs close to my ear.

That's the best advice anyone's ever given me.

Epilogue

Three months later

Lily

"You really want me to move in with you?"

I nod, scooting across my giant bed so I can press my naked body against his. He still has on his boxer briefs but I can feel his erection. If I plan this right, that big cock of his will be inside me in minutes. "Please ease the suspense and just say yes. We're together all the time anyway. If you're not here, I'm at your apartment." But he's in Brooklyn, so we spend more time here. Plus, my apartment is bigger. It also has better security, thanks to Max and the new system he recently convinced them to put in. He's still not sold that Pilar won't pop up out of nowhere and come after me or Violet.

Max chuckles and slips his arms around my waist, his big hands moving down to cup my ass and haul me into him. "I should be like Caden and make you move into my place so we can all be neighbors," he murmurs against my neck as he starts kissing me there. His lips are hot, his tongue wet, making me shiver.

"That would be kind of dumb considering we're opening up our new office downtown next month," I remind him. It's only a few months after I started working with Max and Levi, and business is booming. Word got out that Max now has a team of tech experts working with him and we're almost to the point where we have to turn business away.

Max is currently interviewing for more employees and we recently hired a full-time receptionist. We've kept it quiet that I work with him. I've become more of a silent partner because we don't want to draw any unwanted media attention. Our business is discreet, and potential clients wouldn't like it if they knew a former media darling—or media hot mess, take your pick—was working with them.

And I've had plenty of media attention lately, what with the recent launch of the namesake perfume. I did a ton of interviews along with Rose and Violet, and we did a huge launch at Bloomingdale's. The media especially loves that Rose is hugely pregnant and ready to pop any day now. The Fowler Sisters' perfumes have done amazingly well.

Not that I'm surprised.

In some ways, I've become a completely different person these last few months. I go into work every morning, Monday through Friday, and sometimes we even work on the weekends. Me, the party girl of Manhattan, the troublemaker, the terror, the girl nominated to crash and burn at a young age, has turned into a normal, eight-to-five—or more, to be truthful—working woman.

And I love it. I love waking up with Max, sharing a shower with him before we eat breakfast, gulp down coffee, and head to the office. I love working with Levi, who's intense and smart and enjoys figuring out tricky code as much as I do—maybe even more.

The thing I love the most? Spending every day with Max. I thought we would get sick of each other and he admitted he had that fear, too. Yet I'm not sick of him at all. If anything, I appreciate and love him more and more each day. He's amazing. So smart, so diligent, always wanting to do the right thing no matter what.

All that integrity I thought he didn't have? He possesses it in spades. And it's sexy, too. Everything about him is sexy.

"Yeah, I suppose you're right. We should stay here in your giant apartment versus the box I live in." With his big hands still gripping my ass, he spreads my legs wider, his fingers sinking into my wet pussy, and I inhale sharply, loving the way he knows just how to touch me. "You got enough space in that fancy closet of yours so my clothes can fit?" he murmurs into my neck.

"No way are you getting anywhere near my closet." I start to laugh, but it instantly turns into a moan when he starts to stroke me between my legs in earnest.

"Baby, you are always so wet for me." He moves down my body, his hot mouth burning a path along my skin until he's nestled between my thighs, licking and sucking me into oblivion. "Damn, you taste good," he murmurs against my flesh.

I clutch at his hair, overwhelmed by the way this man makes me feel. How did I get so lucky? And it's not only about the sex, though he certainly knows how to keep me satisfied.

"Max," I whisper, thrusting my hips against his face. He looks up at me, his gaze intense, his tongue circling my clit as he sinks a finger inside me, and that's all it takes. I'm shuddering, the orgasm slipping over me with ease as I cry out. I've never had more orgasms in my life as I do with him.

And I've never felt so loved, so cherished. And it's all because of Max.

It's the way he believes in me. Encourages me. Supports me when I need it and steps back when my freedom is necessary. His instincts are always spot-on and I trust him. He still wants me to be a partner in his business and though I agree, it's a huge step and one I'm not quite ready for.

Which he's fine with. He doesn't push. I appreciate that more than he'll ever know.

He gets along with my sisters and Ryder and Caden. I've met his parents and I really like his mom and dad, though his big brother, Sam, is just as grumpy as Max warned me he would be. He's a police detective in New Jersey, a giant bear of a man with a constant scowl on his face, though he's almost as handsome as Max.

Almost. No one's as gorgeous as Max, at least in my eyes.

"You are loud when you come, princess," he teases as he rises above me, his boxer briefs somehow disappearing.

"I like the way you use your tongue, cowboy," I tease back, sighing with pleasure when he kisses me deep, his tongue thrusting against mine.

"Speaking of cowboy, I think my girl needs to ride me," he murmurs, and then he's flipping me over so I'm straddling his hips, lifting up so I can take his big cock deep inside my body. "Ah, that's it, baby. Start rocking."

I do as he tells me, sliding up and down his cock slowly, rocking into him. I lift my arms and close my eyes, my body swaying as I gather up my hair and pile it on top of my head. I know he likes it when I do this. Putting on a show, thrusting out my chest, my breasts swaying with my movements.

"Pretty view," he encourages as he runs his hands along my waist, over my stomach, then back up to cup my breasts. I drop my arms and open my eyes, smiling down at him, and then he's shifting his position so he's sitting up, his mouth on my nipples as he tongues and sucks first one, then the other.

A shuddery sigh escapes me and I cradle his head in my hands, breathless when he looks up at me with his beautiful blue eyes so full of affection and lust and love. All for me. I still can't believe this man is mine. All mine. "Feels so good," he murmurs. "I love the way you ride my cock."

My pussy clenches around his length and his lids fall to half-mast, as he lets out a low groan. I grind against him, sending him so deep I swear he's touching my very soul.

"Love you, baby girl," he whispers, knowing exactly what his words do to me. He can feel the reaction my body has to his tender endearments. "You gonna come again already?"

I nod, my messy hair falling all around my shoulders. His cock rubs against my inner walls, creating a delicious friction that takes me right over the edge, and he grabs hold of my hair, pulling tight so it stings as he thrusts his face in mine.

"Tell me you love me," he demands.

"Oh, I do. I love you. So much, Max."

He grips my hip with his other hand, increasing his pace, fucking me hard. He's still pulling my hair, his mouth on mine, his tongue thrusting, his cock thrusting, and then I'm coming, milking his cock, his come spurting deep inside me, marking me.

Making me his.

Minutes later I'm in his arms, snug against his side, my head on his firm chest. I can feel his heartbeat, steady and strong, and I trace my fingers over his pecs, unable to stop touching him.

"Maybe we need to start slowing down or something," he murmurs, his fingers in my hair. "All this sex we keep having might kill us."

I lift my head to glare at him. "No way are we slowing down. This is my favorite part of the day."

He chuckles and squeezes my shoulders. "Have I told you that I love you today?"

Only about twenty times, give or take. "Yes, but tell me again."

His expression goes serious and he cups my nape. "I love you. I'm the luckiest man in the world to have you in my life."

"I love you, too," I say, my voice soft, my emotions all over the place.

He stares at me. "Would you give up your closet for me?"

I go completely still. "Are you serious?"

His expression doesn't change and I shove at him, seeing the teasing glimmer in his gaze. "You don't want to force me to choose between you and my closet. I love that closet. At one point I planned to marry that closet and take its name."

"Lily Closet? That was your life plan?" His brows lift, looking too sexy for his own good.

"Has a nice ring to it, don't you think?" I poke at his chest with my index finger.

"I think Lily Coleman sounds better," he says.

My mouth drops open and I swear my heart just tripped over itself. "Are you serious?"

He doesn't say a word, just taps the tip of my nose with his finger.

"Really?" I squeak as he starts to draw my head down to his.

"Just say yes, Lily," he whispers.

"Ye—" I start but he cuts me off.

And kisses me.

Acknowledgments

THIS WAS THE HARDEST BOOK I'VE EVER WRITTEN, ESPECIALLY because I wrote it twice. So I want to thank my editor, Shauna Summers, for being so patient with me while I went through this painful process not just once, but two times, all while getting horribly sick—and during the holidays. It wasn't easy, but I believe the second version is a much stronger book, thanks to your suggestions, Shauna. It's a true joy working with you.

I want to thank everyone at Bantam/Random House for all your support of The Fowler Sisters series. A big shout-out to Kati Rodriguez and Autumn Hull for all that you both do to keep me straight. Lots of love to Katy Evans: my friend, my critique partner, my confidant. I seriously couldn't do this without you.

And thank you to all the bloggers and readers out there for your never-ending support. I write my books not only for me, but for you. This is my dream job, one I've wanted to do since I was a teenager and writing either Duran Duran or *Days of Our Lives* fan fic (so embarrassing, but I'm admitting it like a badge of honor). It's still hard for me to believe that this writing thing I'm doing is my actual career. I'm a lucky girl. So to all the dreamers out there: Don't give up.

Playlist

MUSIC ALWAYS PLAYS A MAJOR PART IN MY WRITING PROCESS. I create a playlist on Spotify for almost every book I write (look me up on Spotify—just search Monica Murphy). Here is a list of some of the songs that inspired me while writing *Taming Lily*.

"Hawaii" by Meiko
"Chandelier" by Sia
"Bad Girl" by Madonna
"This is What Makes Us Girls" by Lana Del Rey
"Lemon" by Katy Rose
"Crave You" by Flight Facilities

PHOTO: © CHRIS MEYER PHOTOGRAPHY

New York Times and *USA Today* bestselling author Monica Murphy is a native Californian who lives in the foothills of Yosemite. A wife and mother of three, she writes new adult contemporary romance and is the author of the One Week Girlfriend series and the tie-in novella, *Drew + Fable Forever,* as well as the Fowler Sisters series.

monicamurphyauthor.com
missmonicamurphy@gmail.com
Facebook.com/MonicaMurphyauthor
@MsMonicaMurphy

About the Type

This book was set in Sabon, a typeface designed by the well-known German typographer Jan Tschichold (1902–74). Sabon's design is based upon the original letter forms of sixteenth-century French type designer Claude Garamond and was created specifically to be used for three sources: foundry type for hand composition, Linotype, and Monotype. Tschichold named his typeface for the famous Frankfurt typefounder Jacques Sabon (c. 1520–80).

F Murphy Monica
Murphy, Monica.
Taming Lily :
22960001126613

2/16

NO LONGER PROPERTY OF
ANDERSON COUNTY LIBRARY

WAFI